# Readers love *The Windup*
## by KATE MCMURRAY

By KATE MCMURRAY

Published by DREAMSPINNER PRESS
http://www.dreamspinnerpress.com

# Thrown
# A CURVE

KATE McMURRAY

Published by
DREAMSPINNER PRESS

5032 Capital Circle SW, Suite 2, PMB# 279, Tallahassee, FL 32305-7886 USA
http://www.dreamspinnerpress.com/

Thrown a Curve
© 2015 Kate McMurray.

Cover Art
© 2015 Aaron Anderson
aaronbydesign55@gmail.com.
Cover content is for illustrative purposes only and any person depicted on the cover is a model.

ISBN: 978-1-63216-969-3
Digital ISBN: 978-1-63216-970-9
Library of Congress Control Number: 2015902240
First Edition June 2015

Printed in the United States of America

This paper meets the requirements of
ANSI/NISO Z39.48-1992 (Permanence of Paper).

# Acknowledgments

I want to thank Marsha Auguste for her help on this book and for putting up with me talking about it all the damn time while I was working on it. Shout-out to Laura, too, for being my enthusiastic supporter through this whole series. And lots of love to every fan whose face lit up when I mentioned I was writing about baseball again.

# Chapter 1

MASON SIPPED his beer and watched Odell mack on some girl. She was pretty, with smooth, dark skin and a petite frame. Not Mason's thing, but he could see the appeal.

He turned his attention to the TV over the bar, which was showing *SportsCenter*. The hot topic of the evening was the Yankees and their abysmal season to date, a discussion Mason could have done without. When the show broke for commercial, he looked for the bartender, who fortuitously seemed to be headed back in his direction. The bartender was a cute, dark-haired white guy with a gym-sculpted body, obvious under the black tank top he was wearing. Mason kind of wanted to lick his arms, just because they were there. He smiled at the bartender and motioned that he wanted another beer. The bartender winked.

That was more like it.

Of course, just as the bartender slid another pint toward Mason, Odell leaned over and slapped Mason on the back. "And this here's my brother, Mason," he said to the girl. "He used to be a Yankee."

And here they went. Mason was mostly unfazed by people using his past notoriety for their own personal gain—this certainly wasn't the first time they'd done this act so Odell could pick up a girl. But still, it grated on him a little.

"You used to be a Yankee?" said the girl, her eyes wide. "Do you know Derek Jeter?"

Mason sighed. "I played with him for a couple of seasons, yeah. But we're not, like, best friends or anything."

That seemed to satisfy the girl, who nodded and hooked her arm around Odell's. "Jeter is so hot," she told Odell, who probably didn't care. Then she turned back to Mason. "Why did you stop playing? Did you get injured?"

Mason had answered this question many times in the four years since his contract had ended. For whatever reason, people thought it was noble to give up a career as a professional athlete because of an injury.

Odell shot him a warning look, but Mason didn't much care what he thought and also hoped Odell would go away so he could flirt with the cute bartender.

"I did get injured," Mason said. "It wasn't debilitating. I fell badly when I was running toward first base during a postseason game. Tore up the tendon in my foot." He pointed at his foot as if that would be enlightening. "It healed pretty well and I probably could have played a few more seasons in the minors at least, but I left when my contract was up."

"Why?" asked the girl. "How could you give that up?"

This was where it got dicey. For one thing, most people assumed that if you played ball professionally, you must have made millions of dollars. That had never been the case for Mason, who had been drafted right out of college and bounced around the minor leagues until he got called up to the Yankees. His first contract wasn't bad, and he'd made enough smart investments to keep him supplied with beer at sports bars with cute bartenders well into the future, but a millionaire he was not.

Also, Odell was now giving him the "I don't know what this girl's deal is, so tread carefully" look.

Fuck it, though.

"Well," Mason said, "I decided not to re-up my contract so that I could come out of the closet."

Odell rolled his eyes and gave Mason the finger behind the girl's back.

The girl's eyes went wide. "You're gay?"

It was hard to read her tone of voice. Surprised, yes, but it was not clear whether she thought this piece of news was good or bad. Mason inwardly braced himself for either possibility.

"Yes," Mason said. "I'm gay."

The bartender was hovering and seemed very interested in this piece of information.

The girl turned back to Odell. "It's really cool that you have a gay brother and that you two get along so well."

Score one for Odell. He grinned. "It *is* cool."

They flirted, so Mason turned back toward the bartender.

"My shift is up at ten," the guy said, sliding Mason a bar napkin. The name *Travis* was scrawled across the top above a phone number.

"Excellent," said Mason. "I live three blocks from here."

"How convenient," said Travis.

"I'm Mason, by the way."

"Yeah, I got that." Travis smiled. He had a dimple in his right cheek.

"I need to powder my nose," the girl said. "I'll be right back, sweetie."

When she was gone, Odell turned his triumphant smile back on Mason. Travis slid down the bar to help another customer.

"That could have gone badly," Odell said.

"Or it could have gone the way it did, which is that now your lady friend thinks you're sweet and sensitive because you're friends with your gay brother."

"Hmm."

"And honestly, do you want to go out with a girl who hates gay people?" Odell shrugged. "Date, no. Hook up with tonight, doesn't matter."

Mason suppressed a tired sigh. "What's the girl's name?"

"Bettina. Pretty name, right?"

"At least you have that much figured out."

She came back a few minutes later and smiled beatifically at Odell. When Odell suggested they leave, he gave Mason a fist bump and wished him luck with the bartender. Once Odell and Bettina were gone, Mason turned back to watch Travis work.

This guy Travis was basically every guy Mason had dated since last summer: athletic, muscular, too much testosterone. Every last one of them had been unfailingly wrong for him. Mason's friend Nate kept suggesting it was a sign that Mason should stop dating meatheads. He had a fair point; the parade of butch guys had not helped him forget that he'd had the best sex of his life in the bathroom at a gay bar in the East Village with a small, femme-y guy named Patrick the summer before. Mason didn't have high hopes that Travis would break the slump, but it might be fun to try anyway.

Still, the central problem was Mason thinking he should be with a guy like Travis but his dick thinking he wanted a guy like Patrick.

Mason's family had had a hard enough time with the gay thing, completely mystified that a guy as masculine as Mason could possibly be gay. Odell was better than their mother and her extended family, for the most part, but he grudgingly approved of guys like Travis. What the hell would any of them say about a guy like Patrick?

Patrick didn't lack athleticism. Hell, they'd met because they both played baseball in the Rainbow League, an LGBT amateur sports league in New York City. But Patrick had piercings and tattoos, and he talked too much. So even though that encounter had been awesome, once the baseball season had ended, Mason had—literally—kissed Patrick good-bye. They hadn't seen each other since. Mason had never bothered to reach out.

And in Mason's defense, Patrick hadn't tried to get in touch with him either.

So when Travis's replacement showed up and Travis shrugged into a very nice leather jacket, Mason was game, though he knew this couldn't last.

"Did I overhear you say you used to be a Yankee?" Travis asked as they walked outside.

Mason hated trading this bit of trivia about himself in exchange for sex, but since it was only for the night, he nodded.


THE WOMAN at Patrick's station had amazing hair. It was thick and wavy, naturally a bright caramel color, the sort of hair many women spent a lot of money trying to achieve. It made the crimes perpetrated against her hair such a shame.

He ran his fingers through it. God, it was healthy and silky too. If only all of his customers took such good care of their hair.

"They really butchered you," he said.

"I know. I said to leave it long in the front and short in the back, which is the opposite of what happened, and the layers are so uneven. Last time I'm going there."

"You came to the right place, girl. I can fix it. It'll be on the short side because I have to cut a lot to fix these uneven layers, but it'll look great, I promise."

"Cut as much as you need to. You are a lifesaver," said the woman. She frowned. "I literally cried when I looked in the mirror after I got home from the salon."

Her name was… Michelle? Patrick was terrible with names. He tended to remember his customers by their hair, and he liked to remember some bit of trivia about each so he could bring it up with his repeat customers. This one, with the thick caramel-colored waves, was a first-timer, here to fix the wretched haircut she'd gotten at some discount salon. Dimensions, where Patrick worked as a stylist, wasn't cheap, but it was a fantastic salon.

He spent the next twenty minutes repairing Thick Caramel Waves' hair, giving her a kicky bob that was trendy enough to be interesting but not so edgy that corporate America would balk. He learned as he was cutting her hair that she worked as a paralegal at a huge law firm in Midtown, so nothing too strange for her.

As he was finishing, his next customer—Black Dye Job, Color #315—came in. The whole day had been this way, back-to-back appointments, which was great for Patrick's wallet, but he was starting to get tired.

After he got Color #315 set up at a sink to get her hair washed, he checked in at the front desk. Valerie was on the phone, but she said, "Oh, he's right here, hang on." She put her hand over the mouthpiece and said, "You free next Tuesday night? It's for Melissa Schneider."

He had no idea who that was. It was irrelevant, though. "Baseball starts Tuesday. So, no, I'm not free."

Valerie tilted her head and looked at him quizzically. "Oh, right. I keep forgetting you do that baseball thing." Patrick knew his appearance didn't exactly scream "athlete."

He couldn't deny that he'd put on a few pounds over the winter, but not enough that he'd gone to waist. His fatigue was making him irritable, and he knew it, so he opted not to get defensive. "Well, I put my schedule in the computer, so the days I have games or practices should already be marked."

"Can you see Melissa on Friday, then?"

"Yeah, that's fine."

He left to go check on Color #315 and then slipped into the back room to mix up the color. It was nice to get out of the salon for a few minutes, although the mention of the impending baseball season was a reminder of what else this summer could bring. He was most looking forward to seeing Mason again, although he was a little worried about that too. Mason had made it pretty clear at the conclusion of their encounter at Barnstorm, the East Village bar Rainbow League members frequented, that it was a one-time thing. Which was a damn shame, because sex with Mason had been mind-blowing.

So, okay, they'd gotten off on the wrong foot. Patrick had put that foot right in his mouth, saying some pretty stupid things. Mason had rightly called him on something racist he'd said. Patrick had wanted a second chance, especially after he'd availed himself of Mason's amazing body. But then the season had ended without them exchanging contact information.

Patrick had pushed the encounter out of his mind. He'd spent part of the winter warming his bed with a sexy personal trainer who worked at the gym up the block from Dimensions, but that had ended as soon as the snow finally melted.

And still Patrick hadn't been able to stop thinking about Mason.

Which was really fucking stupid, because all they'd had was a quick fuck—a spectacular, sensational fuck, but a quick one nonetheless—in a bar bathroom, and yeah, Patrick had never had a hotter encounter, and Mason was so goddamned sexy, but they didn't know each other at all.

Probably they had nothing in common. And at the end of the day, what business did Patrick have with an ex-Yankee?

Patrick sighed and finished with the dye. Then he rejoined the chaos in the salon.


CARLOS WATCHED as Aiden did… whatever the hell he was doing. Pacing? Strutting? Looking for his underwear?

Carlos himself was on the bed in Aiden's apartment, the big down comforter pulled over his groin, but otherwise just as naked as Aiden, who, yes, was displaying his spectacular body, but also was kind of freaking Carlos out.

So Carlos said, "Uh, what are you—"

"Sorry, I have a lot of nervous energy."

Carlos sighed and sank back into the pillows. He'd learned a lot in the not-quite-a-year he and Aiden had dated, so he knew that this was one of their strange incompatibilities. For whatever reason, a good orgasm always made Aiden want to run laps, while Carlos just wanted to curl into a ball and fall asleep.

On the nightstand, his phone buzzed. Carlos grabbed it. A text message from his best friend, Nate, flashed on the screen: *You see that play?!*

"Hey, if you're going to skulk around, can I put the game on?"

Aiden turned toward the bed and tilted his head. "Uh. Game?"

"The Yankees?"

"Yeah, sure, whatever."

Carlos crawled across the bed to grab the remote on Aiden's side table. He flipped on the TV and cycled through the channels until he found the Yankees game. Luckily they were still showing a slow-motion loop of the play Nate must have texted about. A clean double play had ended the inning. The Yanks were up by three runs.

Carlos picked up his phone and texted back: *Yeah, that was great!*

Aiden sat at the foot of the bed and stared at the TV for a moment. When the game went to commercial, he turned around and looked at Carlos. "How can you watch this?"

It took a lot for Carlos not to make a sarcastic comment. "Uh, dude. We both play in a hobby baseball league. If you were not aware that I was a baseball fan, I don't know what to tell you. You should have seen that coming."

Aiden turned back toward the TV. Carlos took a moment to admire the line of his back. Then Aiden spoke again. "TV baseball is so boring."

Not the first time they'd had this argument, so Carlos just said, "Disagree," and turned up the volume.

Aiden announced he was going to go for a run, so Carlos spent the next forty minutes watching the game and texting Nate.

When Aiden returned, he jogged right through the bedroom and into the bathroom. Then he stuck his head back out. "You just gonna lie there?"

Carlos shrugged. "Game's almost over, *papi*. I figured once you were done working through your energy burst, I'd talk you back into bed and we could...." He waggled his eyebrows.

Aiden laughed. "You're insatiable."

"True."

"Let me just hose off some of the sweat from my run."

"You're just going to get sweaty again."

"I know, but...." He pointed back into the bathroom. Then he went inside and closed the door.

Carlos rolled his eyes and went back to his text conversation discussing the relative hotness of the Yankees' rookie outfielder.

Carlos and Nate had never had anything like romantic feelings for each other, so Carlos had made a habit of keeping his relationships with Nate and Aiden in separate boxes. Maybe that was a problem, given that he'd seen a lot less of Nate since he'd started spending more time with Aiden. Carlos made a note to make it up to Nate soon, though.

As the game ended with a Yankee victory, Carlos texted, *Gotta go. As soon as Aiden is out of the shower, I expect to be too busy with other things to look at my phone. ;)*

*Gross* was the reply.

Then: *Have fun. Go Yankees!*

And that about summed things up.

# Chapter 2

MASON FREELANCED as a writer for Sports Net, covering primarily stories relating to gay athletes. The job made him feel pigeonholed sometimes, but the pay was pretty good. He suspected his ex-Yankee status had secured him a higher paycheck than he might have received otherwise, but he didn't question it with his boss, Jim, who was the website's head features editor.

Jim was also a member of the Rainbow League, the second baseman for the SoHoMos. He'd been the one to tell Mason about the league to begin with, lo those many years ago when Mason had recovered—more or less—from the whirlwind in which a torn tendon had ended his season and then a decision to tell the truth had ended his career. Mason had been adrift back then, happy to be out and proud of what he'd accomplished, but mourning the end of his career and the game he'd loved so much. When Jim had offered the job at Sports Net, it had come with the information about the league, in Jim's backward way: "By the way, there's a gay baseball league in New York. It might be your speed."

So Mason would always be grateful to Jim for giving him baseball back, even if it was in an amateur league.

When Jim called in June, just before the new season started, and asked Mason to lunch, Mason agreed. He steeled himself for work talk as he walked down the block to the sushi place in Midtown Jim had chosen. He assumed Jim wanted to talk about the fact that Mason's story about an up-and-coming baseball phenom was late. The kid was currently playing for the Rice University Owls and had just sent an earnest e-mail to all of his classmates in which he came out of the closet; one of the classmates had forwarded that e-mail to Jim's assistant. Mason had flown to Texas the week before to interview the kid, who had proven to be a rosy-cheeked, soft-spoken nineteen-year-old with a cute blond boyfriend, and he kept repeating the old standby lines like "I'm living my truth" and "I just want to play baseball." Mason had thought, *Yeah. I've been there*.

But he'd hit a brick wall when writing up the story, primarily because he was getting tired of how repetitive this news had become, partly because he'd stopped believing gay athletes should be considered notable or newsworthy. Athletes were athletes, gay or straight. This poor kid didn't want to be the feature of a story on a big-name sports website any more than Mason wanted to have a tooth pulled, and as soon as that became clear, Mason lost interest in writing it. Still, if he expected to get his next paycheck, he needed to write *something*.

Jim was already at the restaurant when Mason arrived. Jim was one of the Rainbow League's older members, in his midforties if Mason's guess was right. He had thinning blond hair and a softer belly than many of the other players in the league, but he could run fast and throw hard. Mason liked him; they had made these lunches part of their routine, meeting every other week or so to discuss stories since Mason didn't like working in the office and had enough clout to get away with not being chained to a desk.

As Mason walked across the restaurant, Jim alternated between perusing the menu and looking at his phone. Mason didn't think he was late, but he felt a pang of guilt for making Jim wait. He walked over to the table and slid into a chair.

"Oh, hey," Jim said, glancing up from his phone. Then he looked back and typed something with his thumb. "Sorry, Ken is upset about something. I'm not really sure what. I think it has to do with the apartment renovation."

Mason chuckled. The renovation of Jim and his partner Ken's Upper East Side apartment had been a comedy of errors since the beginning, starting with the fight they'd gotten into with their co-op board about renovating at all and followed by the incompetent contractors Ken had hired and the colony of mice living in their kitchen walls. The last time Mason and Jim had eaten lunch together, Jim had been ready to have the city condemn the whole building.

Jim sighed and put his phone down. "How are you, Mason?"

Mason shrugged. "I'm all right."

"Ready for the new baseball season?"

"I suppose."

Jim waved his hand. "Oh, you are. Don't play nonchalant with me. You've been itching to play again since last season ended."

This was true, although a great deal of pain in his left foot and leg had hampered his ability to play; he'd gone through surgery again in December to repair a tear and had gotten a stern lecture from his doctor about overdoing it. So while he wanted to play baseball again, he was worried about further injury. Maybe, at thirty-two, he was just too old.

That was a depressing thought.

"I'm excited, yeah," Mason said.

Jim smiled. "We got a new guy on our team this season, just signed up last weekend. He played in the league in Boston."

Mason grimaced. "Is he a Sox fan?"

"'Fraid so, but I figure that will just fire him up when we have to play your team." Jim picked up the menu. "I'm feeling daring today. You want to order the chef's special and play Russian roulette with our taste buds?"

Mason agreed, so they ordered and Jim asked about the piece about the kid from Rice. Mason tried explaining his issue but felt like he wasn't clearly articulating what he felt.

"This is the fourth time a kid on a college sports team has come out in this academic year," Mason said, "and to make matters worse, the semester's almost over. This kid, I don't know. I believe he's sincere, but it feels so safe to come out at the end of the season."

"Yes, but he's only a sophomore. He's still got next year to think about."

Mason sighed. "I suppose he's giving his teammates the summer to think about it."

"They still have to play together. NCAA finals aren't for another week."

Mason nodded. "Anyway, my point was really that this is the fourth coming out like this since September. The first for baseball, sure, but these college kids… I think these stories will go the way of coming out on the cover of *People* magazine."

Jim tilted his head. He knew well that Mason himself had appeared on the cover of *People* magazine soon after he'd publicly come out.

Jim frowned.

"I think," Mason said, "that for college athletes, the way we should handle these stories is to profile the top athletes and then, if they happen to be gay, that's a sixth paragraph mention. Like, 'Joe Smith attributes some of his success to his support network, including his boyfriend Bob,' or whatever. That gets the message across without making the kid's sexuality the story."

"Is that how you want to play this one?"

The waitress plopped a bowl of edamame on their table, so Mason helped himself. "Maybe," said Mason.

"I mean, Rice made the NCAA finals this year. Their team is solid. A bunch of the seniors are bound for pro teams. I've seen the scouting reports, Mason, and just up and down, this team has got the goods. Brian Fox is notable because he's only a sophomore, but he's already good enough to compete alongside this group of athletes. You want that to be your story, go with it. But I want you to include something about the kid's coming out without getting too preachy about it."

"Too preachy?"

Jim tilted his head again. "I just don't want a feature article to become a referendum on how we should cover gay athletes. You want to write an editorial about the subject, I'll see if I can talk my boss into running it, but leave that out of this article, okay?"

"Yeah, fine." Mason let out a breath. He knew he had Jim's support, he was just tired of this particular narrative. So maybe he'd call everyone's bluff and play down the gay stuff.

"Anyway," Mason said. "He's a nice kid. Good head on his shoulders. He was nothing but polite the whole time I talked to him. And he's got a hell of an arm. I haven't seen anyone so young throw a ball so hard in a long time. I've got enough for a story, just, you know."

"Yeah. I know."

Their lunch arrived on a cutting board shaped like a large fish. There were a dozen pieces of sashimi and four different rolls arranged symmetrically on the fish. The waitress, in a thick accent, identified everything, but Mason couldn't understand half of what she said. He picked up a piece of what he thought was tuna.

As they ate and the conversation drifted over to the Yankees—Jim and Ken were season ticket holders and Jim was always eager for Mason's opinions on the team's current lineup, even though Mason only knew a few of them personally—Jim's attention suddenly got snared by something behind Mason. Then he sat up a little straighter and waved. "Oh, hey, Patrick."

Mason turned, figuring it was another Sports Net staffer coming for lunch. But no. It was actually *his* Patrick. Crazy-haired, tattooed, pierced, twinky Patrick, who, Mason only now remembered, played for the same Rainbow League team as Jim.

He had a canvas backpack slung over one shoulder, and he hoisted it slightly as he walked to the table. He shot Mason a wary look and then turned toward Jim. "Uh. Hey," he said.

Jim smiled. "What brings you to the neighborhood?"

"Oh, I, uh, was just going to get takeout. I'm taking a class at the salon up the block and they only gave us twenty minutes for lunch."

"Oh, that's too bad. I would have invited you to join us. You know Mason Brooks, right? He plays in the Rainbow League for the Hipsters."

Patrick gave Mason a little smirk. "Yeah, we've met."

Mason felt that in his chest, in his cock. This guy was still incredibly sexy. He was a lot of cocky swagger packed into a lithe little body that had been carefully decorated. Today he wore fairly mundane clothes—a pristine white T-shirt and a pair of jeans with tears across the thighs that had probably been sold that way—but he looked clean and that T-shirt pulled across his chest in a way that didn't make Mason work too hard to picture what was underneath it. His hair was a riot of colors—blond, pink, purple, blue—fanned out in a quasi-mohawk with the longest bits falling into his face. He had a ring in his eyebrow and several in each ear, which caught the bright light of the restaurant. A number of different tattoos went up both of his arms, all of them colorful too, though they blended and fit together in a way that made the shapes seem indistinguishable. Mason imagined he could spend all afternoon studying those tattoos and still not see every detail.

Mason found the whole package unspeakably hot, but he told himself to calm down because this was certainly not the sort of man he had any business fooling around with. Even though he totally already had.

"Nice to see you again, Patrick," Mason said.

"I'm sure it is, honey," said Patrick.

Mason didn't think he imagined how electric it was between them, how parts of Patrick seemed wired to parts of Mason. That damned smirk made Mason's cock as hard as if Patrick had access to an On/Off switch in Mason's body.

Dear Lord. Everything about Patrick was the opposite of what Mason needed. He didn't picture himself with a guy like Patrick, not in the long term. He would have been lying if he said he didn't want Patrick, but he certainly did not need this nonsense in his life. Not to mention that before their super hot encounter in the men's room at Barnstorm, Patrick had let slip from his mouth a number of mildly offensive things. Mason needed to stop fantasizing about this guy, because they had no future.

He took a deep breath. He was trying to come up with something clever and flirty to say, if only to give Patrick a taste of his own medicine, but then the guy working the host stand said, "Patrick?"

"My order's ready," Patrick said. "Toodle-oo, boys. I'll see you at practice, Jim. Mason, I guess I'll see you when the new season starts. I think our teams are playing each other the first week."

"All right. I'll see you," Mason said.

Patrick sauntered over to the host and grabbed his food and then sauntered out.

"Patrick is a character," said Jim.

"Yeah," said Mason.


PATRICK TOOK his sushi back to the salon, where he planned to shove his spicy tuna roll in his mouth in the back room before resuming this refresher class on cutting layers with a razor. Dirk, the owner of Dimensions, made each of his stylists take a class like this every six months or so to keep their advanced skills up. He considered it "professional development." Patrick could have cut circles around the other stylists in the class and generally thought this one was a waste of his time, but he was spending the day in one of the best salons in the city and working with hair models instead of real clients, so it wasn't awful. It was on Dirk's dime. Patrick figured he'd make the most of it.

Except that he'd randomly run into Mason eating lunch with Jim of all people, and now he'd lost his appetite. Was it a date? Didn't Jim have a boyfriend? And wasn't he, like, ten years older than Mason? What the hell was that about?

Was Patrick jealous?

He pushed into the employee break room at the back of the salon, where a few of his classmates were shoveling food in their mouths. He sat down at the big table and started unpacking his sushi rolls.

"Uh, Patty, you okay there?"

Patrick looked up. Sitting across the table was a stylist named Brooke, who Patrick knew mostly from these classes. She worked at a high-end salon in the Meatpacking District and also probably could have cut circles around the rest of the stylists in this class. She was pretty and a little chubby and had light brown hair with purple streaks in it.

He was too dazed to say anything but the truth. "Just ran into this guy I hooked up with last summer."

"Ah," said Brooke. "I hate when that happens."

Patrick laughed and shook himself to try to get back in the right mindset to eat his sushi. He picked up a little packet of soy sauce. To Brooke, he said, "It's kind of an opposites-attract thing. I don't know why I'm so hung up on him. We have nothing in common."

Brooke nodded sagely. "Been there."

"Yeah?"

She tilted her head. "I had a boyfriend in college. He was from Russia originally. He'd lived in the US long enough that he didn't have much of an accent, but he never quite got the hang of US culture."

"Okay."

"Smart guy, great in bed, but he had some backward opinions about women. Called all women 'chicks.' I wondered if it was an English-as-a-second-language thing, like maybe he'd heard someone else say 'chicks' and didn't understand how that came across, but then I figured out that he was more concerned with having a girlfriend who behaved in certain ways than having an actual relationship. And obviously, I am not the sort of conformist girl he was looking for." She ran her hand through the purple streaks in her hair as if to emphasize the point.

Patrick took a moment to admire how gorgeous her hair really was. It was something he noticed on people. Many hairdressers he knew actually had really rough hair, which puzzled him. Maybe they spent so much time on other people's hair they couldn't be bothered to make their own look nice. His coworker Deenie, for example, had recently gone green, but her hair was so dry it looked brittle and frizzy all the time. Not a great look. But Brooke had healthy, glossy hair that fell just past her shoulders.

But he was getting off track. "I mean, not that it even matters," Patrick said. "It was just a one-time thing."

"Is he hot?"

"Very. But again, doesn't matter."

"So what happened?"

Patrick shrugged, regretting having brought it up at all. He supposed he had wanted to talk about Mason, but he really didn't know Brooke well. "Just now or—"

"Last summer. One-night thing? And just now you had an awkward encounter?"

"Yeah, basically. He was having lunch with another guy."

"That sucks."

Patrick laughed. "Yeah. We hooked up once last summer, it was awesome, but then we lost touch. I'd like to do it again, but I don't know if that'll happen."

Brooke smiled. "You're not going to track him down and declare your love like in a romantic comedy movie?"

"Well, I don't have to track him very far. We play in the same baseball league. I'll see him again soon enough."

Brooke narrowed her eyes. "You play baseball?"

Patrick sighed. "I know. I get that a lot. But, yeah, I do. In a gay baseball league."

Brooke laughed. "What won't they think of next?"

Sensing she was going to make a joke based on her perception that everyone in the league was a femme-y twink like he was—and he'd heard it all before, including from guys who thought it was funny to be lispy and fey while miming hitting a ball and running around the bases—Patrick shoved the last of his sushi roll in his mouth, barely tasting it, and then started packing up his trash.

And he realized how he was reacting.

"I should try again with him," Patrick said, mostly to himself.

"I agree," said Brooke. "I don't even know this guy, but if you're this hung up on him, I think you owe it to yourself."

"Yeah." Patrick looked at the wall clock. "Well. Let's go cut some hair."

MASON'S CELL phone rang as he was walking back into his apartment a few hours later. He had to drop his grocery bags to fish his phone out of his pocket. He grumbled a little when he saw the caller was his agent.

It wasn't even like Mason heard from his agent much anymore. But he kept the man on retainer because the rare endorsement deal did still get thrown his way, and he liked having a filter between himself and the media. It had been a good long while since he'd gotten anything like an interview request—he'd been out of both the major league and the closet for coming up on four years now, so he was old news—but it made him feel better to let someone else field those calls.

He presumed that was what was happening here.

"How do you feel about Columbus?" Davis asked.

"The explorer?"

"The city in Ohio."

Mason sighed, trying to pick his grocery bags up with one hand so he could at least carry them to the kitchen before the ice cream melted all over his nice wood floors. "I've never been."

"The organizers of Columbus Pride want you to be the grand marshal in their parade in three weeks."

Mason managed to wrestle his grocery bags onto the kitchen counter without dropping the phone. "Was I their fifth choice or what?" he said. It wasn't the first sort of invitation he'd received—hell, he'd been a headliner on a float at New York Pride the year after he'd come out—but it still seemed unlikely that a has-been such as himself would be picked for anything.

"No, actually. The guy I talked to said they wanted you from the start. I think he's got a crush."

Mason stopped what he was doing and leaned on the counter. He liked Davis, but Davis had a way of making any attention Mason was getting these days sound lecherous and inappropriate. Maybe Mason was projecting because he wasn't comfortable being publicly objectified— perhaps he should have been flattered—but still, this bugged him. He probably never would have been a Hall-of-Fame-worthy player, though he'd been batting .260 his last season and had hit a hundred home runs over the three seasons he played for the Yankees. Nothing to sneeze at. After he'd torn up that tendon in his foot during a bad slide into first base during the ALCS his last season, though, his doctor started making noise about him never being able to run fast enough to play professional baseball again. And so he'd made a decision.

"Yeah, okay," Mason said. "I'll do it. But, and no offense to Columbus, do you think this is a downgrade?"

"You want to stay in the spotlight or not?"

"Not, actually."

Davis let out a long-suffering sigh. "Look, you want to keep your fancy Manhattan apartment, you're going to need more endorsements. I'm working on one now for pain ointment that could be pretty lucrative, but only if you get your face out there enough that people remember who the hell you are."

Davis had a point, but…. "Ugh, pain ointment? What am I, an old geezer?"

"You're a retired athlete, Mason. It's not like you can get Gatorade or Nike anymore."

Mason groaned.

Davis clucked his tongue. "Look, you should be glad that we've come far enough as a society for you to still be getting endorsements at all. Ten years ago you would have been finished the moment you announced you were gay."

"I know." Mason knew that better than anyone.

"I'm just saying, I can get you a good deal, but I need you to do these little public appearances. You really should reconsider the talk-show circuit. Especially with all these kids coming out. You hear about this baseball player at Rice?"

Mason rubbed his forehead and considered hanging up. "Yeah, yeah, I hear you."

"If that kid gets signed by a major league team, he could be the first out gay baseball player since Iggy Rodriguez."

Mason sighed. He had nothing but respect for Rodriguez, who had come out two years after Mason had. And, if nothing else, all the fanfare around that had taken the focus off Mason—much to his delight and Davis's chagrin—because Rodriguez was both still active and far more talented than Mason could ever wish to be.

Still, grand marshal of a Pride parade, even if it was in Columbus, was not too shabby. He glanced at his foot and figured he was lucky to have been able to play baseball in Yankee Stadium at all.

"So think about the talk shows," Davis was saying.

"I'm writing about the kid from Rice in my column."

"That's not enough. You want this endorsement deal, you need to at least make a couple of daytime talk-show appearances. The company wants a spokesman that people actually recognize. Most of America probably can't pick you out of a lineup."

Mason winced. He couldn't think of anything he wanted to do less than be on TV. "I'll think about it."

"That's all I ask. Anyway, the Columbus Pride people offered to handle your airfare and hotel, so I'll let them know you're in and to be in touch with the details. All right?"

"Fine."

Mason got off the phone and started putting away his groceries, feeling a little rattled now. He hated the business of being an ex-Yankee, and it was something he had hoped would go away with time.

He'd made the decision to come out in a short amount of time, in the scheme of things, even if it had felt like it had been years in the making. He'd played college baseball on scholarship and put up good numbers, but he never expected to get drafted by the Yankees. He'd cried like a baby when the news came down.

At the time, he'd been so far in the closet, he hadn't seen a way out. He'd been—mostly—celibate in college in order to keep anyone from finding out the truth. Getting drafted felt like higher stakes, so he'd kept it in his pants when he was in the minors too, aside from a brief affair with the Staten Island Yankees' pitching coach, which only worked out because of the hovering threat of mutually assured destruction. But that hadn't lasted, and then Mason had been called up to the majors.

Sexual frustration and loneliness had plagued Mason through a lot of his career as a Yankee, but he overcompensated by going out with his teammates a lot and cultivating an active social life. He hit on women when his teammates were around, but he never took any of them home and developed a reputation for being kind of a prude. That was fine with Mason, until the night he met another closeted athlete who got his heart racing.

That hadn't really worked out either—how could it have?—but it was mere weeks after that affair had ended that Mason ripped up his foot.

He'd been lying on an uncomfortable bed in the hospital with his leg in traction when everything seemed to come into focus. His contract was up at the end of the season and the Yankees seemed disinclined to renew it, and though a few teams had put out feelers, Mason had no firm plan in place for next season. Probably Davis could have negotiated something, but being a free agent meant Mason wasn't obligated to play the next season. Not that he would be able to, because the doctor had pretty much forbidden him from doing anything athletic in the offseason.

So fuck it, Mason had thought while lying on that bed. He'd had a good run. He'd lived his dream, even if it was only for a short time. The foot injury was bad enough that the doctors thought it would always bother him, and maybe he could have done a few seasons in the minors, but likely he'd be out altogether by his thirtieth birthday.

He had a vision of finally having the freedom of movement retirement would grant him—in his head, anyway—and being in his thirties, long past his prime. So what would be the greater regret? Spending the rest of his twenties celibate or trying to eke out a career despite a bad foot and long odds that he'd ever get called back up to the majors?

Maybe it had been the painkillers talking, but he'd known what he had to do.

He'd called Davis the next day and said, "I'm done. I'll wait out this contract, but then I'm coming out of the closet and saying good-bye to baseball."

"You're gay?" Davis had spluttered.

But he'd gotten over it, thankfully. Davis had actually been the one to urge Mason to go public, and at the time, Mason had enough rage and frustration that finally putting everything out there had felt like the best course of action. He didn't regret it, exactly, but he didn't like the public attention.

Now he was living off the money he'd made by smartly investing his Yankees salary, supplemented with the occasional product endorsement deal, because even the decent salary he made writing features for Sports Net wasn't quite enough to keep Mason in the life he was accustomed to. For a while Davis got him commercials and endorsements primarily because he'd been a novelty, but lately clothing brands were giving him the most attention. Davis argued that even if he didn't play baseball professionally, he still *looked* like an athlete. Of course, Davis thought he should develop a second career as a model, but Mason had hard limits about how often he could stand to get his picture taken.

Anyway, if he never got another endorsement deal, he'd figure it out. He'd sell his second house or move to a more modest apartment. He didn't really *want* to do those things, but weighed against the prospect of posing in front of a camera....

He sighed. Now that he'd saved his ice cream from certain destruction and he'd put away the rest of his groceries, Mason walked back to his living room and plopped down on the sofa. The phone rang again before he could flip on the TV.

It was Odell.

"I was thinking for Mom's birthday that we could go to that seafood place in the Bronx she likes," Odell said.

"What place?"

"You know, the one with the crab on the sign? We went there a couple of years ago."

Mason sighed. "The one on City Island?"

"Sure." Odell didn't sound confident. Probably he had no idea where the place was.

"Yeah, that's fine. When? Next weekend? Should I call and make a reservation?"

"Nah, I'll do it. Uh. Do you have the number?"

"They have this thing called the Internet now. You can use it to find phone numbers."

Odell scoffed but grumbled that he'd take care of it. Mason decided to change the subject. "How'd it go with the girl from the bar?"

"Bettina? I'm seeing her again on Friday."

"That's good."

"And you and the bartender... I mean, not that I even want to know, but you hooked up with that guy, right?"

"Yeah. Not sure if I'm seeing him again."

"That bad?"

"No, just… you know how it is."

"Sure."

Mason wondered if Odell actually did understand. Probably he did. Odell's last girlfriend dumped him when she discovered Odell had been seeing one of his coworkers on the side, so it wasn't like Odell was sheltered or oblivious.

"Anyway," Odell said, "I'll make a reservation at this place and text you the time."

"Thanks."

"Mom is, uh, doing pretty well these days, yeah?"

Mason wasn't sure what to make of the question. "She was the last time I talked to her."

"Oh, it's probably just me being dumb, then. She was kind of weird when I called her to tell her to save the date for her birthday dinner."

"Weird how?"

"Like she didn't want to go."

That was odd. Mason's mother had always made time for her sons, despite the busy work schedule that came with the single-mom territory. She worked fewer hours now that her kids had flown the nest, but she still had some workaholic tendencies. She kept busy and wasn't home much, but Mason had always found she'd make time if he wanted to see her.

"Maybe she just doesn't want to be reminded of her age," Mason said, mentally calculating how old she was. Fifty-eight, if his math was right. Which meant it had been almost twenty-five years since Mason's father had taken off for parts unknown. Like any of them needed a reminder.

"Maybe," said Odell. "Well, anyway. I gotta go make this reservation. I'll see you this weekend, all right?"

Once Mason hung up, he turned off his cell phone and put it on the coffee table. Then he leaned forward and put his head in his hands.

# Chapter 3

MASON WALKED to the field, feeling limber and ready to play baseball.

All Rainbow League games took place at the ball fields in East River Park, in the shadow of the FDR Drive and the Williamsburg Bridge. It got noisy sometimes with the buzz of cars whizzing by on the street, but the ball field where they usually played was right on the water, which muffled the car sounds. The park was a little out of the way, in that it was a fair distance from public transportation, but Mason had always liked it. That, and it was a convenient few blocks from Barnstorm in Alphabet City.

When Mason arrived at the field, everyone was talking at once. Nate and Carlos were tossing a ball back and forth while jabbering about the previous night's Yankees game. Ty and Ian seemed to be having some kind of argument. Mason couldn't tell if they were being playful or not. He walked a little closer to eavesdrop.

"First of all," Ty was saying, "as I already told you, I don't want to leave Brooklyn. Second, your apartment doesn't have space for all my stuff. We'd have to at least get a two-bedroom so I can have an art studio."

"But your place is so far from my job," said Ian. "And you're the one who thought I should sign a longer lease on my apartment. There are still five months left on it."

"Boys," Mason interrupted, "we're supposed to be friends and teammates. No time for fighting. Take your domestic quarrels off the field."

Ty shot Mason an astonished look. He waved his hand. "Whatever, dude."

Ian rolled his eyes. "It's not really a domestic disturbance. This is *supposed* to be good news for us. The lease on Ty's apartment is up soon, so we've decided to move in together, but where we move is a sticking point."

That felt like big news—Ty and Ian had only been dating about a year, and now they were thinking of moving in together?—but Ian rattled it off as if it were just the normal course of things, like telling Mason they were going out for ice cream after practice.

"Don't you like Brooklyn?" Ty asked Ian.

Ian patted Ty on the shoulder. "I like it fine, Texas. But Mason is right. We should take this argument off the field."

Ty shrugged. "How are you, Mason? Long time no see."

"I'm good. Happy to be playing baseball again."

"Aren't we all?"

Ian playfully punched Ty in the arm. "Weren't you just complaining about all the weight you always put on in the off-season?"

"Actually, I weighed myself yesterday. I didn't even gain a pound." Ty made a bodybuilder pose. "I guess it's all that, ah, working out I did this winter." He elbowed Ian.

"More information than I needed, guys," said Mason.

"Like you haven't had your pick of the beefcakes," said Ty.

Mason shrugged. He had gone on a second date with that bartender Travis, but he wasn't really feeling it. Their nights together were… fine. Travis was objectively hot, but they didn't have much chemistry. "Who are we playing tonight?"

"Was the glitter not a giveaway?" Ian asked, pointing.

Mason silently cursed himself for forgetting that he already knew. His team, the Brooklyn Hipsters, was playing the SoHoMos, a team that reveled in its queerness. Their uniform shirts this season were electric blue and their team name was scrawled across the front in a frilly script font above a picture of a unicorn. A bunch of the players had body glitter on their arms or faces or in their hair. Mason thought the whole thing was a little silly, but this was not his primary concern.

Patrick played for the 'Mos.

Patrick of the swishy walk and ridiculous hair. Patrick who had given him one crazy night in the men's room at Barnstorm. Patrick who Mason had been unable to stop thinking about. Patrick who Mason had no business being attracted to. Though he was. So much.

He did a quick scan of the field and saw the man in question preening for one of his teammates. His hair was as crazy as ever, though gelled into spikes now. His delicate features belied an athletic body, and though he was short and pierced and tattooed and talked too much, Mason was thoroughly and completely in lust.

The Hipsters' manager, Scott, started barking out orders so the game could get underway, thus saving Mason from thinking further on the matter.

PATRICK SPENT most of the game trying to decide if he should talk to Mason, and thus he spent the entire game not talking to Mason.

He knew he'd screwed up before. In a bad attempt at flirting, Patrick had asked if it was true what they said about black men. Mason had gotten offended. In his defense, Mason did have a big cock, so the guessing he did based on his skin color was perhaps gauche, but proved accurate.

Still, he'd gotten the impression that Mason didn't like him much beyond the sexy bits—which Patrick felt confident all parties could agree were completely awesome—and that was a damn shame, because Patrick was pretty cool, if he did say so himself, and Mason was so very smoking hot. If Patrick was honest with himself, he could admit that the part of him that craved validation wanted some sign from Mason that he wasn't completely worthless. He certainly wanted a round two. Maybe in a bed this time.

The 'Mos lost the game fairly spectacularly, which was a bummer but not really a surprise. The team cleared the field pretty fast after the last out, and Patrick fell in with his teammates on the walk to Barnstorm. Most of the Brooklyn team lingered, chatting and taking their sweet time getting their gear packed up. Patrick gave Mason a quick parting glance and then followed his team to the bar.

Barnstorm was kind of a dive, but it had a certain charm. It was the official bar of the Rainbow League for coming up on a decade. It was vaguely baseball themed, with sports paraphernalia everywhere and one wall adorned with photos of Rainbow League games and retired jerseys from players who had moved on. Barnstorm's owner, Tom, often worked the bar on game nights. He was a big, jovial man who seemed to love baseball and men with equal measure; he kept a photo of himself and his late partner at a Pride parade hanging on a wooden column near the bar. Although it wasn't the sort of place Patrick would have frequented otherwise, he liked Barnstorm and had a lot of happy memories of the place. It was a great spot to get a drink after a game.

He was halfway through his Cosmo when the bulk of the Hipsters arrived. Patrick couldn't really remember anyone's name, besides Mason's, obviously. Hot Ginger and Dishwater Blond were clearly a couple. Brown Dad Cut had on a wedding ring. Puerto Rican Buzz Cut came in with his BFF Auburn McGee. They were all one big, chummy unit.

So Patrick bided his time, sucking down a couple of cocktails and chatting with his teammates. Most of the Hipsters only stayed for a round or two before departing. That left Mason by himself at the bar. Patrick steeled himself and decided to make a move.

He walked up to Mason and said, "Hi!" Then he mentally rolled his eyes. All wit and class, that was Patrick.

"Hi," said Mason. "Uh, how are you?"

*Deep breath*, he told himself. *Just put it all out there.* "It's okay. You don't have to pretend. Just, see, the last time we were alone, I pretty much put both feet in my mouth. We don't know each other and you may not even want to know me, but I can't help but think that people who connect so well physically may connect just as well in other ways, so I'd love it if you gave me a second chance."

Mason stared for a long moment. He took a sip of his beer. Then he said, "Okay."

"Okay? That's all? Just okay?"

"Isn't that what you want to hear?"

Patrick grunted. He put his martini glass on the bar and then hopped onto the stool next to Mason. "So, okay, yeah, I guess it is. I mean, mostly I want to have sex with you again, if we're being honest, but I have a hard time getting it up for guys who hate me, no matter how hot they are."

Mason smiled at that. "I don't hate you."

"I get the impression you don't like me much."

"So change my opinion."

Wow, Mason really wasn't giving much away. He sat so still, cool as a cucumber, not even remotely as ruffled as Patrick felt. "I'm sorry for what I said and I totally get why it was wrong and I want to start over." Patrick ran a hand through his hair, making sure it stuck out the way he wanted it to.

"You're forgiven. It really wasn't... my back was up that day, is all. I was more defensive than I might have been otherwise. I mean, you should be careful about what you say sometimes, but... I forgive you. Forget it. Let's start over."

Patrick smiled, feeling giddy and relieved. "I'm Patrick. I'm a hairdresser. I think you're super sexy."

Mason held out his hand. "I'm Mason. I write about sports. I also think you're super sexy."

"Oh. Good."

"I mean, I'll be honest." Mason leaned forward a little, closing the space between himself and Patrick.

Patrick could smell him. The scent was male musk and baby powder, salty sweat, dirt, man. It was heady. Patrick took a deep breath to inhale more of it. Mason's scent seemed to permeate Patrick's skin everywhere, making him tingle, making him hard. It was as if all he needed was the memory of that one dirty encounter to make his body react, yearn for more.

He had nothing in common with Mason, not really. Just mutual attraction and baseball.

But did it matter? If they were hot for each other, didn't they kind of owe it to the gods of good sex to see that through?

"What?" Patrick said softly, remembering that Mason had said something.

"I said, I'll be honest. You're not my usual type."

"Oh." *Fuck*.

"But I have not been able to stop thinking about you since last summer."

Mason placed one of his big hands on Patrick's shoulder. It was warm and close, and suddenly Patrick could imagine being folded up in those strong arms, being held, being kissed, being fucked.

"Me neither," said Patrick. "Well, I mean, I think about me all the time, but I haven't been able to stop thinking about you either, and that's weird for me."

Mason leaned even closer, so Patrick slid off the barstool and stepped forward until their faces were mere inches apart. With Mason sitting on a stool, their heights were close to even. Mason's lips were *right there*, and Patrick wanted to kiss him but wasn't sure how cool Mason would be with that.

"So not my type," Mason muttered. Then he kissed Patrick.

Patrick didn't have to be persuasive. He didn't have to use words or debate. All he had to do was kiss Mason, because surely Mason felt how incredible this was. The kiss was concrete evidence that *something* good was between them. The kiss had perfect pressure, was warm and tingly and just right, and Patrick couldn't get enough of Mason's salty taste. When Patrick felt a big hand on his back, he stepped closer, pressing his chest against Mason's and snaking his hands around Mason's waist.

It was over all too soon.

"Of course, we're in a bar," Mason said.

"A gay bar."

"Sure, but we don't have to give everyone here a show."

Patrick considered their options. He wasn't that excited about the restroom—the one at Barnstorm was clean, but they'd already done it there that one time, and because they were somewhat outmatched size-wise, it was hot but required some tricky gymnastics.

"Where do you live?" Mason asked. "I'm in Hell's Kitchen, but if you're closer…."

Patrick almost died. He recovered and said, "Well, darling, I live on Stanton, just a few blocks from here, but my three other roommates are probably there just waiting to see what kind of hunk of man I bring home this time."

Mason raised his eyebrows. "Do you bring home a lot of hunky men?"

Patrick grinned. "Well, not a *lot*. Just, my roommates are nosy. I think Wendy is actually keeping a running log so that, when faced with some sort of transgression such as leaving the toilet seat up or drinking the last of her beer, she can confront me with the fact that I am an unrepentant slut, as if that were evidence of my being a bad roommate. But I suspect that sleeping with anyone would make me seem slutty to her. As far as I can tell, she doesn't even masturbate."

Mason wrinkled his nose and shook his head. "I have a hell of a time following you sometimes."

"Just wait, darling. We're only beginning to get to know each other."

"So what you're telling me is that we should go to my place."

"I mean, if you want to."

Mason put a few bills on the bar and slid off his stool. He stood a good six or eight inches taller than Patrick, but Patrick could work with that. On a bed. Which was where they were headed.

"You really have three roommates?" Mason asked as he started to walk toward the door.

"Cutting hair is not the most lucrative profession."

Mason put his hand on the small of Patrick's back, which Patrick found somewhat endearing. He smiled up at Mason, who smiled back.

"Let's get a cab," said Mason.

# Chapter 4

PATRICK WAS impressed. Mason's Hell's Kitchen apartment was in a high-rise building with marble floors in the lobby and a doorman and everything. Mason waved at the doorman as he walked in. Patrick could do nothing but trail behind him into the elevator.

They got off on one of the upper floors—Patrick missed which number it was, but it had two digits—and okay, it wasn't the penthouse, but it was still a very nice apartment that Mason escorted Patrick into. It was clean and a bit spartan, masculine but not aggressively so. Patrick imagined Mason had a cleaning lady and got his groceries delivered and wallowed in the luxury his old pro-ball salary afforded him.

Mason didn't seem particularly interested in giving Patrick the tour, though. Instead, he tugged Patrick into a bedroom—just as neat as the living room he'd just walked through; the bed was made, even—and, oh, Mason was taking his shirt off. Jesus.

Patrick backed up against the wall for a moment and closed his eyes. This was overwhelming. It was one thing to fuck Mason in a bathroom stall because they were hot for each other and needed to get off, but it was another to be in Mason's space, part of his world. Patrick's apartment was sheer chaos, full of more stuff than actually fit and more roommates than should have probably been there and overnight guests and Wendy's underwear hanging to dry in the bathroom and all of the daily life insanity Patrick was used to. It wasn't this neatly ordered, clearly expensive life that Mason led.

Patrick felt Mason hovering over him.

"You okay?" Mason asked.

"Yeah, just needed a second." Patrick opened his eyes and gazed at that chest. Well, if he needed an incentive to push all his own nonsense aside, here it was. Mason's chest was something to behold, muscular and broad and brown. Mason was sweating a little, which lent his skin a healthy sheen. Lord, those pecs and those abs were incredible. Patrick couldn't keep his hands off, and he pressed his palms against Mason's nipples. He touched all that skin, felt the ridges of muscle, the roughness of Mason's little curly chest hairs, the sheer unblemished perfection of Mason's skin.

"Wow," Patrick breathed.

Mason chuckled. "Like what you see?"

"Oh, come now, honey. You can't be so modest that you don't know you've got it going on." Patrick shifted his exploration to cupping the round muscles of Mason's upper arms. "Oy."

"I'll show you more if you strip for me."

Patrick was suddenly self-conscious. Yes, they'd been together once before, but it had been a quickie without either of them taking their clothes off. Patrick had some strength in his body, but he was scrawny compared to Mason. "Hey, we have all the time in the world, right?" Patrick said. "Why rush it?"

"All right."

Mason ducked his head and kissed Patrick hard, drawing Patrick's attention entirely to the way their lips slid together—so tasty and perfect—and although Mason's hands were under his shirt, Patrick didn't figure out what he was up to until Mason broke the kiss and pulled off Patrick's shirt.

"Hey!"

"I want to see you naked," said Mason. "I mean, that was the point of you coming here, right?"

"Well, sure." Patrick laughed. He looked down at his own chest—flat, not especially muscular, but not fat or fleshy either—and looked at Mason's. His muscles had muscles, geez.

"Patrick?"

Patrick looked up and met Mason's gaze. He had dark eyes, with little flecks of lighter brown in the dim bedroom lighting. Those eyes really were pretty amazing now that Patrick was looking at them. Patrick laid a hand at the spot where Mason's neck met his back, cupped the ridge of his spine, and kissed Mason again.

Really, Patrick decided to let himself be manipulated. He'd take these hot kisses in exchange for losing his clothes. There had to be some kind of trade-off.

Mason put his hands on Patrick's waist and dipped his fingers into the edges of Patrick's baseball pants. Those fingers were warm and calloused and rough against Patrick's delicate skin, and then Mason got more assertive, shoving his hands down to cup Patrick's ass.

Mason moaned. "Oh, your ass. I've been wanting to touch it like this all night. Please lose the pants."

"Well, since you said 'please.'"

Patrick was nervous, but he wanted to be with Mason. Since last summer, he'd wanted to get Mason naked, wanted to see all that flesh exposed, wanted to fuck him again. If getting naked was part of the bargain—especially since Mason seemed to want it so bad—then so be it.

Patrick took a step back. He kicked off his sneakers, pulled off his socks, and stood up. Mason's own pants were unbuttoned—had Patrick done that?—and the bulge behind the fly was... significant. Patrick remembered that cock, salivated at the idea of getting near it again. It had gotten Patrick in trouble last time, sure, but Mason *did* have a big cock and had let Patrick fuck him anyway.

Arousal moved through Patrick, flushing his skin and making him hot everywhere. He took a deep breath and pushed down his pants, tugging the jock he still had on with them, exposing himself to Mason's gaze. He stepped out of the pants and stood before Mason completely naked. He looked up, worried about what he'd see in Mason's gaze.

Mason gazed back hungrily.

Okay, then.

Patrick stepped forward and grabbed for the fly of Mason's pants. He reached into Mason's underwear and felt that big hard cock.

Mason put his arms around Patrick and pulled him close again. He kissed Patrick and gnawed a little on Patrick's lower lip. Patrick pushed Mason's pants down his hips, exposing Mason's cock to the air, and then he thrust his hips forward until they pressed together.

Yes, that was it. That was magic right there. Mason groaned into Patrick's mouth and thrust his hips against Patrick's. Patrick grabbed both of their cocks and gave them a few hard strokes. That seemed to sizzle. It sent flames of pleasure and arousal through Patrick, made his skin dance and sing, made his brain short out.

"On the bed," Patrick said, pushing Mason toward it.

Mason sort of fell-sat on the edge of his bed, tugging his pants off as he did it. He pulled off his shoes and socks and then lay back on the bed, his legs splayed, his cock hard, his whole body hard and beautiful and *ready*.

Dear Lord.

Patrick crawled up the bed and sucked that big cock into his mouth.

Oh, that was perfect, the way Mason fit in his mouth and the salty taste of him. Patrick wrapped his fingers around the base and stroked a few times as he sucked. Mason moaned and panted and thrust his hips up toward Patrick's mouth. Patrick savored it, all of it, the scent of Mason, the taste, the way their proximity and this act sent all the blood in Patrick's body rushing south. He reached between his own legs with his free hand and stroked himself, not that he needed that stimulation to stay aroused.

He couldn't decide if he wanted to fuck Mason or to just spend all night sucking his cock. He kept stroking as he moved to take one of Mason's balls into his mouth, and he sucked, loving the feel of it, the size and shape and soft texture, and loving, too, the way Mason writhed and groaned his approval.

Patrick sucked on Mason's balls until Mason was panting and grabbing large swaths of the bedding in his fists, and then Patrick took Mason's cock back into his mouth. He sucked hard and traced patterns with his tongue. Then he licked the tip and pressed his tongue into the little space behind the head.

"Christ," Mason said. "I'm gonna come."

That was perfect. Patrick wanted that. He wanted Mason's come in his mouth, wanted to know what it tasted like. He stroked Mason's cock with long, smooth movements and sucked on the head. He kneaded Mason's balls. Mason's legs twisted and moved, his toes curled.

Patrick took Mason's cock deeper into his mouth. He relaxed his throat and swallowed the whole thing. He held there for a moment, his nose pressed against Mason's pubic hair. He moved back, licking a long line up the length of Mason's cock as he went. Then he licked the head again and sucked on it, and Mason's body went stiff. Mason shifted his hips up one last time and suddenly the bitter taste of Mason's cum burst on Patrick's tongue. Mason moaned and sighed and emptied into Patrick's greedy mouth.

Patrick held him there until the twitching and moaning stopped. He lifted his head and swallowed, and then he gave Mason's softening cock one last, slow lick.

"Come here," Mason said.

Patrick crawled up his body and kissed him, thrusting his now very hard cock against Mason's hip. Mason wrapped his hand around Patrick's cock, tugging and stroking.

Mason said, "Do you want me to—"

"No. I'm close. Keep doing that."

Mason leaned up and kissed a line from Patrick's jaw to his ear and then sucked Patrick's earlobe as he stroked Patrick hard and fast. The intensity of that, of being surrounded by Mason, of still being able to taste

Mason on his tongue, proved overwhelming. Patrick thrust his hips forward, meeting Mason's strokes, grunting as he did so, because he was... almost... there....

Mason wasn't quite getting him to the finish line, though. Desperate to come, anxious to do it, Patrick slapped Mason's hand out of the way and then stroked himself the way he needed it. He crawled over Mason again and sucked on one of Mason's nipples as he brought himself off.

Suddenly he got there, flashbulbs going off behind his eyes, so he shifted up and aimed his cock at Mason's. He came hard with a long groan and pressed his forehead against Mason's chest as he came all over Mason's soft cock.

Spent, he rolled onto his back and panted.

Mason looked down. "Jesus, that was hot."

"I know."

Mason chuckled. "You're hot too. Your mouth can do magic."

Patrick smiled. "I've been told as much."

Mason reached for his face and stroked down Patrick's cheek. Then he pressed his lips against Patrick's for a soft kiss. "Magic," he said.

Patrick backed away. He grabbed a couple of tissues from the side table. "Here, let me clean you up. Then we'll snuggle and you can tell me more about how awesome I am while we rest up so we can do it again."

Mason laughed. "Deal."


MASON WOKE up with the certainty that something was different or out of place, but he couldn't figure out what that was. Then he rolled onto his side and saw a patch of blond hair with colorful streaks peeking out from under his quilt.

*Oh. Right.*

So he'd done that, and he didn't regret it, but now he had to figure out the next step.

Patrick stirred and rolled onto his back, pushing out a little from under the covers. He blinked a few times and looked up at Mason. "Don't stare at me, honey. It's creepy."

Mason laughed. "Sorry."

Patrick shimmied back toward the headboard and sat up. "It's fine. I know I'm gorgeous." He preened.

Patrick's hair stuck out every which way, blond and pink and blue spikes pointing in all different directions, flattened a bit on one side. His pale skin was flushed. Mason couldn't see anything below Patrick's belly button, but he could easily picture Patrick's lithe little body, pink with arousal. God, he still wanted Patrick.

"So the tattoos," Mason said.

Patrick smiled. "I will confess that not all of them were acquired through fully rational decision-making." Patrick stroked his own arm. "Actually the dragon here is covering up a snake tattoo I got as a tribute to my college boyfriend. His name was Steve, but everyone called him Snake. Probably because he was a slithery bastard."

"Okay."

And then Patrick took Mason on a tour of his body graffiti. "I think the symbolism of the scissors is obvious," he said. "Some of these here were just because I liked the designs. This bird was designed by a friend of mine." He pointed to the tattoos going up his arm. "I also, well, I mean, I started getting tattoos in college and just kept adding." He indicated the sleeve that went up his arm. "My mother was horrified, but I figure I'll never have a corporate job anyway."

Mason reached over and traced with his finger the lines of the dragon on Patrick's bicep. "I like these."

"And you just have the one tattoo." Patrick picked up the sheets and pointed at the Yankees logo on Mason's hip.

"Well. Once a Yankee," Mason said. Under Patrick's gaze, Mason's already-stiff cock got harder.

"If you'd stayed in the majors and got traded, what would you have done?"

"Probably get a tattoo of whatever team I got traded to right next to it."

Mason pulled the sheets away from Patrick's body. In all, he had tattoos up one arm and mostly covering the other. The most prominent tattoo on the less-decorated arm was a big green shamrock. Mason's gaze kept getting drawn to it. A flock of blackbirds went across one of his pecs, and three stars adorned his hip. He had some kind of swirly pattern going up the outside of his left leg from his ankle to his knee. But a lot of Patrick's skin was smooth and unblemished.

"I never really felt strongly enough about anything to get it permanently inked on my body until I got called up to the majors," Mason said. "I thought I should commemorate the occasion, which I figured would be short, you know? I mean, I've been playing baseball since I was five years old. It was my dream to play for the Yankees. Then I got to do it. I still don't believe it happened sometimes. The tattoo was like evidence. I don't know."

Patrick ran his hand over it. The tattoo was about the size of his palm. "You'd get another tattoo? If it was meaningful, I mean?"

"Yeah, maybe."

"That'd be hot." Patrick snort-laughed. "Ha, listen to me. I mean, I think tattoos are hot, obviously. I'm not gonna lie, some of the sleeve is just narcissism because I like how it looks. Maybe I'll regret it when I'm eighty."

"You'll just have to stay hot."

"Sure, I'll work on that."

Mason laughed and touched more of Patrick's tattoos, then gave up all pretense and ran his hands over Patrick's skin. Patrick closed his eyes and leaned into the touch. Then he surprised Mason by dropping his head and kissing the Yankees tattoo, which was dangerously close to Mason's cock. Mason's body came to full alert.

That blow job earlier in the night had been a work of art, and Mason wouldn't have minded another, but though he was hard now, he had something else in mind. He reached for Patrick, grabbed his hair, and tugged gently. Patrick looked up with a grin. He surged up and met Mason's lips, kissing him hard.

Mason ran his hands over Patrick's arms. He trailed kisses from Patrick's mouth down his jaw, down his long neck. He nibbled on Patrick's collarbone, pressed his palms against Patrick's shoulder blades. He held strong when Patrick threw his head back, and then he kissed lower, tasting Patrick's salty skin, sucking one of Patrick's nipples into his mouth. Patrick squirmed against him.

The blow job had been perfect, but Mason wanted more.

He gazed at Patrick's tattooed body. Then he leaned forward and licked the swirls on his arm, made his tongue trace those long lines, the colors, the shapes. He touched the pictures, ran his finger along the dragon and the birds and all of it. Patrick grabbed Mason's head and held him there for a moment, then ducked to kiss him. They wrestled with their tongues for a moment and Mason's brain stopped working.

But then he remembered his real objective.

"I want you to fuck me."

"Yeah, Jesus, okay."

Because that was what Mason needed right now. He needed it to hurt a little. He needed to feel Patrick pushing against him, filling him, moving inside him. He wanted Patrick's big cock and he wanted to be driven crazy. He wanted that perfect moment he'd achieved in the bathroom at

Barnstorm last summer when Patrick had fucked him against the stall door and he'd come so fucking hard he thought he'd melt.

Mason shifted on the bed and pulled open the drawer in the side table. Patrick raised an eyebrow but grabbed lube and a condom. Mason took the condom from Patrick and tore open the wrapper. Patrick poured lube on his hands and wrapped those slick fingers around Mason's balls, squeezing them gently for a moment, before he moved his fingers farther south and stroked at Mason's entrance.

Mason spread his legs and leaned back as Patrick touched him; Mason wanted that touch bad. He stroked his cock and shifted his hips up to give Patrick better access. He gazed at Patrick's cock, hard and jutting out from his body, and he stroked that too. It was perfect, really, nicely shaped, pink with arousal, curving up slightly. Mason took the condom and rolled it on that perfect cock, his heart racing with the anticipation of having it inside him.

"God, I want you."

Patrick nodded and thrust his cock against Mason's hand. "Add some lube."

So Mason picked up the bottle and poured some of it on Patrick's cock as Patrick thrust his fingers into Mason's hole. It felt amazing, a little painful but mostly pleasurable as Mason's body stretched to accommodate Patrick's fingers.

"So fucking good," Mason said, "but I want your cock."

"Of course, babe. Hey, get up on your hands and knees."

"Yeah."

Yeah, that would be hot. His pulse kicked up as he imagined Patrick pushing into him from behind and the sheer pleasure that particular angle brought him. He rolled onto his stomach and then lifted his ass in the air.

"Oh, baby," Patrick moaned. "Do you have any idea how sexy you are?"

"Shove that big cock in me."

Patrick laughed, though it came out a little choked. "If you insist."

Mason couldn't see Patrick, but he felt Patrick's thighs brush against the backs of his own. Patrick grasped Mason's ass and dug his fingers in as he pushed the cheeks apart. Then something wet at his hole surprised Mason. He gasped as Patrick pressed his face between Mason's cheeks and licked and rimmed the entrance to his body.

Was it possible to be any more aroused? Each lick sent an electrical charge through Mason's skin. He grabbed a rung on the headboard and held on for dear life as Patrick plundered and kissed him and reduced him to a whimpering mess.

"Please," Mason groaned.

"Please what?" Patrick asked against one of Mason's asscheeks, the words vibrating against Mason's skin.

"Please fuck me, Patrick. Fuck me hard. Make me come. Come in me."

"With pleasure," Patrick said, moving away.

Patrick pressed the blunt head of his cock at Mason's hole. Mason moved back, wanting it like he wanted nothing else in this life. He was crazy with wanting, and Patrick's teasing was making him frantic.

But then, wham, Patrick pushed forward.

Mason moaned at the sudden penetration; it hurt but it was so fucking good. He shifted back, encouraging Patrick, moaning so Patrick would move because he couldn't make the words to tell Patrick what he needed. Instead, Patrick seemed to sense it. He started slamming forward and fucked Mason hard and fast, and it was just right. It was *so good*. It was exactly what Mason needed, pain mingled with the pleasure of that big cock moving in and out of him and nailing his prostate. He shivered, bit into the pillow to keep from screaming, and pressed back, wanting more, wanting this forever.

They didn't speak, but they didn't need to, because Patrick knew just what to do, pushing in and out, running his hands over Mason's ass, his lower back, his thighs. He kept up his onslaught, Mason groaning the whole time. And then, just when Mason was about to put some effort into speaking again so that he could tell Patrick to grab his cock and stroke him off, Patrick pulled him onto his side. Patrick didn't even pull out, just pressed the whole length of his body against Mason's back until they were spooning. Patrick somehow kept up his pace, hooking an arm around Mason's leg and pulling it up. Mason grabbed his own cock and stroked, pleasure everywhere, until he thought he might fly apart.

Then he *did* fall apart, his body screaming as he came. Patrick kept slamming into him fast, his pace a little frantic now, indicating he was getting close too. Mason thrust into his own hand, spurting out seemingly everywhere, long ropes that landed on his leg, his stomach, the sheets. It was a mess, but he didn't care because Patrick kept going.

Patrick dug his fingers into Mason's skin and thrust forward a few more times. Then he groaned, and Mason could feel him shake as he came, still pumping into Mason's body fast but eventually losing momentum.

The two of them collapsed into a tangle.

"God, that was perfect," Mason said.

Patrick pressed his face against Mason's shoulder. "Your body is really something. I could spend all day groping you and still never get enough."

Mason rolled over to face Patrick. He kissed him hard and wrapped his leg around Patrick's hips. They were both soft now, but they were sticky and messy, and it was so great to be stuck together this way.

"Mmm," Patrick said, pulling away. He slowly took off the condom and dumped it in the wastebasket beside the bed. "Really, I think we owe it to each other to keep on having sex on a regular basis, because I haven't met anyone I am nearly so compatible with."

"You talk a lot," Mason said with a yawn.

Patrick smiled. "Yeah. We made a mess too. Should we clean it up?"

"Probably. Let's just lie here for a minute, though."

Patrick kissed Mason's neck. "All right." He pulled Mason into his arms. They lay together like that for a long time, Mason savoring every moment of it, until at long last he got itchy and had to get up.

"Shower with me?" Mason asked.

"You don't even need to ask, babe."

# Chapter 5

THE ACHE in Mason's leg bothered him. He rubbed at his knotted calf muscles in vain, worried this was a bad omen for the rest of the summer. He had bad days sometimes, days when his foot throbbed or his knee spasmed, though he'd had fewer of those since his surgery over the winter.

"You okay?" asked Scott.

Practice buzzed around them. The Hipsters held their practices in Prospect Park in Brooklyn, and on weekend afternoons, the area surrounding the ball fields was intensely crowded, especially since the weather was beautiful. The chaos of practice itself on top of the chaos of the park on a Sunday afternoon had started to feel overwhelming.

Mason had asked for five minutes when his ankle buckled, but batting practice was carrying on without him.

"Tight," Mason said to Scott.

"It hurt?"

"Not terribly. It's kind of throbbing now."

Scott nodded grimly. "You going to be okay to play? I can get Zach or Eddie to take shortstop during Tuesday's game."

"I think I'll be all right." Mason managed to feign confidence, though he didn't feel confident at all. "I just need to ice it and stay off it for a little while."

Scott nodded. "I'll tell Eddie to be ready, just in case."

Mason cursed his bad leg. He hated to sit out a game, though he knew if it didn't feel better by Tuesday, he'd have to. He pushed too hard and he could hear his doctor scolding him as he rubbed his ankle.

It wasn't even like he'd hurt his leg doing anything strenuous. He'd felt agile as a teenager when Patrick had slept over. This morning, though, getting out of the shower, he'd stepped on his left heel too hard and it was like a lightning bolt had gone up his whole leg. It hadn't been quite right since then, and after the weird quasi-yoga warm-up exercises Scott had them do and a couple of laps around the ball field, Mason's leg had started screaming.

But it was better now, a little less tight and twitchy. He flexed his ankle, and though he didn't have full range of motion, it wasn't quite as bad as it had been a few minutes ago.

"I'll live," Mason said, standing back up.

"You want to hit a couple of balls?"

"Nothing wrong with my arms."

Scott chuckled and gestured toward the backstop, where Ian was currently failing to hit any of the baseballs Nate hurled at him. Mason nodded and limped over to the line.

He watched his teammates struggle to hit anything Nate pitched them—Nate was on top of his game, hurling fastballs right through the middle of the strike zone—and thought of Patrick again. It was insane how awesome that had been, and though they'd talked in the abstract about doing it again, they hadn't made any firm plans. They hadn't even exchanged phone numbers.

Mason supposed the odds of them running into each other again were pretty good. He could probably get Patrick's number from one of the league organizers. He could just imagine Josh's glee at Mason being interested in another league member—Josh was happily married and seemed determined to help the rest of the league achieve the same status—but he wasn't quite ready to take that step yet.

Besides, it was just an infatuation. It didn't mean any—

"Mason! Get your head in the game!"

Ty was standing in front of him, holding up a bat. "Earth to Mason."

"Sorry," Mason muttered.

"Don't apologize, just get your head out of the clouds," Ty drawled. "I hope he's hot."

Mason tried for a smirk. "Oh, he is."

"S'all that matters. You're up, lover boy."

Mason stepped up to the plate and wondered if that was all that mattered. If Mason liked Patrick, did what he looked like matter? Did the tattoos, the hair, the career, did any of it matter if Mason liked him?

Well, they *mattered*, as all those things were a part of Patrick, and Mason really liked those things about him, but what would everyone else think?

No, he couldn't possibly ask Josh about—

A ball whizzed by his face.

"Look alive, Mase!" Nate shouted from the mound.

So Mason pushed aside all thoughts of Patrick and focused on hitting the ball.

At a Park Slope gay bar after practice, Mason debated popping a pain pill or just having a beer—he knew from experience that bad things happened when he did both—and then reasoned that if he was hurting enough to contemplate a pill, it was probably time to just admit something was off.

He ordered a Coke and took a pill.

Ty slid onto the chair next to him and said, "So your leg hurts again."

"Your powers of observation are keen."

Ty grinned. "Well, you know. Are you all right?"

"I will be. But I'm thinking about sitting out Tuesday's game. Maybe I need a break."

Ty's eyes widened. "It's that bad?"

"It hurts some, but nothing some rest won't cure. I just need to take it easy for a few days." Mason thought about the best way to achieve that rest. "Maybe after I finish my current work assignment, I'll go to my house on Fire Island for a few days."

Ty laughed. "I forgot you owned that house, Mr. Major League Salary."

"The renovation just finished. I actually haven't been out there since just after Hurricane Sandy."

Ty nodded. "That'll be good. To see the house again, I mean. It got pretty beat up in the storm, didn't it?"

"Yeah, it did. Renovations weren't cheap, but we came in under budget, so." Mason took a sip of his soda. "But yeah, I mean, hard to go wrong with a few days of beach and boys, right?"

Ty smirked. "Sounds like a great vacation to me."

It definitely had potential. Mason would be happy to finally be rid of the Brian Fox story, submitting an article that was a straightforward portrayal of a Rice baseball star, though the mention of his sexuality made it into the third paragraph. Mason wasn't quite satisfied with the story, but he knew he'd have to let it go soon.

The Fire Island idea had been a fleeting one, but he had been meaning to go take a look at the house now that renovations were finished; he'd left everything in the hands of his very capable architect. If he had to sit out a few baseball games, maybe now was the time.

"Lots of distractions on Fire Island in the summer," Ty said with a wink. "Or would that conflict with the hot guy you were dreaming about during batting practice?"

"The hot guy I was thinking about was a one-nighter almost a week ago." Well, it had been more of a two-nighter now, hadn't it? Still, Mason wasn't exactly ready to go public with a relationship.

"But you're still thinking about him?"

"Maybe. Doesn't really matter. I'm happy to let the boys of Fire Island distract me."

"I haven't been there in a while, but I remember that area of the Pines near your house being kind of a man buffet, especially in the bars."

"Yeah, it certainly was the last time I was there. Lot of couples, though."

"And so it goes." Ty smiled a private sort of smile. He looked toward the bar, where Ian was waiting for their drinks. Their gazes connected and Ty's smile broadened.

"So that's going well."

"It is. Housing situation notwithstanding. I've been trying to get Ian to spend more nights with me in Brooklyn to see how well he copes with the commute. It's farther from his job, yeah, but he won't have the job much longer. Then he thought we should wait to move in together until he figures out what he's doing next." Ty rolled his eyes. "We'll figure it out. I'm not really worried."

"That's good."

"Yeah. What can I say? I love him, even when he's being stubborn."

"And you're being stubborn too."

Ty winked. "Sure." He sipped his beer. "Well, if you decide to skip town, I hope you have a good trip. Better take care of that leg. We'll need you at the game against the Mermaids in a couple of weeks."

"You sure do need me," Mason said with a laugh. "Rachel could beat the rest of you all by herself."

Ty grimaced. "Don't remind me."

THE WOMAN in Patrick's chair looked like she'd bathed in henna.

"You did this yourself?" he asked, running his fingers through her bright orange hair.

"Yes! Isn't it fabulous?"

It had that first-day-after-henna neon brightness that Patrick knew would fade in time. It was an interesting color, Patrick could give her that, but it was an odd choice for a woman over sixty. The texture of her hair was odd, dried out. He wondered if she'd gone completely white under all the henna and that was part of why it looked so orange.

"It's nice," he said, not wanting to piss off the customer.

"I know it's intense, but the woman at the store insisted it would make my hair look like it was naturally red."

Patrick wanted to point out that no one her age had hair this bright, even natural redheads, whose hair tended to fade a little over time. He just nodded and tried to work out how best to cut her hair. "What do you think about layers around your face? Or do you want to keep it long?"

"Long. I love this hair! It makes me feel so young."

Patrick got to work, and though he was focused on what he was doing, his mind wandered a little. He was doing the sort of trim he could do in his sleep, just making sure the ends of this woman's hair were all the same length.

He thought about Mason. Of course he thought about Mason. He'd done little else but think about Mason, even over the winter when he'd dated that gym bunny, even now that he'd gotten another taste, which, if anything, had only made him want more.

He'd made the critical error of leaving Mason's apartment without exchanging phone numbers. Of course, he knew where Mason lived now and could just show up. And he had no doubt that they'd run into each other sooner or later.

Patrick hoped sooner.

But eh, maybe he shouldn't get his hopes up. Mason played in a different league, so to speak. He was hot and wealthy and Patrick wasn't entirely sure his family would approve, not that he cared.

"Maybe I should get bangs!" said Orange Henna.

Patrick shook his head and tried to pay attention to what he was doing. "Bangs would make you look younger," Patrick said.

"Perfect. Let's do it."

So Patrick focused on cutting bangs for Orange Henna, and he gave her a cute haircut that still kept a lot of the length. He was pretty proud of the cut, and it did help her look younger, but man, that hair was bright. And Patrick had purple and blue streaks in his hair; he knew all about bright.

After Orange Henna paid and left, Patrick stood over at the front counter near Valerie. He opened his mouth to complain about how bizarre their clients had been all day when Dirk made one of his rare appearances at the front door.

Dirk had founded Dimensions when he and his partner, Sean, had moved to New York City from Arizona—Tucson, Phoenix, Patrick could never remember—and they'd both cut hair for years before starting to hire other stylists to take on their overflow of clients. Eventually the stylists who rented chairs at the salon had more or less taken over; Patrick and Valerie probably put in more hours than anyone else.

"Afternoon, Dirk," Patrick said amiably.

"How are things?" he asked.

"Going pretty well," said Valerie. "Can we do something for you?"

"I actually thought I might get a trim. Would you like to do the honors, Patty?"

He didn't want to. Thoughts of Mason still rattled him a little, and probably no crime was worse than fucking up your boss's hair if you were a hairdresser. But he couldn't exactly say no either. "Yeah, all right. Do I have an appointment now?"

"Not for another half hour," said Valerie.

"Sure, Dirk. Come on back." He prayed he wouldn't fuck it up. Any of it.

# Chapter 6

A WEEK later Carlos stretched out his arms and did his cooldown stretches as practice wrapped, feeling pretty good. As Ian packed up his stuff, Carlos said, "We're going to Spokes tonight."

The gay cowboy bar in Prospect Heights was Carlos's favorite postpractice cooldown spot for two reasons: it was close to Prospect Park, where the team practiced, and it was near Aiden's apartment.

Ian smiled and said, "Fine by me. I like that place. Brings out the Texas in Ty."

Carlos laughed.

Aiden was already at the bar when the team rolled in. Carlos walked up to him and gave him a kiss. Aiden smiled. "Hey, babe."

"Hey, *papi.* How are things tonight?"

"Good. How was practice?"

"Pretty good. Nate was pitching like it was game six of the World Series for the second week in a row, though, and nobody could hit anything. Scott can't seem to decide if he should praise Nate or yell at the rest of us for being so inept at bat."

Aiden looked up and at something behind Carlos. He said, "Hey, Nate."

"Uh-huh," Nate said.

"Aw, come on, be nice," said Carlos as he turned around to look at Nate. "You just pitched amazingly. Are you not at least happy about that?"

Nate let out a breath. "Yeah, sorry. Hi, Aiden. I hope you're well."

Aiden seemed to take it in stride, smiling and offering Nate a hand to shake. Nate took it briefly and then turned to the bar. He held up his hand and waved at the bartender. "Geez, what does it take to get a beer around here?"

Irritated now, Carlos hooked his hand around Nate's arm and led him away from the bar. "Talk to me a sec."

When they were out of earshot of Aiden, Carlos said, "Dude. What the fuck is up with you?"

All the tension seemed to drain out of Nate's body. "Sorry. It's nothing. I'm just being an ass."

"Yeah, you are." Carlos glanced back at Aiden, who by all appearances had turned his considerable charm on the bartender; Aiden was all smiles and bashful hand gestures. When Carlos looked back at Nate, Nate was grimacing again. "You hate Aiden."

Nate sighed. "I don't hate Aiden."

"You don't like him much."

Nate bit his lip. "He's fine. I have no reason to hate him."

"I know. That doesn't seem to have stopped you."

"This is not the time or place to have this conversation."

Carlos crossed his arms and figured he'd wait and see if Nate confessed what was in his head. He was apparently in for a long wait, because they just stood and stared at each other for a minute.

Finally Nate said, "Are you happy?"

"I'm not happy that you hate my boyfriend, but I am happy with Aiden."

"That's all that matters, then. I'll… I'll try, okay? He just… rubs me the wrong way. I don't know why. But I'll try."

"Fine."

"Fine."

Ty walked over and slapped Nate on the back. "Hey, help me and Ian eat a plate of hot wings."

Nate raised his eyebrows at Carlos, shrugged, and followed Ty to the other side of the bar. So Carlos went back to sit next to Aiden.

"What was that about?" Aiden asked.

"Nothing. Nate's just got his panties in a wad about something. He'll get over it."

"Can I get you a drink?"

"Or six. Yeah."

"Mason here? I didn't see him come in with you guys."

Carlos shook his head. "He ditched us to spend a week on Fire Island. The nerve, yeah? Just 'cause his leg was bothering him. I'm surprised Scott didn't tell him to push through the pain. One of the spare pitchers is manning Mason's position until he gets back. It's not the same."

Aiden nodded. "Too bad. He seems like a good guy. Fun to hang around with."

"Sure. He is. All these guys are."

It was weird, like a test. Aiden seemed to be gauging his reactions to his other teammates too, asking after all of them in turn. But it wasn't until later that Carlos really got blindsided. That was when Aiden said, "Maybe you should spend less time around Nate."

"Heh?" Carlos was too flabbergasted to make an actual word.

"I don't even get what you like about him. He's such a surly bitch sometimes."

"He's my best friend. And actually, he's only that way around you. He acts like a normal human most of the time. You seem to bring out the worst in him."

"Is he jealous?"

Carlos laughed because the idea was so absurd it didn't merit thinking about. "No. That's crazy."

"I think he might be. Maybe he hates me because he's in love with you."

"Nate? In love with me? No, that's insane. He's like a brother. Our friendship is purely platonic, I promise."

"You sure about that?"

"Yes. Absolutely."

Aiden nodded. "Well. He's still a surly bitch. Maybe if that's how he's gonna be, you should give him some space."

It seemed like reasonable advice. Carlos didn't want to abandon his best friend, but maybe Nate needed some consequences to his being such an asshole. Maybe Carlos wouldn't see him until he worked through whatever the fuck he needed to work through.

"Yeah," Carlos said.

Aiden waved his hand. The bartender slid a beer in front of Carlos. "Forget about him for now," Aiden said. "You want to come back to my place later?"


MASON STOOD at the stoop of his summer house in the Pines on Fire Island. Jerome, the architect who had overseen the house's renovation after it had sustained some serious damage during Hurricane Sandy, yammered on about reinforced this and flood protection that. Mason cared insofar as he wanted his house to be livable, but he'd gotten Jerome's report the previous month and his eyes had glazed over every time he'd tried to read it.

"The flood damage in the basement?" Mason asked in an effort to sound like he was paying attention.

"Better. After we gutted it, we laid down new drywall and...."

And Mason's brain checked out again.

He waited for Jerome to stop for breath and then said, "Can we take a look?"

"Oh. Yeah. Of course."

Jerome led the way inside and then proceeded to give Mason a tour of his own house.

It looked good; Mason could say that for the place. He'd have to move some of the furniture around; he'd picked out what he'd needed to replace the furniture that was destroyed when the house flooded, but he'd left it up to Jerome to decide where to put it as it was delivered over the winter. Still, the furniture was all to Mason's taste, modern and somewhat utilitarian, and it was certainly better than the beachy, overcolorful couches and chairs that had come with the house when Mason had bought it right after his retirement.

He therefore viewed the so-called superstorm and all of its resultant flood and wind damage as kind of a blessing in disguise. He'd bought the house before Sandy and rented it out most of the time, but hadn't gotten around to doing much with it until a storm nearly destroyed it. That had been fairly traumatizing; he'd sat at home, somewhat thankful he'd escaped the week-long power outage that hit all of Manhattan below Thirty-Fourth Street, and watched the news reports describing how the wind had ripped large swaths of oceanfront property to shreds. He'd felt impotent watching that footage and thinking about his little house on the island. But it had worked out in the end. He supposed he was lucky to have had the money on hand to cover whatever insurance hadn't, although it had taken a healthy chunk of change to repair the damage. The end result was that he finally had a summer home that felt like his.

"How long do you intend to stay?" Jerome asked. "You moving out here for the summer?"

"For now? I'm just here until the end of the week." His leg felt better, but he figured a week out of the city would do him good. "I've got too much going on at home to stay away too long, though. I might rent the house out again. It would be a shame to leave it here empty, I suppose."

"Such a great location," Jerome said. "Really, it was a pleasure to work on it."

"I'm glad."

"It would make a nice little love nest too. You bring one of those city boys out here for a few days of sand and surf and he'd be putty in your hands."

Mason laughed. He tried to imagine one of the guys he'd dated recently but couldn't quite picture him in this space.

But then, like a vision, he saw Patrick sitting on the sleek modern sofa in the living room, perusing his books or magazines, yapping about shells he'd collected or parties he wanted to go to. Maybe he'd be mostly naked on that sofa, his tattoos on display, his crazy hair standing in contrast to the straight lines of the room's design.

Mason wanted that. He wanted it so bad he could practically taste Patrick's skin.

"I'll keep that in mind," Mason said.

He shook hands with Jerome and bid him good evening. He walked through the house himself, inspecting it more closely, looking for water damage that might have been overlooked but not finding anything. Jerome was talented and he'd been thorough. The house had been in good hands.

Mason wanted to spend the night in his new house, sitting on the new furniture, being surrounded by it, but he was anxious too, kind of itchy. Perhaps the best thing for it would be to hit up one of the gay bars up the road, at least to look. He didn't really intend to pick anybody up.

He decided to walk. The sun was still up, but the evening air was getting cooler. Mason loved the smell of the beach: salt, sand, the vague scent of fish. The air was thick and damp, a little muggy for Mason's taste, but the night was also nearly cloudless, so he couldn't complain too much. He shoved his hands in the pockets of his jeans as he walked. Other people walked toward the bars too, mostly young men. Mason wasn't shy about checking them out, but none of them did much for him; most of the guys he saw were generically handsome and too young for Mason.

He was feeling pretty mellow when he got to his chosen bar. He figured he'd go in, get a beer, look around, and walk back.

But then who should be there, standing by the electronic jukebox in the corner, but Patrick.

Mason bypassed the bar and walked straight to him.

He let Patrick exist in his little world where he didn't know Mason was behind him for a few moments, but then he reached over and touched Patrick's shoulder.

Patrick turned around. He started and laughed. "Oh, Mason, honey. Fancy meeting you here."

Mason smiled. "Likewise. Unless you make a habit of hanging out at jukeboxes in the bars that I frequent."

"I assure you, this is entirely a brilliant coincidence." Patrick glanced at his companions, a pair of guys Mason didn't know, both Patrick's age, which Mason had estimated was roughly "young," or at least more than five years younger than Mason. Both were kind of cute but didn't hold a candle to

Patrick. Patrick grinned. "I just like to ensure the music in all places I frequent is danceable."

"Can I buy you a drink?" Mason asked.

Patrick's grin widened. He curled his hand around Mason's elbow. "Absolutely. Lead the way."

Patrick ditched his friends and followed Mason back to the bar, where they sat beside each other on stools. Mason ordered a beer and Patrick a Cosmo.

"So," Patrick said brightly, a wide smile on his face.

His hair seemed to have more blue in it today, though he still had the mohawk situation. His dark roots were starting to show, but everything about his hair was deliberately messy, from what Mason could tell. Patrick had round onyx studs in both ears. The tank top he was wearing showed off his tattoos nicely. Mason wanted to explore all that, to get a closer look, to get Patrick naked and in his bed where he could lick all those tattoos again….

Yeesh, what the hell was wrong with him? They weren't even dating. Time to rein it in.

"So," Mason said.

"Of all the gay bars on Fire Island, you just had to stroll into mine."

"I own a house up the road."

Patrick laughed. "Of course you do. I keep forgetting you were, like, super famous."

"Well, not super famous."

"*People* magazine, right?"

Mason sighed.

"I just mean, of course you can afford a place on this island. Sam and Gus over there, the three of us are renting a house with three other guys. I can only afford to stay, like, two days, so I figured I'd make the most of it. Just as well. There's a limit to how much I enjoy overhearing my friends and their tricks."

Mason shook his head. "Oh, to be young."

"What are you talking about, honey? You are not that old, girl, first of all. Plus, you are smoking hot. You could have any man in this bar."

"Well, thanks for that." Mason lifted his beer in a toast.

Patrick grinned and clinked his glass against Mason's. "So this house of yours," said Patrick. "It's nice?"

"You want to see it?"

Patrick leaned forward and rested his elbow on the bar. He gazed at Mason dreamily. "I thought you'd never ask."

"I figured you might like to have a night with more space. You'd just have to share with me, not five other guys."

"That sounds swell to me." Patrick touched Mason's shoulder. Then he ran his hand down Mason's chest. "God, this body. It's like you were made from a mold."

Mason put his hand over Patrick's and held it against his stomach. "Your friends won't worry if you don't go home with them tonight?"

"Oh, Mason. The whole point is to not go home."

Mason laughed, though he had a strong adverse reaction to the idea of Patrick going home with just any random guy.

He sighed.

Patrick turned his hand against Mason's until their fingers were laced together. He put their joined hands in his lap. "You know, if we don't stop running into each other like this, one of these days, we'll be a regular thing."

Mason swallowed hard. He knew Patrick was kidding around, but part of Mason really wanted to see Patrick regularly. He nodded. "Do you... do you want that?"

The grin on Patrick's face suddenly vanished. He sat up a little straighter. "Well. Yes, if I'm honest. I wasn't sure that was what you wanted."

Mason wasn't sure what he wanted either, but he could be honest too. "I don't know, but I can say the thought of you going home with somebody else makes me want to throw this glass at the wall." He picked up his pint glass.

Patrick leaned back. "Possessive. Interesting."

"Just saying."

"Sure. I like it." Patrick leaned over and kissed Mason's cheek. He moved away again, but Mason snagged him, hooking an arm around his shoulders and bringing him back for a kiss on the lips.

When they parted again, Mason said, "You want this to be a regular thing?"

"Yes. And maybe not even a sex thing. Maybe we, like, go out together and get to know each other." Patrick gasped exaggeratedly. "I know, perish the thought, but I thought whatever is sizzling between us might merit a more romantic approach."

"Are you serious?"

"Of course, darling. I'm always serious." Patrick grinned cheekily at Mason. "How long are you on the island for?"

"Through the end of the week."

"Then we better get going, honey. We're wasting precious time."

PATRICK SOAKED in the Jacuzzi in Mason's bathroom, letting out a deep groan as the jets massaged his body, a little sore from the athletic sex they'd been having for the past day. They'd really only stopped long enough to shove some food in their faces and for Patrick to text his vacation roommates so they didn't think he'd been abducted. Patrick supposed the ache in his lower back was a sign he was getting a little older—or that he was just out of shape—but he liked it. It was like a reminder.

"There room in there for one more?" Mason asked, walking into the room.

Patrick leaned his head back on the edge of the tub. "Looks that way." The tub was huge. Four people could easily have fit in it. Mason had mentioned earlier that it had come with the house, which Patrick supposed made sense since this seemed super luxurious, even for former pro athlete Mason. Mason struck Patrick as not especially frugal, but not extravagant either.

Mason climbed in across from Patrick and let out a groan as he settled into the hot water. "Oh, that feels good."

"A guy could get used to this." Patrick kept his eyes closed, content to slowly boil in the hot tub, but he reached over with his foot and ran his toe up Mason's calf.

"It is pretty nice. It feels good on my sore leg."

Patrick looked up, concern lancing through him. "Are you okay? I know I got pretty aggressive that last time, but did I hurt you?"

"No." Mason shifted in the tub a little, putting his leg up on the bench next to where Patrick sat. "The leg has been bothering me some lately. Pushed myself too hard at the last practice I went to. It's why I decided to come out here this week. Figured I could use a rest."

"This is the leg you injured before you left the Yankees?"

"Yeah. Torn Achilles, some other damage. I pulled a tendon toward the end of last summer and had to have surgery in December."

"Ugh, that sucks. I thought you said the injury wasn't that bad."

"It wasn't. But it *was* bad enough to take me out of the game. Even if I hadn't left, I probably would have been tossed back to the minors. My Yankee career was done."

"Oh. Does it hurt?"

"It's throbbing a little. The hot water is helping."

Mason took a deep breath, hard enough for his chest to rise and fall. He shook out his shoulders and then rested his arms on either side of the tub. He really was perfectly made. His long arms stretched out that way made his wingspan look impressive, like that of a swimmer, and his arms were still firm with round, corded muscles. Patrick even liked the little tufts of black hair at his armpits; he'd spent some time licking there just an hour ago.

"Anyway," Mason said, "I saw the doctor the day before I came out here. There's some swelling, but it wasn't bad enough that he was concerned. I've been instructed to take it easy."

Patrick rested his hand on Mason's foot experimentally. When Mason wiggled his toes and smiled, Patrick left his hand there. "I'm afraid I've kept you from taking it easy."

Mason laughed. "Hell, you kept me off my leg."

Patrick laughed too. He rubbed Mason's ankle, which pulled a groan from Mason's parted lips. Patrick picked up Mason's foot and put it in his lap. He started to slowly massage up Mason's leg.

"Do you miss it?" Patrick asked. "The majors?"

"I do, yeah. Those three years I played for the Yankees, they were really tough in a lot of ways. I don't think I ever worked harder in my life. But I was playing at the top of my game and having a hell of a lot of fun doing it." Mason murmured something soft as Patrick continued to massage the knots in his calf. "Still, those years weren't great for my personal life. Being a closeted athlete is not a life I can really recommend. So it was a trade-off. Oh, yeah, right there."

Patrick laughed softly and kneaded the muscle. "You have a crush on any of your teammates?"

Mason laughed. "What? No."

"It's okay to tell me, honey. I won't say anything."

"If I said a name, would you even know who I'm talking about?"

Patrick didn't follow professional baseball. He knew a few of the big players, but otherwise he probably wouldn't have been able to pick most of the active players out of a lineup. "Nope."

"Well." Mason shook his head. "No, none of my teammates. I found a few of them attractive, I guess, but you develop this weird kinship with the other guys on your team. I bet it's kind of like going to war, only lower stakes, I guess. These guys, they're your brothers. But there was a catcher for one of the Midwest teams. God, he's so hot. If he'd crooked his finger at me, I would have followed him. Married to a woman, though."

"I'd hope she was his beard for your sake, but I'm afraid I've got the same possessive streak you do and I want you for myself."

Mason smiled. "Oh good. That feels awesome, by the way. Next time I throw out my knee, I'm calling you."

"I'd come in a heartbeat."

"Oh, I'll help you come all right."

Patrick laughed. The goofy look on Mason's face told Patrick he was kidding, but Patrick liked a dirty joke. He liked, too, that Mason seemed so relaxed, so happy and carefree, even though his leg probably was quite sore. Now that Patrick was looking at it, he could see that it was a little discolored and swollen, that there were thin scars crisscrossing the otherwise smooth skin near Mason's knee and ankle. He could certainly feel how tense Mason's muscles were.

"This was fun," Patrick said. "This last day, I mean. I'm glad I ran into you."

"Yeah. I'd been starting to wonder when I'd see you again."

"Let's not leave it to chance." Patrick leaned forward and touched Mason's chest. "Don't let me go back to the city without giving you my phone number. Anytime, Mason. You can call me anytime."

"Yeah. Same goes. I'll take you out when we're both back home. There are some great bars in my neighborhood."

"Okay, deal."

They grinned stupidly at each other for a moment, and Patrick felt safe and happy. This man was sexy and strong and seemed to genuinely like him. He was good in bed, he was smart as hell, and, as Patrick had learned earlier that day, he even knew his way around a kitchen. Patrick could heat up frozen dinners, but that was basically the beginning and end of his cooking prowess.

"I almost wish I didn't have to go back to the city," Mason said. "I wish we could just stay here indefinitely."

"You'd get tired of me eventually. They all do."

Mason shook his head. "Not possible. I'd never get tired of you."

Patrick couldn't help but smile at that. "So how long can I soak here before I turn into a prune?"

"I say you've got another ten minutes or so."

"Great. Then for the next ten minutes, we do not talk about the city or going home. We just enjoy this soak in the tub."

Mason grabbed Patrick's hand. He laced their fingers together. "Sounds perfect."

# Chapter 7

"VALERIE WAS so impressed," Patrick said, "but I still had no idea who this lady was. I guess she's a Broadway actress who has done a few TV shows."

"Okay," said Mason as he looked across the room.

"Like, blonde hair, kind of a long face, mole over her left eyebrow?" Patrick pointed to the spot over his own left eyebrow where the mole would be, but Mason wasn't looking.

"Uh-huh."

"If I watched more TV I'd probably know who she was, but I don't even have cable. Maybe you would have recognized her. Either way, Valerie was going crazy because a *celebrity* came to our salon for a haircut."

"Sure."

Mason was there, in that he was sitting with Patrick at a bar near his apartment in Hell's Kitchen, but he wasn't really there, because his attention was clearly not on Patrick. They were in a gay bar and the whole fucking world knew Mason was gay, but he was acting eerily similar to the closeted guy Patrick had dated a few years before. That guy had been a Wall Street something-or-other who was convinced that if a soul found out he was gay, his annual bonus would be less money, or something like that. He and Patrick had gone out occasionally at Patrick's insistence—he figured "if you want to get with me, you have to be willing to be seen in public with me" was a pretty low bar to clear—but when they'd been out together, they'd always sat a foot apart, they never touched, they never talked about sex or their relationship. Patrick had summarily dumped that guy once he grew tired of that, which didn't take long.

So that was how Mason was acting. They were sitting across from each other at a tall table in a hunky meat market sort of gay bar, both sipping from colorful cocktails. Mason's was the color of grape soda, not the sort of beverage a man worried about the integrity of his masculinity usually drank. In fact, Mason was wearing a Human Rights Campaign T-shirt, a tight one that stretched tantalizingly across his chest. He had a rainbow-beaded bracelet around his wrist. He might as well have been wearing a sandwich board declaring "I'm gay!" So why the distance?

Or why did he act like they were just mismatched buddies and not two men on a date? That was the vibe Patrick was getting. Like they were just casually hanging out and Mason intended to go home with one of these overdeveloped meatheads and not with Patrick.

It was especially weird given how great things had felt between them on Fire Island. They'd had a lot of sex, sure, but it felt like they'd really connected when they were out of bed too. Patrick couldn't figure out why Mason would act so distant now, unless he had regrets or was embarrassed by Patrick or something like that. Wasn't the first time a guy had acted this way. Patrick had thought Mason was different, but maybe he was wrong.

"I have to replace my baseball glove," Patrick said, trying to engage Mason. "I mean, I bought it secondhand anyway, so it was really only a matter of time. Now it's all frayed on the fingers. Who knew that could even happen?"

"Well, they do wear out eventually. But you don't want a brand-new glove. They're too stiff."

"That's what she said."

"What?" Mason's gaze was on a guy flirting with the bartender on the other side of the room, a guy shaped like an inverted triangle in a sherbet pink T-shirt.

*Oy vey.*

Was this just one of Patrick's recurring issues? Was he destined to continue to fall for guys who didn't really get him? Unavailable guys? Even openly gay unavailable guys?

"So should I leave, or…?" said Patrick.

"What?"

"I feel like I'm just sitting here talking to myself. I'll leave if that's what you want."

Mason turned and met Patrick's gaze. "No. No, that's not what I want. I'm sorry."

"Is it the hair? Because it grows back."

"It's not the hair."

Patrick felt self-conscious suddenly. He fingered the piercings in his ear, ran his hand over the tattoo sleeve on his arm. "Is it all too much for you? Should I start taking steroids?"

"What?"

Patrick huffed out a breath. "Do you think the muscle-head over there is hotter than I am?"

"No." Mason answered immediately, with no hesitation. So that was something.

"I feel like I don't have your undivided attention."

Mason leaned on his elbow. "I'm sorry. I'll try harder."

"Is it me? Am I really not your type?"

Mason shook his head. "You're exactly my type. You're the hottest guy in this bar."

Okay! Patrick sat up a little and smiled. "Oh, hush. No need to butter my ego."

"I'm not. I'm being honest. Maybe more than I would have been if this wasn't my third... what the hell is this drink called?"

"Purple Rain," said Patrick, feeling better over the undercurrent of annoyance.

"Yeah. No, I was just thinking about something unrelated to you."

"Well, honey, if we're on a date, I would appreciate if you thought more about things related to me."

"Yes. I will."

"Because I was starting to think I embarrass you."

Hesitation this time. "No."

"I get that we're pretty different. Like, basically as different as two people can be."

"I figured that was what made things interesting."

"It is." Patrick nodded. "Maybe I'm projecting, but I can't help but think...."

"I'm sorry I haven't been very attentive. There's a lot on my mind."

"Are you sure that's all?"

"Yes."

"Do you want to talk about it?"

Mason shot Patrick a wary look. "Not... especially. Not here, anyway." He lifted one finger and gestured around the bar.

"I'm used to guys thinking I'm ridiculous. I had a guy tell me once *to my face* that he hated queeny twinks. Blanket statement, across the board. Just because I'm thin and look young doesn't mean I'm shallow."

"Well, if he didn't like guys like you, you shouldn't have been with him anyway."

Patrick frowned. Something that he didn't understand was definitely going on here. He still didn't feel like Mason's focus was on him—indeed, Mason seemed to have a wandering eye, or at least a habit of darting his gaze around a room that Patrick had never noticed before—but Mason was saying all of the right things.

"I gotta go to the little boys' room," Patrick said, sliding off his tall chair.

He left Mason to gaze at all the hot guys in the bar and went to the restroom. After he took care of business, he splashed some water on his face and fluffed up his hair. He'd just added green streaks and liked the effect. And that was what he tried to remind himself now: he liked how he looked. He put effort into cultivating his look. He had self-conscious moments, sure, but he had pride too, and he wasn't going to let his parents or society or Mason tell him not to be himself.

He nodded at the mirror. So affirmed, he went back to the table.

Mason was sitting there looking at something on his phone. Patrick didn't bother going back to his chair. Instead he walked right up to Mason, hooked a hand behind his head, and pulled him in for a kiss. He was essentially marking his territory.

Mason was receptive, but the full-on passion they'd indulged in before wasn't there.

What had changed?

Unfortunately, Patrick couldn't put his finger on any explanation, and if Mason was going to remain tight-lipped—figuratively and literally in this case, since he wouldn't open his mouth to deepen this kiss—then answers wouldn't be forthcoming.

Patrick pulled away. "Maybe I *should* just go home."

Mason groaned and rubbed his forehead. "No, please don't. I'm sorry. Let's just… let's get out of here. Go back to my place. I'll close out the tab."

That didn't feel like a real solution, but Patrick was willing to go with it. Maybe out of this public place, Mason would actually talk about whatever it was that had made him all weird.

"Okay," Patrick said. "Let's go."


A MAN at the bar looked alarmingly like a more polished version of Odell, which had made Mason's head spin with worry and confusion. He could just imagine Odell's reaction to a guy like Patrick. Odell had a particularly expressive face and had never been able to hide his emotions, so Mason knew well how pinched eyebrows or a small frown could mean revulsion or bafflement or confusion or "What the fuck?"

He'd known it wasn't fair to Patrick to keep comparing him to the guys he usually dated, the sorts of guys who met Odell's standards for masculinity.

It shouldn't have mattered.

But as Mason walked Patrick out of his building the morning after they'd had drinks at the muscle bar, it did matter to Mason what his family thought. He shouldn't have worried about the weird-colored hair or the sleeve of tattoos or the piercings, since he found all these things incredibly sexy, but he could hear Odell or his mother whispering in his ear that this sort of man—if he could even be called that—was not the right sort of man for Mason.

Mason hated himself for these thoughts. Hadn't he spent a good portion of his twenties coming to terms with the fact that he was still a man despite lusting after men? Hadn't his grandfather and his uncles and whole swaths of the Brooks family essentially said something was so wrong with him he couldn't be a part of the family anymore? Hadn't Uncle Gary essentially said he was throwing away his career for some cock, and nothing could have been more disgusting?

Mason gave Patrick a quick peck on the lips at the subway entrance, knowing perfectly well how dissatisfied Patrick probably was with that but unwilling to do more. Fire Island had been one thing—and what a marvelous thing it had been, especially after Mason had talked Patrick into staying an extra day—but now that they were back in the city and back to their real lives, Mason was suddenly self-conscious, aware in a way he didn't want to be of everyone looking at him.

He went about his day, working out of his favorite cafe on Tenth Avenue and finishing the article about the gay baseball player at Rice University, though he didn't like it much either. He called Jim and asked for another day.

That night he met Odell for dinner at a restaurant in the West Village Odell had been wanting to try.

Odell had recently taken over management of a sporting goods store in Midtown called Action Sports that specialized in urban sports equipment and Yankees memorabilia. It had put enough spare change in his pockets to do fancy dinners with Mason once a month or so, usually at whatever restaurant was the hot new place.

Mason was proud of his brother. Odell worked hard and had been steadily working up the ranks from a sales associate to a shift manager and now to managing the whole store. The owners had two others in the city, but

Odell's location was on Fifth Avenue, just down the street from Saks and Rockefeller Center, so it saw a lot of tourist traffic, specifically the sorts of tourists who had money to burn on vintage jerseys and signed baseballs. But the store sold a good range of high-quality baseball equipment, so Mason referred his Rainbow League teammates there all the time. Since taking over management, Odell had offered discounts to the Rainbow League players at Mason's urging, which had been a boon to both the league and the store. So it wasn't that Odell was homophobic or unsupportive. Not really. Right?

So what was Mason getting his panties in a bunch about?

He sat across from Odell at a table in a pretty high-visibility section of the restaurant. Mason wondered if it was coincidence or if he'd been recognized. It still happened sometimes that he got special favors—a gay sports bar in Chelsea let him drink free most of the time, for example—but those times were waning as people forgot.

Odell looked snazzier than usual in a shiny blue suit and a tie with silver thread woven through it. Mason had put on a shirt and tie, but it was way too hot out for a jacket.

"You look fancy," Mason commented as he sat.

"I had a meeting today with the guy in charge of merchandise for the Giants."

"And?"

Odell pointed to himself with his thumbs. "Who just secured a deal for selling officially licensed merchandise at his store?"

"Congrats!"

"Thanks. The owners have been wanting to do this for a while, but I finally took some initiative." Odell did a little chair dance, lifting his shoulders and snapping his fingers.

Mason laughed. "Seriously, that's great."

"Thanks, little brother. Now, let's look into getting some chow."

After they ordered, Mason asked, "You talk to Mom recently?"

"Yesterday," Odell said, breaking a roll in half. "She called. Wanted to see about using my employee discount on some golf clubs for Uncle Gary for his birthday. Even with the discount, though, they're still kind of out of her price range."

"She seem okay?"

"Yeah. I know I said she was being weird about her birthday, but she seemed just fine when I talked to her yesterday."

"Okay." Mason was still a little worried, but he knew he should talk to his mother himself rather than relying on Odell. Maybe she'd never been out of sorts. Maybe she still was. He'd been afraid to confront her lately, concerned she'd judge him for some of the choices he'd made recently. He made a mental note to call her the next day and then otherwise put it out of his mind.

They were pretty well into their main course when a gay couple walked in and sat at the table next to them. The couple consisted of a skinny South Asian guy with glasses and a blond twink wearing a lot of eyeliner. They looked adoringly at each other. Mason thought it sweet and smiled to himself.

Odell leaned across the table and said, "What the hell just sat next to us?"

"A couple?"

Odell raised his eyebrows. "I don't get it with these girly boys," he whispered.

"What's to get?" Mason's hackles were raised now.

"Thank God you're not one of *those* gay guys."

Mason put his fork down. If he hadn't shaved his head recently, he imagined the hair on the back of his neck would be standing straight up now. "One of *what* gay guys?"

"You're still a man, bro. You're not like one of those, you know." Odell raised his hand and let his wrist drop while he pursed his lips in a move Mason guessed was supposed to look fey. "I mean, no offense, but I just… those guys?" Odell shook his head.

Mason glanced at the next table to see if the couple had heard anything. As they were still just gazing at each other as if nothing else in the world existed, Mason supposed not.

"And, like, I don't really get it, you and the guys you date, but at least you've always gone after real men, you know? Not girly boys."

"What if I did, though?" Mason asked, his back up now. The force of his anger surprised him, but it was there and he grabbed on to it, feeling offended and righteous.

Odell shrugged. "Why would you? You're not into that, are you?"

Odell sounded so grossed out by the idea that Mason bristled. He thought of poor Patrick. No, not "poor" Patrick, *sexy as fuck* Patrick. Gorgeous, proud, colorful, exciting Patrick. The guy who really got Mason's motor revving, more so than the acceptable-to-Odell sides of beef Mason usually brought home.

"No. Why would I?" Mason could hear the bitterness in his own voice. "But what if I did? What if one of these days, I brought home a guy who didn't measure up to your standards of masculinity?"

"You're being weird."

"I'm serious, Odell. And what would you do if *I* started doing some of those things? If I dressed better, spoke with a lisp, got my ears pierced?"

Odell goggled at Mason as if he had grown an arm out of his head. "Stop being an idiot."

Mason sighed, still frustrated but wanting to let it go. "Let's talk about something else. Tell me more about this merchandise deal."

Odell's face lit up. "So the manager was this stuffy guy in a shark suit, you know?"

# Chapter 8

WHEN MASON woke up, Patrick was sitting up in bed, looking at something on his phone. The ink on his arms seemed to stand out in strong contrast to his pale skin in the bright white light of the morning.

Mason reached over and ran a hand down Patrick's arm.

Patrick turned and smiled. "Good morning, babe."

"Morning. What are you looking at on your phone that is so interesting? It's not porn, is it?"

Patrick burst into laughter. "Sweetheart, if I wanted to see naked men, I'd just pick up the sheet." He turned his phone toward Mason. "No, I was looking at this tattoo design website."

The screen showed a photo of a man's arm with a phoenix tattooed on it. "Are you getting another tattoo?" Mason asked.

Patrick shrugged. "It's been a while. I was contemplating it. I dunno. I can't really afford it right now, at least not something with this kind of color work." Patrick gazed at the photo and then shut off his phone. "Sometimes I just like to look. Like window shopping."

Mason laughed softly and hooked his arm around Patrick's waist to pull him back down and against him. Patrick laughed and jerked as if he were ticklish. He continued to giggle as Mason tucked him against his body. Patrick took a deep breath and relaxed as Mason kissed the back of his head. Mason liked the way Patrick's body fit against his as he held Patrick close.

"So what do you think? Should I get a tattoo?"

Patrick put his hand over Mason's where it rested on Patrick's belly. "It might be hot, depending on what it is. On the other hand, your skin is so gorgeous, you don't need any ink to make it better."

Mason wondered about that. Had Patrick gotten tattoos to cover up something he didn't like? Or did he think the colors enhanced him? Maybe some of both. He wasn't sure he could ask the question delicately enough not to offend Patrick, so he kept his mouth shut. Instead, he said, "Maybe I should get the Hipsters logo tattooed on my hip."

Patrick giggled. "That glasses-and-beard thing? Oh, hell no. I mean, I get it, but can you imagine some future boyfriend coming along and asking about it? You're about the farthest thing from a hipster that I can imagine."

Mason snuffed a laugh, but something about the prospect of "future boyfriend" pinged him the wrong way. Why should he think about one when he was here in bed with Patrick? Sure, the odds of their having a future were not great, but also not completely out of the realm of possibility. Right?

Patrick settled against Mason. "That will probably be my next tattoo, actually. Not of the hipsters, but the unicorn from the SoHoMos logo. The only reason I haven't done it yet is that I keep thinking, 'Gee, getting a unicorn tattoo, how gay am I?' You know. But who cares. I'm me."

"I like you," Mason said. The words sounded lame as they tumbled out of his mouth, but he meant them. He did like Patrick just as he was.

"Mmm," Patrick said. "Well, I like you too. And don't get a tattoo just because you think I'd think it's hot. I mean, I totally would, but you should be yourself too."

Mason pressed his face into Patrick's hair and then said, "We're so different."

"True, but don't say it like it's a bad thing. I like that we're different. It keeps things interesting. I mean, how creepy are those twin couples?"

Mason laughed. He pulled Patrick closer against him. He could totally picture two men who looked essentially identical but were clearly dating; he'd seen them all over Hell's Kitchen in the years he'd been living there. And Patrick was right; there was something creepily incestuous about those couples.

"So you're saying we should embrace our differences," Mason said.

"You bet, babe. Although I'd like to embrace some other things too." Patrick growled and then burst into laughter. "Man, that was cheesy."

"I like that about you too," Mason said, because it was true. Because if they couldn't make silly innuendos and laugh with each other, there really was no hope.

Patrick rolled over in Mason's arms. It was a little awkward, but when he settled back against Mason, he grinned and then kissed Mason, and suddenly things were not so funny. But they were still good, so Mason decided to go with it. He put his arms around Patrick and held him close and kissed him until they had to come up for breath. And then they were laughing again and holding each other, and it was magical.

THE HIPSTERS suffered a somewhat embarrassing defeat against the Mermaids, the runner-up team from the previous season's play-offs. Nate had pitched very well. Mason had gotten two hits and batted in Ty in the seventh. The Hipsters still lost by four runs. Mason didn't want to feel embarrassed that they'd lost to a team of girls, but it seemed particularly humiliating to lose to the Mermaids.

Ty and the Mermaids' first baseman, Rachel, taunted each other most of the walk to Barnstorm, but in a good-natured way. Ian held Ty's hand as they walked and just grinned.

*Must be nice*, Mason thought.

He spared a thought for Patrick, aware that he was going to have to make a decision soon regarding the man. And then who should be in Barnstorm but Patrick himself.

Mason headed straight for the jukebox, where Patrick and a couple of his teammates were hanging out. "What are you doing here?"

Patrick raised his eyebrows. "Well, honeybunch, last I checked this bar was open to the public. Or at least to all Rainbow League members."

Mason sighed and tried to push away the tide of emotion he was feeling suddenly. He was elated to see Patrick. He was also caught off-guard and utterly mortified both by the recent loss and his excitement about seeing Patrick. It was making him feel stiff and uncomfortable.

Patrick was mad. Mason didn't blame him. He knew he'd been acting like an ass. Part of him wanted to kneel at Patrick's feet and beg for forgiveness. He wasn't ready to analyze why exactly. Mason hadn't really been given to great feats of monogamy and commitment before.

No, all he really knew was that he wanted Patrick in his life, that something about just a glimpse of the crazy hair and everything made Mason happy.

"I'm sorry," Mason said. "Let me start over. I'm glad to run into you, although you aren't usually here on nights when your team is not playing. What brings you here?" He thought he'd achieved a pleasant tone.

Patrick smiled. "Well, since you asked nicely, we had to move our usual practice night from Thursday to tonight because a critical mass of our players have other engagements this Thursday. So we practiced uptown and a few of us decided to come here afterward. I saw your team was playing tonight, so I figured I'd see you."

"Oh. Okay."

"I'm not, like, stalking you, or whatever it is you're thinking."

"No. I know. I didn't think that. I was just surprised, is all."

"And now you're talking to me like a normal person, which I appreciate. Of course, your teammates will see us together."

"So?" Mason tried to sound flippant, though that was a concern. It shouldn't have been, but he wasn't entirely ready to have their relationship become public knowledge. Again, he didn't want to analyze that instinct too closely.

Patrick nodded slowly. "All right. So you're not a total closet case."

"I'm not a closet case at all. I came out on the cover of *People*, remember? There are drag queens more in the closet than I am."

Patrick raised an eyebrow. "Are you sure about that? Because based on what happened last week—"

"I'm sorry about that too."

"You don't exactly seem thrilled to be seen with me, is all."

"I'm here now, aren't I?"

A slow smile spread across Patrick's face. "Yes, you are."

Mason hooked his hand around Patrick's elbow and pulled him a little away from the jukebox. He wanted to speak without being heard, which he supposed proved Patrick's point, but this was between them and nobody's business. "I am really happy to see you. You probably don't believe that."

"I don't know what to believe, babe. You give more mixed signals than a drunk with a telegraph machine."

"What?"

"Just be honest. Do you want to be with me?"

"Yes. Yes, very much."

"Are you ashamed of being seen with me?"

"No."

It was the truth, which surprised Mason at first. The way they made a mismatched pair appealed to him, though, and honestly, Mason's desire to be with Patrick, to have Patrick at his side, outweighed his shame at being seen with a man who was colorful and effeminate. Because Mason found, as the summer progressed, that he desired Patrick above all other things, that this quirky man made his pulse race and his cock hard, that he'd been fooling himself by thinking he was supposed to be with a particular kind of man when the man he wanted to be with was right here.

"No, I'm not ashamed," Mason reiterated before ducking his head and kissing Patrick hard.

Patrick smiled against Mason's lips and put his hands on Mason's shoulders. Then he opened his mouth and let Mason in, really let him in, snaked their tongues together, and seemed to relish in the kiss.

Patrick leaned back a little. He kept his hands on Mason's shoulders as their gazes met. "That was a persuasive argument."

Mason worried for a moment that a lot of people had probably just seen them kiss, but then he decided it was worth it. He looked at Patrick and met his gaze. "I really am sorry if you thought… or if I gave you the impression that… well. I think we both know what happened. I kind of got up in my own head. I am genuinely sorry about how I behaved."

"Mason, can I point out something really obvious to you?"

Mason smiled, though he worried Patrick was about to say something he wouldn't like. "Go ahead."

"Everyone makes snap judgments. Right? I mean, I imagine any number of people I walk by on any given day look at me and think I'm shallow or ridiculous. A man came into my salon last week with his daughter and kept mumbling to her all 'Get a load of this guy, eh?' like I couldn't hear him speak. And I know I bring it on myself. I wasn't born with green streaks in my hair or a sleeve of tattoos. But this is who I am, you know? I express myself with my body."

"Okay."

"That first night we met, you made no such snap judgment. You saw me and thought I was hot. I mean, that's what happened, right?"

"Yeah. I still think you're hot."

Patrick grinned. "And I think *you're* hot, but you know, I'm sure people look at you and make assumptions based on your skin color all the time."

Mason jerked, a little offended, but Patrick held firm. He went on, "I don't say that to be racist or to be an asshole, I'm just saying that people walking by you on the street or in a gay bar or out on a baseball field see you and make snap judgments about you because of what you look like. You have no control over that, I know. And I'm just some white kid from the suburbs, so you can tell me to shut the hell up. You *did* do that when we first met, as I recall, because I make snap judgments too. But I know what it's like to have people make judgments about things I can't control, like how high my voice is or how small my body is. And because of what I've done to my body, people make snap judgments based on my appearance all the fucking time. I figured you might understand what that's like."

Mason did. If not the obvious things, like his skin color, then the smaller issues, like every sports reporter who had interviewed him and commented on how articulate and well-spoken he was, the "for a black guy" left silent. He still cringed whenever he remembered a recent encounter with a salesperson at Macy's who had steered him away from the cashmere sweaters he was admiring by actually saying the words "These blends are much more affordable," as if a black man couldn't possibly have pulled in a good enough salary to afford a goddamned cashmere sweater, or worse, because she thought he'd steal one. And he knew what it was like to be treated like a sex object because the men who picked him up wanted to "taste a little chocolate" or whatever the fuck. Mason had often felt that the way other men viewed him—as a pro athlete, as a black man—trumped what was going on in his mind, in his heart, because the guys he usually dated couldn't see past that.

Although that was not true for Patrick.

So yes, Mason knew what that was like. "I do understand," he said. "It's why I'm apologizing."

"So I figured," Patrick said, tilting his head and making his grip on Mason's shoulders a little more firm, "that we'd see each other this summer and get to know each other as people, see if we're compatible in more than just the sexy ways, and take it from there. What do you think?"

"I think that sounds good."

Patrick leaned a little closer. "Good, I'm glad that's settled. So when are you taking me on a date?"

Mason laughed. "*I'm* taking *you* on a date?"

"I've seen the way you dress when you're not wearing a uniform, darling. I know you must have some of that Yankee money squirreled away. We've gone out to bars or whatever, but how about you wine and dine me properly? I'd treat, but I can basically afford fast food and maybe a movie if you don't get popcorn. Maybe you can come up with something more elaborate."

"Who's making snap judgments now?"

"I'm not gold-digging or whatever. I just thought—"

"Are you free Friday night?"

Patrick smiled. "I sure am."

# Chapter 9

PATRICK WAS deeply skeptical of all the Yankees paraphernalia in the vestibule in front of the host stand of the restaurant he'd just walked into with Mason. This place seemed suspiciously like a sports bar, which meant Patrick, who had been led to believe he'd be going to an upscale eatery, had dressed entirely incorrectly. Hell, he played baseball. Even though the only time he saw a game was if it was on in a bar or it was the play-offs, he could pass for a sportsy guy if he had some warning. Instead he'd put on a black button-front shirt and a purple tie and had been prepared to pass for a guy who could afford to eat in one of Manhattan's high-end restaurants. And yet.

Then again, Mason was overdressed too, in a dark suit that looked like it had been tailored specifically for his big body. He smoothed his hand over the electric blue tie as he flirted with the hostess. She giggled and said she'd look into their table.

"You are shameless," Patrick said.

Mason shrugged.

"So are we here to eat hamburgers and cheer on your former teammates or…."

"What?"

"Is this one of those trendy sports bars that serves bland fare to tourists? Because that's what it looks like."

"Oh. No, no. I mean, it's owned by Julio Ramirez."

Patrick had no idea who that was. He stared at Mason blankly.

"Former Yankees right fielder? Retired two years ago? Nothing?"

Patrick held up his hands. "You're the former Yankee, honey."

Mason shot Patrick a flirty half smile. "Right. Well, anyway, Julio and I are friends. We were in the trenches together back in the day. He opened this place last summer. Apparently his two life-long ambitions were to play baseball and open a Latin bistro."

That seemed promising. Patrick took a closer look at the memorabilia on the walls and realized most of it was Ramirez-specific—a framed jersey, a signed ball, a signed bat, a ton of photographs. And oh, a photo of Ramirez and Mason standing together in some stadium graced the wall, too; both of them looked quite resplendent in their uniforms. Mason had lost a little weight since leaving the majors, but man, him in a real uniform, that was something. Patrick wondered briefly if he still had that uniform and if he'd be willing to….

"Gentlemen, your table's ready."

Mason held his hand out for Patrick, so Patrick took it. The hostess led them to a table in the restaurant proper. Here, at least, things were classier, everything dark wood and brass. The walls were dark and uncluttered. No sports detritus here at all.

"The lobby is deceptive," Patrick said. "And narcissistic."

Mason grinned. "I think all professional ballplayers are a bit narcissistic."

"You included?"

"Sure. I probably mentioned that I used to be a Yankee the first time I met you."

"You did. I don't find that impressive." Patrick leveled his gaze at Mason. The truth was he did find it impressive; Mason was a gifted athlete who had once had the ambition to pursue a professional sports career.

"You were more impressed that I was on the cover of *People*, right?"

"Knowing you is surreal sometimes."

"Shall we order some wine?"

It became clear quickly that Mason was an old hat at this fine dining thing, probably from all those years of making multimillion-dollar salaries or whatever—Patrick didn't know how much he'd made, but he assumed even playing one season with the Yankees would net a guy more money than Patrick would ever see in his lifetime—so Patrick let Mason lead the way through dinner. Mason ordered wine, explained a few foreign words on the menu, and then ordered a small feast when the waiter came by.

"Now I'm impressed," Patrick said as the waiter walked away.

"Because I can order food?"

"You have smooth confidence. You just walk in here like you own the place and order all this food and know what you're doing. I feel like a fish out of water."

Mason's eyebrows came together, making him look puzzled. "But you blend right in here too. I like your tie, by the way."

"Thank you." Patrick was temporarily knocked off-guard by the compliment. "Well, anyway. I don't get to eat like this… well, ever. So if your goal for tonight was to impress me, well done."

"My goal was to have a romantic dinner in which we got to know each other better."

"All right. Let's do that, then." Patrick leaned forward a little. "Tell me about yourself. And I mean real stuff, not the dumb stuff I can Google."

Mason laughed. "Well, I don't know. I grew up in the Bronx."

Patrick pulled his phone out of his pocket. He brought up the browser and searched for "Mason Brooks." "Okay, here we go. 'Mason Brooks is a former professional baseball player. After three seasons with the New York Yankees, he made headlines by retiring and then coming out of the closet.'"

Mason rolled his eyes. "Yeah, yeah. I know all that."

"Brooks was born in the Bronx," Patrick kept reading. He quickly did the math on the listed birthday and realized Mason had recently turned thirty-two years old. "Oh, happy birthday."

Mason laughed. "It was over a month ago."

"Still. Let's see, what else? Baseball scholarship to the University of Virginia. Drafted by the Yankees in the sixteenth round. Played first base. Uh-huh."

"Are you just going to sit there and read my Wikipedia page?"

"I'm saving us some time. See, your whole life is here on the Internet. I'm more mysterious."

Mason rolled his eyes and sat back in his seat.

"Apparently you've been paired romantically with Bobby Jetson."

"I don't even know who that is."

Patrick laughed, temporary jealousy abated. "He's that pop singer who won *American Voice* a couple of seasons ago."

Mason continued to stare at him blankly.

Patrick sang, "'I Wanna Be the Man For You.' No? That's his hit song."

"No clue," said Mason.

"Good to know. Also it says here you've been linked with a wrestler. Gary Brown?"

"Oh, I did date him for a hot minute two years ago. You want to know some gossip?"

"Yes." Patrick leaned forward.

Mason smiled. "He's a walking PSA for not taking performance-enhancing drugs. Couldn't get it up."

"So you dumped him?"

"A man has needs."

Patrick laughed. He reached over and squeezed Mason's hand where it lay resting on the table. "Aren't you glad I can get it up."

"Very."

Satisfied, Patrick went back to reading. "So, it says here you tore your Achilles as well as some ligaments in your knee and had to have surgery, and that's effectively what ended your career."

"You already know about that." Mason waved his hand dismissively. "The bum leg and the fact that I got tired of being paranoid all the time that I was about to get outed were the big things in my life at the end of that season. So I did it myself before anyone else could."

"Why not out yourself and continue playing baseball?"

A brief pained look came over Mason's face. "I didn't think I could. I… I never wanted to be a trailblazer. I didn't want that much attention. I just wanted to live my life."

Patrick appreciated that. He nodded. "There's an image of your *People* cover, on which you look quite fetching, and some other photos of you in uniform and… in a bright blue suit at the ESPN Espy Awards. Yikes. Don't ever wear that color again." Mason looked good in the photo, but the color of the suit was so bright it made Mason's skin look a little green. "That's it for information on the Internet. So what else have you got?"

"I was raised by a single mom. She still lives in the Bronx. I have a brother named Odell who lives not far from here."

"Older brother? Younger?"

"Older. He manages a sporting goods store. You know Action Sports?"

"Oh, yeah! I just bought my new glove there. There's a discount for Rainbow League players."

"Who do you think made that happen?" Mason pointed to himself.

"Well, look at you!" Patrick laughed. "Nicely done."

The wine arrived. Patrick let Mason taste it. He'd said it was a sweet red, but that was the sum total of what Patrick knew about wine. After Mason tasted it, he nodded, and the waiter placed a large wineglass before Patrick.

After the waiter poured the wine and left them again, Mason said, "You've pulled a lot from me. What about you? All I know is that you're a hairdresser and you like tattoos and weird music."

"Weird music?"

"You're always fiddling with the jukebox."

Patrick grinned. "Well, honey. I grew up in Yonkers, so not very far from the Bronx, and my parents are still married but barely talk to each other. I have three sisters, and my father is convinced I grew up to be so colorful because my mother let them dress me up when I was a kid. You and I know that's horseshit, but this is what my father believes. Uh, I got an English degree from Purchase College, and then I moved to the city and went to beauty school." For good measure, Patrick sang a few bars of "Beauty School Dropout," but Mason looked mystified by that.

"See? Weird music. Is it really called beauty school?"

"You're looking at a graduate of the Empire State School of Cosmetology."

"Wow."

"And I'm good at what I do, by the way. If you had any hair on your big bald head, I could make it look lustrous."

"I'm sure you could." Mason topped off the wineglasses. "You like what you do?"

"I love it. I don't love all my customers, but I like working with hair. It's my canvas. Well, okay, sometimes I get a guy in who just wants me to buzz the sides, and sometimes I get, like, a corporate dragon lady who wants something old-fashioned, but my salon is pretty edgy. I do a lot of color."

Mason smiled. "You are a lot of colors."

Patrick smiled back. "I know. You like that about me."

"It's true. I do. What is your real hair color?"

"Eh. Kind of dark brown, I guess. I started bleaching my eyebrows too, so it wouldn't look so striking." Patrick touched his hair, on which he'd used pomade that morning to make it stick out just so. "I haven't seen my real hair in a while, I'll admit. It's pretty dry as a result. I could grow it out, maybe, just to be subversive." He smiled. "Or not."

The first course arrived then. Patrick had never eaten some of the food on offer. This was Latin cuisine, but like nothing Patrick had ever had before; this place did not serve burritos or quesadillas. This course included a roasted corn dish with cheese that proved to be quite delightful and some kind of potato and chorizo thing. Mason explained the dishes in a way that was a delight to listen to; he didn't really have any sort of accent, but he sometimes hit a consonant in a hard New York-y way, and his voice had a certain rhythm to it that Patrick found appealing.

So they ate, and they ate well, and they talked about their respective childhoods, which really weren't that different.

When they were most of the way through their main course, a man in a slick gray suit arrived at their table, all smiles.

"Mason!"

Mason stood and embraced the man, but in a straight-guy, back-pat-heavy way. "Hi, Julio, how are you?"

"Good. Glad to see you. You're enjoying the food?"

"Yeah, it's great. Oh, Julio, this is my boyfriend, Patrick."

Patrick almost died right then. They hadn't really been on many real dates, but Mason had just introduced Patrick to his former teammate as his boyfriend.

It took him a moment to catch his breath and slide out of the booth. He shook hands with this Julio fellow and managed to make his mouth form the words to some pleasantries. He nodded when Julio asked if he enjoyed his meal.

So much for being in the closet.

"So you do like me," Patrick said as they sat back down after Julio left.

"Yeah. Was that not clear?"

"You just introduced me as—"

Mason grabbed Patrick's hand. "I know we haven't had a conversation about it or anything, but maybe we, I don't know, we could consider seeing just each other for a while. Like, exclusively. Make it a real thing?"

Patrick laughed. "You wanted to have a big romantic meal, and nothing about this has been especially romantic. The food's good and I like talking to you, but I felt like we were just talking. Then you had to go and introduce me to your teammate as your boyfriend. I think 'make it a real thing,' said the way you just said it, is maybe the most romantic thing anyone has ever said to me."

Mason squeezed Patrick's hand and smiled. The gesture went a long way toward calming Patrick's nerves. Because underneath everything, Mason impressed Patrick, and Patrick wanted to be with this man not just because he was sexy but because he was interesting and smart and funny and completely unlike anyone Patrick had ever met.

"So what do you say?" Mason asked.

"I say yes. Let's make it a real thing."


MASON HELD Patrick against him, nestled together in the postcoital glow in his bed, in his apartment that was only a little narcissistic. Sure, a couple of his old uniforms still hung in the closet, like a reminder that the three years of his life he'd spent as a Yankee were real. It almost didn't feel that way these days. He wondered if anyone would even remember.

He was a blip in the long legacy of the team, a player who had done all right but was hardly Hall of Fame material. Probably if anyone remembered him, it would be for coming out and not for the thirty home runs he'd hit his second season or the five RBIs he'd gotten in one particularly glorious game.

In the scheme of things, Mason's legacy was not that significant, and he'd been flying under the radar for a while and the stakes were low. Maybe that was why it had made sense in his head, as illogical as it was, to introduce Patrick to Julio as his boyfriend. Not "my friend," not even "my date for this evening," but "my boyfriend." He wanted it to be true. Patrick had seemed happy about that.

Mason had been wasting his time in the limelight, doing what he thought was appropriate and not what he really wanted to do. The uniforms hanging in the closet were a symbol of that.

He spared a thought for poor Davis trying to procure Mason more endorsement deals. Pride parades were one thing, but Davis wanted Mason to talk about his experiences as a gay baseball player on some morning show now that, in the aftermath of the NCAA finals, the phenom from Rice was making headlines again. Mason's article on Brian Fox had brought a ton of traffic to the Sports Net website, but Mason still wasn't quite comfortable with how it had all played out.

Not much he could do about it now that the article was out there. He'd been politely declining TV appearance opportunities because he just didn't want to be in the spotlight, especially now that he was with Patrick. Why should he be the expert on being a gay athlete? He was only one man.

He stroked Patrick's hair. Could he be seen around town with a guy like Patrick on his arm? Why the hell not? Why was he always tying himself in knots about what people might think? If he never got another endorsement deal, he'd survive. He could make money in other ways than shilling for some product.

Because being with Patrick made him happier than he'd been in a long time, and he was just so content, lying here, holding the colorful sleeping man in his arms. And tonight he'd apparently made a decision to get over himself and really be with Patrick instead of pretending and keeping him at arm's length.

So he pulled Patrick harder against him until Patrick's little butt settled against his belly, and he kissed the back of Patrick's neck, and he sighed happily when Patrick leaned into him.

"Are you awake?" Patrick asked sleepily.

"Having one of those middle-of-the-night train of thought derailments."

Patrick laughed softly. He put his arm over Mason's. Mason played with the soft hair on Patrick's belly.

"What are you thinking about?" Patrick asked.

"Product endorsements."

"Eh?"

Mason sighed. "That's how us has-been athletes continue to keep our swanky Manhattan apartments, or this is what my agent tells me. I get paid a lot of money to do ads for products, basically."

"Are you going to be in commercials?"

"Hard to say. Probably just a couple of magazine ads. That's all I've really done in the past."

"You're very handsome, you know. You'd look good on TV."

"Yeah, well. Washed-up athletes don't tend to get a lot of screen time."

"There's that one former Yankee that shows up in those ads for the car dealership in Brooklyn."

Mason smiled. That was true. One of the best players from the Yankees late-nineties dynasty had somehow been convinced to read stilted dialogue for a car dealership fifteen years after his retirement. Mason wondered if the dealership owners knew him or if he was just that hard up for money. Or both.

"I don't like attention," Mason said.

"So why do the big splashy coming out?"

Mason pressed his face into Patrick's weird, stiff hair and inhaled, mostly taking in the acidic scent of the hair products Patrick used, but underneath was soft and baby-powdery and very Patrick. "I was so mad."

"What do you mean?"

"I was mad." Mason closed his eyes, inhaled again, and remembered. "One of the pitching coaches called us all girls at practice one afternoon. Just lost his mind and started shouting all this nonsense. Stop wasting time braiding our hair and talking about dresses. Maybe if we weren't taking it so hard up the ass we could run like real men. That kind of thing. I got pretty good at letting it roll off my back, but that afternoon, it just hit me the wrong way."

"There's a right way to take that?"

Mason smiled at the indignant tone in Patrick's voice. "No. There really isn't. But being a closeted professional athlete means you suck it up and laugh nervously from the sidelines even though you're a mess inside.

But this time, I got really angry. I just snapped. Yelled at Coach to cut the homophobic crap. He just got even more on my case and kept calling me a faggot." Mason hated this memory. He felt the bile rising up now, as if he could redo that whole afternoon and go punch Coach in the face, as he'd wanted to at the time. "Anyway, at the time I was casually seeing a guy on the down low, another closeted athlete. The relationship was stalled because we didn't dare tell a soul we even knew each other. We broke up just before I got hurt."

"That must have sucked."

"It did. A lot. All of it. Then the postseason rolled around. Did I tell you about how I injured my foot?"

"Torn Achilles tendon. That's all."

"Game two of the ALCS, I hit a grounder toward third, and as I was running for first base, I put my foot down hard and it got twisted. I dove for the base and landed wrong. The pain was blinding. I couldn't even stand up. I had to be carried off the field in a stretcher."

"God."

"Yeah. And I remember lying there, my whole leg feeling like it was on fire, and I thought, 'I can't do this anymore.' This was only a few weeks after that bad practice and the end of my relationship with the athlete."

"So you quit."

"I quit, yeah. I mean, you saw, my leg still bothers me sometimes. A tough practice or a long Rainbow League game can set me back for a couple of days. But I was so angry that, I don't know, I felt like I needed to shout out the truth. Finally."

They were both quiet for a few moments. The silence disturbed Mason until he realized their breathing had synchronized.

Eventually Patrick said, "I think you're brave."

"No."

"No, you are. A lesser man would have stayed quiet."

"A greater man would have come out and kept playing."

"Don't dwell on regret. All you can do is look forward. Live your life the way you want to now that you're out and live it to the fullest."

Mason smiled. That seemed like a sound philosophy, one that Patrick admirably lived up to. "I will," Mason said. He wasn't sure if he could do it, but he wanted to. "Come here."

He tugged at Patrick and turned him around. Then he laid a soft kiss on Patrick's lips, drawing it out slowly. Patrick still tasted of toothpaste and sleep.

When Mason pulled back, Patrick smiled. "Do I figure into your life-living plans?"

"Definitely."


IT WAS too good to be true.

Patrick was fully aware that a hormone-and-wine-fueled romantic date did not erase whatever issue Mason was dealing with, but it was nice to pretend for a while. And in a moment early that morning, Mason had held him and kissed him tenderly, and Patrick felt safe and cared for. He didn't often feel safe, it was true; he was too strange, tended to draw too much attention to himself. But with Mason, he always felt a little like he had a guardian teddy bear hanging around.

Mason really was a teddy bear, after all. He was big and huggable and cute in his way, for all his muscular athleticism. Patrick really liked the look of him, obviously, but the whole package drew him. Except for this nagging sense that Mason was ashamed to be seen with him.

As Mason kissed him good-bye in the morning and Patrick took the elevator down and walked out of Mason's building, he wondered if his unease was habit, if he just expected people to dismiss him or think he was too weird to be around, or if he was reacting to something Mason had actually done. It was hard to tell.

It wasn't the first time Patrick had fallen for someone unavailable. His past had closet cases, and guys with serious cases of internalized homophobia, and a guy who didn't get around to telling Patrick he was married until the third or fourth time they slept together. Patrick was starting to wonder if he had a sign on his forehead that read "Got issues? Apply here."

He took the subway home, feeling like his nice clothes from the night before helped him blend in rather than acted as a sign saying "Walk of Shame." When he got home, he showered quickly, tried to make his hair behave, and then slithered into a pink T-shirt and skinny jeans so he could go cut some hair.

When he got to Dimensions, Valerie was self-manicuring her nails, but the rest of the salon was quiet.

"Huh, you're early," she said.

"I was up on the early side. Figured I'd get ready for my first client instead of making her wait. It's Can't-Commit-to-Purple, right? Think she'll go for it today?"

Valerie chuckled. "No. Better go mix up the red."

He thought about getting started on the color mixing. Instead, Patrick plopped into the chair next to Valerie. He huffed out a breath.

"Okay. What's going on?" She raised an eyebrow. "Talk to Mama Val."

Patrick smiled. "So I'm dating a guy, right? And he's, like, the most closeted out gay guy I've ever met."

"Huh?"

Patrick sighed and rubbed his face. "Why do I always fall for the guys who are ashamed of being attracted to me?"

Valerie nodded. "Oh, he's one of those. Is he super masculine?"

"Yeah. I have a type, I guess."

"So he can go fuck himself. If he doesn't like you for who you are, then he doesn't deserve you."

Patrick smiled, glad to have a defender. "That's not quite the issue. He does like me for me. He'd never ask me to change. He's hot for me as I am." Those things were all true, and Patrick knew that in his gut. It was part of Mason's appeal. But.... "He hates himself for being attracted to me."

"Why? The hair?"

"And the tattoos. And my voice. And the fact that I like to wear eyeliner and have extra holes in my ears. And that I'm small and kind of effeminate. The whole package. I think...." Patrick paused to work out what he'd learned of Mason so far. "I think he thinks he should be with a guy more like himself. He portrays a certain image. It's okay for him to be gay if he's also really butch. I throw him off. And honestly, I think that's what he likes about me, but it's all tangled up."

"Sounds like a lot of work," said Valerie, unscrewing the cap of a bottle of topcoat.

"Yeah. Can you do my nails next?"

"Sure, sweetie. What are you going to do about this guy?"

"I don't know. Keep seeing him and wait for him to get over it?"

"You think he will?"

"I don't know. That's the risk."

"Love is a risk."

Patrick rolled his eyes as he moved to the chair across from Valerie. He grabbed a cotton ball and started swabbing his own fingers with polish remover. "Love? Who said anything about love? This is just fucking. On a regular basis."

"Boys." Valerie rolled her eyes. "If this were just fucking, you would not be this bent out of shape."

Patrick could acknowledge the point but didn't want to. He walked over to the nail polish display and picked a particularly garish shade of yellow. "What do you think I should do?"

"Do you like him?"

"Obviously. But I always like the unavailable ones. Just like you always like the crazies."

Valerie nodded. "I do like them mentally unbalanced."

This wasn't actually true; Valerie just coincidentally only dated guys who were total head cases. Well, *Valerie* said this was a coincidence.

"Is there any hope?" Valerie asked. "Do you think he could turn it around?"

"Yeah, I think so. Maybe. With time. But do I want to wait for that?"

"That's up to you."

Patrick sighed and handed her the yellow polish. "You're no help."

# Chapter 10

MASON WORRIED about how much his leg throbbed as he finished jogging a lap and arrived back at the ball field where the Hipsters were having their Sunday afternoon practice. He walked over to the backstop, propped his hands against it, and attempted to stretch out his leg.

"You all right there?" asked Ty in his slow Texas drawl.

"Yeah. Little sore. Foot's acting up again. I think I stepped on it wrong." He looked at his leg, frustrated with it. He wanted to run, to do well in practice, to have a leg that worked all the time, but instead he'd hit his heel on a rock or something and pain so sharp and hot it felt like his bones had shattered had gone up his leg. Fortunately, after another few steps, it subsided. Now it just ached, but it was still worrisome. Mason rubbed his ankle.

And thought about Patrick massaging his foot in the tub at his place on Fire Island.

He shook his head and coughed to cover up the illicit thought, sure suddenly that Ty could tell what he was thinking about.

But that was silly. Mason wondered if he was losing his mind.

Ty tossed a ball in the air and said, "You coming out after practice?"

"Yes. If I can still walk."

Ty smirked. "We'll carry you if we have to."

Mason nodded. "No, I'm going. I invited the guy I've been seeing."

Ty's eyebrows shot up. "Oh, really?"

It was time, Mason figured. It would be a gesture of good faith to Patrick, a sign that Mason was serious about their relationship. The prospect of introducing Patrick to his friends had Mason's stomach tied in knots, but he knew it was the right thing to do. "Yeah," he said. "I mean, he plays for the SoHoMos, so you probably already know him, but I figured I should formally introduce him to my friends."

"Aw, that's adorable. Is it serious, then?"

Mason didn't know how to answer that. "Yeah, I guess."

"Ooh. Is it that beefy outfielder? What the hell is his name? Steve?"

"Ah, no. Not Steve. His name is Patrick."

"Which one is Patrick?"

"God, you're as bad as Josh with the matchmaking. You'll meet Patrick soon enough. It's a real thing now."

Ty pursed his lips. "We don't even talk like adults anymore, do we? 'A real thing'? As in, like I have with Ian? My boyfriend who I'm about to move in with?"

Yikes, moving in together. The idea gave Mason hives. "Maybe not that real. Did you find a place?"

"Not yet, but—"

"Quit yakking!" shouted Scott. "Line up for batting practice."

Mason got in the batting line behind Ty and in front of Josh, who stared at him with a giddy expression. "Did I overhear you say you invited your new man to the bar tonight?"

"I did, yeah."

Josh was practically bouncing. "You never even told me you were dating anyone. How long have you been together?"

"I don't know. A month or so? Since the beginning of June?"

"How can you not know?"

Ty rolled his eyes. "Yeah, bro, didn't you know that you're supposed to mark all these things on a calendar so you can celebrate weekly anniversaries?"

"Oh, please," said Mason.

"Ty, you're up!" shouted Scott. "Stop gossiping like teenage girls."

When Mason stepped up to the plate a few minutes later, he realized he was giddy too, and nervous, and a little shaky. His pressed his heel into the sand at home plate experimentally. Nate gazed at him from the mound for a moment and eventually said, "Are we dancing or playing baseball?"

"Throw me the ball, asshole," Mason shouted back.

He got into his batting stance and swung at the ball. He missed and twisted his bad foot in the process. Pain shot up his leg.

"Dammit," he muttered.

"You okay, Mason?" Scott asked.

"Yeah. Let me try that again."

Nate was pitching a little high, so Mason adjusted, and he at least got the bat on the ball the second time, though he sent a wimpy grounder toward first base.

"Again!" shouted Scott.

Mason took a deep breath and tried to remember that this practice had no pressure, that most of his teammates were at practice as a pretense to go out drinking afterward, that whether the team won or lost was immaterial. No batting coach would call him a faggot—they were all faggots, even shouty Scott—and his future career did not depend on him hitting this ball.

It was a hard habit to get out of, caring whether he won or lost. He liked the Rainbow League because it was low-pressure fun and he still got to play baseball every summer. But games had little in the way of competitiveness, and part of him missed it.

He raised his bat again and looked at Nate. Nate lobbed the ball at him, and he hit it again, this time sending it sailing over Nate's head.

"Better," said Scott. "Next!"

Mason handed off the bat to Josh and supposed he could have gotten more indignant, asking Scott where he got off telling a former Major League Baseball player he was hitting okay. Mason had hit home runs—dozens of them!—in Yankee Stadium against pitchers a hell of a lot better than Nate, and Nate was one of the best pitchers in the Rainbow League.

But Mason was retired. The Hipsters considered him their secret weapon, but the truth was that, especially with the bum foot, Mason wasn't major league material anymore. He wasn't even that much better than the other guys on his team.

No matter. As practice wrapped, he got a hug from Carlos, who had plans that night that did not involve his teammates, and a back pat from Ian. Josh practically skipped out of the park, so gleeful was he about meeting Mason's boyfriend. Ty told him to calm down, then took Ian's hand and led the way to the bar with Nate in tow. It was a quick enough walk from the Prospect Park ball fields to Spokes, the cowboy bar they'd been dropping in on after practice in the nearby Brooklyn neighborhood of Prospect Heights. They alternated between it and a gay bar in Park Slope after practice.

Mason was nervous, no denying it. His heart raced as they got closer to the bar. This shouldn't have been so nerve-racking, but suddenly Mason worried his friends would take one look at Patrick and ask Mason what the hell he was thinking. He worried they'd judge Patrick and find him lacking. He was so nervous as they walked the last block that he thought he'd have to vomit into a nearby trash can.

Patrick was already at the bar when they got there, sitting on a stool and looking a little dazed. As Mason approached, he said, "Who knew there was a gay cowboy bar in the middle of hipster Brooklyn?"

"To be fair," said Ty, who lived in the neighborhood, "this is more yuppie Brooklyn than hipster Brooklyn, but point taken. Are you the boyfriend?"

Patrick shot Mason an amused look. "I believe so."

Mason tamped down his nerves and said, "Guys, this is Patrick. My boyfriend. He plays for the SoHoMos, as you may know. Patrick, that's Ty, Ian, Josh, and Nate." Mason pointed. "They're my friends and Hipsters teammates."

Everyone stood there for a long moment staring at each other. Mason's stomach dropped.

But then Josh was on Patrick in an instant, hugging him tightly. Patrick made that same amused look at Mason over Josh's shoulder.

"It's so good to meet you," said Josh. "I mean, for real this time. We've probably met before but never really had a… so did you guys hook up after a game or what?"

"That's about the sum of it," said Patrick.

"This is very exciting. Mason hasn't introduced us to a boyfriend in a while. Not since that one two years ago. The guy with the shoulders. What was his name?"

"Bruce," Mason supplied.

"Right," said Josh. "More like Brute, though. God, that guy was not someone you wanted to run into in a dark alley. But you, Patrick dear, are adorable."

"Thanks," said Patrick, blushing.

Mason's chest swelled a little and he put an arm around Patrick, who likewise put his arms around Mason and gave him a quick hug. It felt… real. Warm and affectionate and real.

"How was practice?" Patrick asked.

"Fine," said Mason.

"Oh, sure, everything was fine until Nate started throwing meatballs," said Ty. "Turns out that slowing down a ball does not make it easier to hit."

"Hey, Scott told me to do it," said Nate, holding up his hands. "Changing pitch speed is supposed to keep you guys on your toes."

Ty walked up to the bar and signaled to the bartender, who gave him a "just a sec" finger. He turned around and leaned back against the bar. Ian moved next to him, as if he couldn't stand to be separated.

"I thought how well you played didn't matter," Ian said.

"It doesn't," Ty said with a scoff. "And this was just practice anyway."

But Ty seemed bothered. Mason wondered if they'd had this conversation before. Ian laughed softly and gave Ty a kiss on the cheek before turning and contemplating the beer taps.

"What are you drinking?" Mason asked Patrick, relieved that things were going okay. Mason knew he should have trusted his friends; they were all decent men. Of all of them, Ty was probably the most judgmental, and he seemed unfazed.

"A Cosmo," said Patrick. He lifted an empty glass. "I gotta go use the little boys' room, though. Be right back, honey."

He stood on one of the rungs on the stool he'd been sitting on and gave Mason a quick peck on the lips. Then he hopped down and walked to the back of the bar.

"He's cute," said Josh. "I want to bundle him up and put him in my pocket."

Ty narrowed his eyes at Josh. "You're such a weirdo."

Josh shrugged.

Ty turned to Mason. "He's not your usual type."

The nerves came back with a vengeance, like a body full of television static, white-hot and moving rapidly through Mason's chest. He swallowed and said, "Yeah."

"Hey, I think we should all be applauding Mason for no longer dating those dumb jocks," said Nate. "Not to be all stereotypical, because you are a beefy jock with a fine head on your shoulders, Mason, but those guys you were going with… I mean, brick walls, all of them, you know?"

That made Mason feel marginally better. "I do know."

"Kind of an odd couple, you and Patrick," Ty said. "Like these guys I saw over on Flatbush Avenue the other day. Clearly a couple because they were holding hands, right? And matching outfits too. Both of them in plaid shirts and navy shorts. But one was, like, six five, and the other was barely over five feet tall. It was kind of amazing."

"And then you spent five minutes trying to work out how they fuck, didn't you?" said Ian.

Ty shrugged. "It crossed my mind. How could it not? The tall guy's legs were at least six inches longer than the short guy's."

"It's all the same when you're horizontal," said Nate.

"I guess." Ty looked at Mason. "Not that I was thinking about you and Patrick…." He waved his hand. His face went red. "Ugh, whatever."

Ian laughed. "I love you, you perv." Ian turned to Mason. "He's the guy we all saw you make out with at Barnstorm a couple of weeks ago."

Had that happened? The memory came back to Mason suddenly, and it made him hot. He'd just gone right in there and kissed Patrick in public because he'd needed to prove he wasn't ashamed. Because he wasn't. And his friends didn't seem to care that much.

"Yeah, dude, we were onto you," said Nate. "But it's fun to see you sweat."

"Wait, where was I?" asked Ty. "I don't remember any kissing."

"He seems nice," Josh said. "And seriously, I want to pinch his cheeks."

"I think your big bear of a husband might object if you stole away with him," Ty said to Josh.

"Tony would want to pinch his cheeks too," said Josh.

Patrick came back then. He looked at everyone. "Uh. What are we talking about?"

"You," said Ian. "All nice things, though."

"Oh. Good."

"So what do you do when you're not solving physics problems with Mason?" Ty asked.

Patrick shot Mason a puzzled look. "Physics problems?"

"He's alluding to our height difference."

Patrick raised an eyebrow but said, "I'm a hairdresser. I work at a salon in the East Village."

"I bet Mason gets a discount," said Ty.

"What?" said Ian.

"Because he has no hair? Ugh, I give up." Ty held up his hands.

Everyone laughed. Mason started to believe everything would be fine.


PEOPLE SEEMED to drift off into pairs, so Patrick settled in with Mason at a table off to the side.

"I like your friends," Patrick said. And he did. He was elated that Mason had thought to do this. Perhaps the situation between them was not so hopeless. Mason had introduced Patrick to his friends as his boyfriend. That held promise. It felt like progress. It felt like a giant leap forward. And Patrick found he was grateful.

Mason gave Patrick a small smile. "Yeah. Thank you. I'm glad you like them. They seem to like you too."

"Good." Patrick rubbed the back of Mason's hand. "I know you were nervous."

"A little. These guys are some of my best friends. I was so busy when I was still a Yankee that I didn't make many friends outside of our own clubhouse. Joining the Rainbow League was almost as much about meeting new people as it was about playing baseball, you know?"

"I definitely do." Patrick looked around at the guys hanging around the bar. "Blondie and Texas are a couple, right? Sorry, I'm bad with names."

"Ian and Ty. Yeah. They've been together a little over a year."

"Ty." That was familiar. Patrick knew a Ty, didn't he? "Like, Ty Arnold? Token Slut Ty?"

Mason laughed. "Not anymore, but yeah. He had kind of a rep for a while there. Ian tamed him, I guess."

"I mean, hey, I am pro slut. No offense to him. Just, I was warned about him when I joined the Rainbow League."

"Yeah, everybody was for a while. I don't think he was actually sleeping his way through the league, but you know."

"Yeah. Leave it to a bunch of queens to amplify the gossip." Patrick smiled. He took a deep breath and relaxed into his seat. "And then the taller brown-haired guy is married to some Italian bear."

"Josh. Yes. His husband is not in the league."

"And Nate is... single?"

"Yup, as far as I know."

"Okay. Like I said, I like them. Not to distill everyone down to their relationship statuses. I am sure they have other things going on in their lives." Patrick smiled. "Thanks for introducing me to everyone. It means a lot that you wanted your friends to meet me."

"You're welcome. The next hurdle is just my family." Mason let out a shaky breath.

Patrick's eyes went wide. "You'd introduce me to your family?" Because that was a shock. They'd barely just started their relationship. Meeting Mason's family? Too soon.

Mason seemed to agree. He frowned and squirmed in his seat. "Well, maybe not yet. I don't... my brother is...."

Patrick held up a hand. "Say no more. It's fine. One step at a time."

"It has nothing to do with you. My family doesn't really like *me* that much sometimes, and, well...."

"Honey, it's fine. We haven't been dating that long. I don't need to meet your family right now. I am happy you introduced me to your friends, though." Patrick smiled. He was genuinely pleased with how the evening had gone. "Most of my non-baseball friends work in my salon.

You should stop by sometime. I know you don't have any hair, but the manicure girls are really good."

"A manicure?" Mason looked mystified.

"Have you never gotten one?" Patrick held up his yellow fingernails.

"Can't say I have."

"Ooh, you could do the whole mani-pedi thing. The salon has this little whirlpool thingiebob in the back where the pedicure customers can stick their feet. It's totally relaxing."

Mason scrunched up his face in distaste. "Really?"

"Yeah. It's basically a foot massage, but then they paint your nails at the end. I wouldn't even make you do a color, just a little clear polish, but it's totally worth it. It makes your feet look awesome."

Mason laughed and shook his head. "I am pretty sure being with you is going to change my life."

"I would count on it." Patrick grinned. "Anyway, Valerie? She works in my salon. She's one of my best friends. She's fabulous and she'd love you. You really should come by sometime."

"All right." Mason reached over and took Patrick's hand. "Maybe I will stop by sometime."

Patrick grinned. "Good."

Mason looked at his beer glass and then up at Patrick. "You want to come home with me tonight?"

"Of course. Although, hey, if I spend any more time at your place, I probably won't have to pay rent anymore. One of my roommates told me the other day that I'd been home so little she'd forgotten what I looked like."

"How could anyone forget you?"

Patrick couldn't help but smile at that. "Aw, sweetie."

A faint blush broke out across Mason's cheeks, and the way his shoulders went up indicated a kind of bashfulness that was, frankly, adorable.

# Chapter 11

MASON GAZED out at the view from a Brooklyn rooftop.

Ty had invited everyone to his friend's apartment for the Fourth of July. Ty had insisted the best spot for viewing the fireworks was from a Brooklyn rooftop. This friend of Ty's, a work colleague, lived in a high-rise building with roof access not too far from the Brooklyn Bridge. Ty had been told to bring friends, so he'd invited Ian, Nate, Carlos, and Mason. When Mason had asked if he could bring Patrick, Ty had said, "Hey, Jack said, 'The more the merrier.' I'm taking it at his word. I mean, worst case, we can ditch the party and just hang out on the roof."

The party was big enough that Ty and his friends seemed to blend right in, and though the apartment Jack and his wife shared was a little cramped, the roof was a wide expanse on which everyone spread out to watch the fireworks. The building was not super close, but Mason could kind of see the East River in the distance, and this was certainly better than competing with tourists for space on the Promenade. It had been a few years since the fireworks were launched over the East River instead of the Hudson, and Mason was happy to take advantage of this spot.

"The awesome thing," Ty said with an arm casually thrown around Ian, "is that from here, you can also see the fireworks in Queens and on Coney Island. They'll be all around us."

"Is he always this much of a know-it-all?" Patrick asked Mason.

"Pretty much, yeah."

The hosts of the party had put out some lawn chairs, but most of those assembled chose to stand. The edge of the roof had a wall that came up to about Patrick's nose, so he kept having to stand on tiptoes to see over it well, but they did have a decent view of South Street Seaport, which was where the fireworks barges would park.

So Mason let out a breath and put his arm around Patrick and tried to savor the moment, which was rather sweet and romantic. It was dark but for the sun setting in the distance. They were up high enough that even the light pollution from the streetlights wasn't too bothersome. Every now and then, a bottle rocket would whiz into the air; kids on the street clearly had some fireworks to send up.

"That's how someone loses a hand!" Ian shouted over the edge of the roof.

Patrick laughed, his body vibrating softly against Mason's. Mason pulled him close and kissed the top of his head.

"Did you know," said party-host Jack, "that I proposed to Melinda on this very roof the last year the fireworks were over the East River? I waited for the crescendo of the grand finale and I got on one knee and popped the question."

Jack's wife beamed at him.

"That's really sweet," said Patrick.

"I thought it was a moment that merited fireworks. Right, honey?"

Melinda smiled. "Good thing I said yes, or the night would have been awfully anticlimactic."

"Hey, they're starting!" said one of the other guests, pointing toward the river.

Mason and Patrick spent the next twenty minutes gazing at the fireworks and remarking about them to each other. Patrick seemed in awe of the view—he kept commenting on how amazing it looked and how cool it was to be able to see the fireworks from this angle—but Mason was more in awe of Patrick. Patrick was dressed well, in a crisply tailored black shirt and dark jeans. He'd put a series of onyx earrings in each ear and wore bangle bracelets that jangled together when he moved. His hair was particularly riotous. He was so fucking beautiful to Mason.

"Kiss me," Mason said to Patrick when the fireworks seemed to be building up to a finale.

"Yes," Patrick said as he leaned into Mason's arms.


BETWEEN THE bang of the fireworks over the East River, the muffled thump of more distant fireworks displays, and the fizzy sparklers and bottle rockets the kids on the street were shooting off, it was all explosions. Patrick thought this might be what a war zone sounded like.

Which made kissing Mason that much more intense. The noise—and his proximity to Mason—made his heart pound.

On top of that, he couldn't help but think about that story Jack had told about proposing to his wife during the grand finale. It certainly was romantic up here on the roof, darkness surrounding them except for the streetlights from below and the faint lights from neighboring buildings. It was hard to make out Mason's features in this light, except for his eyes, which seemed to sparkle even in the dark. Fireworks burst in the distance and a gentle breeze cut through the muggy July heat. The moment was nearly perfect.

*I could really love this man*, Patrick thought, his arm hooked around Mason's torso as they held each other. He leaned his head against Mason's chest and thought about just being with him, how great it was, what it meant. If not for the pesky problem of Mason still sometimes getting caught up in his own weird prejudice regarding masculinity, this relationship could be perfect.

The fireworks seemed to be winding down, but partygoers were standing on various edges of the roof, pointing out other distant fireworks displays.

"Can I ask you a weird, personal question?" Patrick asked.

"Okay?" Mason's voice was wary.

"I just keep thinking about that story Jack told. About proposing to Melinda. It's really romantic."

"I agree."

"This is really romantic too."

"Mmm."

"Just curious. What's your position on marriage?"

Mason stiffened briefly before he repositioned his arm around Patrick's shoulders and said, "Position on marriage? I'm for it?"

"I just mean, you know, some gay guys think marriage is a farce or it's heteronormative or whatever. This guy Hugh on my team? He's been with his partner for eleven years. *Eleven*. I asked him once if he thought he'd get married and he said no, he didn't believe in marriage for himself, but he was happy that people who wanted to get married could. So he personally thinks marriage is kind of a crock, but he believes we should all have the right to it, I guess. So I was just curious."

"Is this a 'where is this relationship going' conversation?"

The idea of that made Patrick's veins feel icy. It was definitely way too soon for that. "No. Just hypothetical."

Mason let out a breath, clearly a bit unsettled to be talking about marriage with a guy he'd only been with for about a month. "Hypothetically, I'd like to get married one day. If I found the right guy."

"Sure. Me too, for the record."

"Yeah?"

"I mean, I know I look like the least likely person on this planet to get fitted for a tux and worry about flowers and cakes and all that, but I always figured, you know, if I found The One, I'd want to marry him."

Mason hugged Patrick tightly and laughed softly. "You're right, you are the last person I can picture in a tux."

"Hey, just because I have tattoos does not mean I'm against monogamy. I've been totally faithful to you all summer. Haven't even looked at another guy."

Mason laughed harder. "Really?"

"Well, okay, maybe I exaggerate a little. But this guy who was all muscles and beard came into the salon for a trim last week. He was pretty easy on the eyes. Not as hot as you, but pretty hot, you know? I offered to trim his beard too, just as, like, a public service? I mean, neckbeard looks stupid on everyone. He let me, and then he asked me for my number. So I said I had a boyfriend. That takes real strength of character, I will have you know."

"Mmm." Mason leaned down and kissed Patrick. Patrick held him there and let Mason suck on his lower lip. When they pulled apart, Mason was grinning. "You did notice how hot he was."

"I have eyes. But like I said, not as hot as you."

"Thanks. I appreciate that."

Patrick turned in Mason's arms toward what he thought might be Coney Island, where fireworks were still exploding in the distance. "Seriously, though, maybe I look slutty, but I much prefer being in relationships. Having one person to rely on. Having that one guy to think about all the time and knowing he's thinking about me too."

"Yeah?"

"Yes. That's what I want."

"Do you think about me all the time?" Mason nuzzled Patrick's temple and then kissed the edge of his hair.

"Yeah. Pretty much nonstop since we hooked up last summer."

Mason moved behind Patrick and snaked his arms around Patrick. "Me too."

"It's getting chilly up here," someone complained.

"I've got more wine in the apartment," said Jack. "I think some of Melinda's red velvet cake is left too. Follow me!"

Their reverie seemed to have ended, so Patrick stepped away from Mason. He took Mason's hand, though, and led him into the procession headed back to the building's elevators.

# Chapter 12

IT WAS a bad season for the Yankees. In Carlos's sillier moments, he attributed their recent downfall to Mason's departure, though realistically, he knew that a weak bullpen and an aging batting lineup were preventing the Yankees from reclaiming the glory of their last World Series win.

Still, he sat next to Nate in his uncle's seats in the upper tier of Yankee Stadium, eating Cracker Jack as Nate leaned forward and stared at the field.

"This is ugly," Nate said.

The Yankees were only down one run, but Nate was right, they were playing sloppy baseball. "I know," said Carlos. "If Sanchez decided to actually pay attention instead of picking his nose, he totally could have caught that last pop fly."

Nate leaned back again and stole a handful of Cracker Jack. "I see now why Tio Felipe was willing to part with these tickets."

"Yanks are still second place in the division. It's not a total disaster."

Nate shrugged. "Okay, it's not all bad. It's still fun to watch the game live, even if they are getting their asses handed to them."

"One run, *papi*. That is hardly an uphill climb. That's more like driving over a speed bump."

One of the Yankee batters stepped up to the plate. Apparently now it was Carlos's turn to lean forward and watch. This batter was a rookie, but Carlos sensed something about him, felt good about the kid's confidence as he lifted his bat and settled into his stance. Carlos glanced up at the Jumbotron, which showed the feed from a camera that had zoomed in on the batter as he got ready to hit. It was almost like he called the shot with his facial expression. The first pitch went foul, but the second pitch seemed to bounce off the bat before it soared in the air toward the bleachers.

"Holy shit!" said Nate, sitting up.

It was a home run. The rookie pumped his arms in the air as he ran—the note on the Jumbotron said this was only his second home run of the season—and the stadium roared with delight as he looped around the bases.

"That was awesome," said Carlos.

"Yeah, it was." Nate held his hand in the air for a high five. Carlos obliged.

"Oh, did you hear? Lourdes is having another baby," Carlos said conversationally after the hubbub died down.

"Yeah, I was on that group text she sent announcing it."

Carlos laughed and shook his head. "At least she told me in person. She is so tacky sometimes."

Nate grinned. "Then Marisol sent me a separate text that was basically an eye roll."

"That's Marisol. I think sometimes that if you weren't gay, I would have tried to set you up years ago. You're like two peas."

"Yeah. I love your sisters like they were my own, though. Even if I weren't gay, that would be a pretty big hurdle. Marisol and I get along great, but in a sibling sort of way."

"Just saying. You're not ugly. I could think of worse fates for Marisol."

Nate rolled his eyes. "Gee, thanks."

"Aw, come on, you know what I mean. You would make someone a good boyfriend. Not Marisol, obviously."

Nate sighed. "Yeah."

"I heard Mason has a new boyfriend."

"He came to the bar after practice a couple of weeks ago. Then Mason brought him to that July Fourth party I went to." Nate let out a breath. It sounded like relief. "Nice guy. Not at all what I was expecting, though."

"In what way?"

"Are we really going to gossip about our friends' love lives like we're fourteen-year-old girls?"

"Hey, you led with the 'not what I was expecting' comment. I'm curious now."

Nate rubbed his forehead. "Well, if you came out with us anymore, you'd have gotten to meet him. Instead you always ditch us after practice so you can go fuck Aiden."

Carlos bristled. "So?"

"So this is the first time I've seen you outside of practice in three weeks!" Nate sounded exasperated. He rubbed his hands over his face. "Sorry. I didn't mean to yell like that. Just pointing out that, you know, we used to hang out all the time, but I've barely seen you since you got hot and heavy with Aiden. I guess I thought, hey, I'm working fewer hours this summer, I'd get to hang around with my friends more, but you're too busy with your boyfriend."

"I'm here now, aren't I?"

"Sure. Fine. Whatever."

"Don't be a dick, Nate."

"I'm not. Sorry. Geez."

Carlos turned to look at Nate seething. He was right that Carlos had been spending less time with his friends of late. But he wanted to spend time with Aiden, who was, after all, his boyfriend. Carlos had a limited amount of free time, and yeah, he prioritized Aiden, but wasn't that what people in relationships were supposed to do?

Then again, he did hardly ever see Nate anymore. There was a time in the not-too-distant past when they'd seen each other nearly every day. But Aiden had asked Carlos to spend less time around Nate, and Carlos had been honoring that request. Carlos figured Aiden would get over this little jealous phase and things would go back to normal.

"I'm not, like, deliberately shutting you out or anything," Carlos said. "Just Aiden—"

"He's your boyfriend. It's fine. I get it."

"He thinks you're jealous."

That was clearly the exact wrong thing to say. Nate jerked upright and scowled at Carlos. So… nope. Not jealous. Okay.

"Fuck that guy," Nate said.

Carlos had thought it would be a funny joke. He and Nate had been friends so long, they were brothers too. Maybe at a certain time in his life, he'd had an eensy bit of a crush on Nate, but Carlos had gotten over it by the time they'd graduated college, and anyway, Nate had never shown the slightest bit of interest. Nate had no reason to be jealous, and he'd never been jealous of one of Carlos's boyfriends before. Nate's aggression where Aiden was concerned baffled Carlos.

"Come on," Carlos said. "He's not actually the asshole you seem to think he is. He's funny and nice and he cares about me. I don't get why you've been such a jerk."

Nate threw his hands up. "I'm not—" He shook his head. "Ugh, sorry. I told you, something about him rubs me the wrong way. I'll shut up about it if…"

"If?"

"If you try a little harder to make time for your friends. I mean, we've known each other forever. You're not someone I ever figured would become my see-occasionally-and-exchange-Christmas-cards sort of friend."

"That's not how we are."

"Not yet."

Carlos closed his eyes for a moment and took a deep breath. The hurt and irritation in Nate's voice rang through bright and clear. "Okay. I'll try harder. You and me, we'll hang out more. Okay?"

"Yeah, deal."

"So tell me about Mason's new boyfriend." That would at least get them off this terrible conversation.

Nate nodded as if he agreed with Carlos that things had gotten too heated. "He's kind of a twink? I mean, if guys in their late twenties are still twinks."

"Sure. I don't know."

"Me neither, man. But he's on the thin side and also has all these tattoos and piercings and really zany hair."

"He's another ballplayer?"

Nate smiled. "Yeah. His name's Patrick. He plays for the 'Mos."

Carlos tried to picture him. A couple of twinky tattooed guys played on the SoHoMos. "I think I know who you're talking about."

"So, like, the opposite of Mason's usual type, right?"

"Yeah, doesn't he pretty much only date really butch dudes?"

"Uh-huh. I mean, hey, the guy is really cute. I understand the appeal. And he and Mason are super into each other. It may just work out for those crazy kids."

"I hope so," said Carlos.

"Oh, Sanchez is up. Let's see how bad he fucks up this time."

Carlos laughed and leaned back. He ate his Cracker Jack and glanced at Nate, who seemed to have calmed down. He'd missed Nate, to be sure, as they'd been apart more often than not lately. It was nice just sitting together at a ball game, even if they were sort of arguing.

Sanchez managed a grounder toward third base, batting in the runner who had apparently gotten on base while Nate and Carlos were not paying attention. That put the Yankees up by two.

"This game may not be a waste after all," Nate said with a sidelong glance at Carlos.

Sensing he meant more than just in terms of the Yankees, Carlos nodded. "Nope. Doesn't seem that way to me either."

THE HELL'S Kitchen bar Mason chose for his date with Patrick was one of his favorites; it was low-key, not too loud, not too much of a meat market. He figured they could snag a booth, have a couple of drinks, make out a little, and then head back to Mason's place a few blocks away. Fun and easy.

He hadn't dated much. So many of his relationships had been cloak-and-dagger affairs, liaisons that required careful discretion and subterfuge so that Mason and his male lover wouldn't get caught together. Even since Mason had come out, his relationships rarely made it past the third date. Having a sustained one was a novel experience.

He thought maybe dates should involve more than chatting and drinking, but he couldn't think of anything he'd rather do than sit and talk with Patrick. And play baseball. If he could have just those two things in his life for a while, he'd be a pretty happy man.

His agent called when he was on the way to the bar. Mason growled at the phone but answered.

"You have an interview with Alison Lowe from *All Sports Weekly* two weeks from Thursday," said Davis with no preamble.

"I… what? Davis, I told you I didn't want to—"

"You said no talk shows. This is a magazine interview. You'll have to pose for a max of two photos. No video."

Anger knotted in Mason's chest. "I really wish you had run this by me first. I never would have said yes to an interview."

"I know. That's why I did this. I can get you this endorsement deal with the ointment brand if you get a little more press. We have to convince them that you're still a viable property. This is pretty low stakes, Mase. I compromised for your sake, you know. This'll be easy. Just answer the nice reporter's softball questions about your life. It'll take forty-five minutes max."

Mason cringed. Davis had a tendency to talk about his clients as if they were commodities and not people, something that had never sat right with Mason. But professional athletes got that treatment all the time, as if they were chess pieces part of a grand strategy and not living, breathing humans with feelings and vulnerabilities. "I'm not really comfortable—"

"You're doing the interview," said Davis. "I'll e-mail you the details. Once it hits newsstands, that should be the leverage I need to get the Lion ointment people on board. Then it'll be ads in *Sports Illustrated* and *All Sports Weekly*, maybe a TV commercial, and—"

"Davis…."

"Think about the TV ad. You probably will just have to stand and flex your muscles a little while the voiceover explains the virtue of the product. Fifteen seconds, thirty max."

"Fine," Mason said. "I'll think about it."

So he was already irritated when he finally walked into the bar. And who should be there but Odell.

Fuck.

A quick glance around the bar indicated that Patrick had not yet arrived, so Mason walked up to Odell, who was sitting at the bar nursing a beer.

"Hey," Mason said.

Odell looked up, his eyes wide in surprise. "Hi. Of all the bars in Hell's Kitchen…."

Mason and Odell had been to this bar together a number of times and it was only a couple of blocks from Action Sports, so Mason supposed he should have been less surprised. "What are the odds? Are you waiting for someone?"

"I had a shit day and didn't want to go home just yet. Figured I'd come here and see if there was anyone I wanted to bring home."

"What happened to Bettina?"

Odell shrugged. "She dumped my ass a week ago."

Mason slid onto the chair next to Odell. "What did you do?"

Odell balked. "What makes you think *I* did something?"

Mason raised an eyebrow.

"Okay, fine. I thought maybe she was only into me because I manage a business and could buy her nice presents. That turned out not to be the case."

"Ah. So you accused her of being a gold digger and she got offended."

Odell nodded and sipped his beer. "Not my finest moment."

"You're a real asshole sometimes, you know that?"

"What brings you here?"

Mason sighed. "I have a date."

Odell smirked. "Oh, really?"

The sly, slick way Odell smiled was off-putting, and Mason's nerves started flitting around like butterflies. Maybe Patrick hadn't fazed Mason's friends, but Odell wouldn't react that way.

"Mom wanted me to tell you she enjoyed her birthday dinner, by the way, so thanks for making that happen," Odell said.

Mason and Odell had taken their mother out for her birthday to a good seafood place in the Bronx. Mason had ended up making all the arrangements after Odell persisted in not remembering the name of the restaurant and then forgetting to call them to make a reservation. Mason wondered if he'd kept putting it off just so Mason would do the work. The dinner itself had been… fine. Mason and Odell had both refrained from discussing their personal lives despite getting quizzed, and their mother had been distant too. A normal Brooks family dinner, in other words. If something was wrong in her life, she was not forthcoming about it.

"I'm glad she liked it. I'll call her tomorrow." He made a mental note to actually call her this time. Mason regretted not keeping in better touch with her, especially since they still lived in the same city, but he'd been avoiding her a bit lately. The last time they'd spoken on the phone, she'd given him a lecture about… well, Mason wasn't exactly sure, but she'd seen a segment on the news about goddamned Brian Fox and his meteoric rise from unassuming college athlete to gay hero, and his mother had thought it was highly inappropriate for a kid to garner headlines for himself that way. Mason had tuned out part of it; the whole thing made him feel weary.

Now Odell was nodding. "So after I talked to her the other day, she gave me the speech about how she's not going to be around forever and I should start seriously considering making her some grandkids."

"Ugh."

"I'm her last hope, you know." Odell shot Mason a pointed look.

"I could get married someday. Remember how I'm about to have a date?"

Odell shrugged. "It's not the same."

Mason nodded. He suspected that somewhere, his mother was worrying herself into a lather about Mason's dating prospects and the odds he'd even have children—he didn't think he wanted them but hadn't ruled them out entirely—and Mason supposed that after thirty-some years of worrying about her children, it was a hard habit to break. Not to mention, Mason having actual biological children would require great feats of science. Would his mother treat an adopted child the same as her own flesh and blood? Mason wasn't sure. He'd been afraid to ask.

"I don't know," Odell said, looking around the bar listlessly. "I'm not ready to get married yet."

"So don't get married."

"Easy for you to say."

The snap didn't do much to ease Mason's already bristly mood. "Odell. Think before you speak. It has only been possible for me to get legally married in the State of New York for the last few years."

Odell looked chastened. "Right, I'm sorry. But the thing is—"

"Hey, Mason!"

Mason turned and a grinning Patrick greeted him by launching himself into Mason's arms and laying a big kiss on him. Mason caught him and got lost for a second. Then he heard the shocked gasp from Odell. He pulled away from Patrick as gently as he could.

Patrick stood there with one hand on his waist. "Who's your cute friend?" he asked.

"Ah, this is my brother, Odell. Odell, this is Patrick."

"Your date?" said Odell, looking astonished.

"My boyfriend."

Odell just stared. Mason found it unnerving.

"Sweetie, I need to powder my nose," Patrick said.

"Back of the bar to the left."

"Thanks. Be right back." Patrick wandered toward the back of the bar.

Odell's eyes were wide when Mason turned back toward him. He hoped Patrick hadn't seen.

"Dude," Odell said.

"What?" said Mason, though he knew.

"All right, let's break it down. One, he's your boyfriend?"

"Yes. We've been dating about six weeks." Mason closed his eyes for a moment, steeling himself for the coming fight. Defensively, he lobbed a cannonball at Odell: "How long were you with Bettina before you called her your girlfriend?"

Odell scoffed. "But that guy? Really?"

Mason knew full well what Odell was implying, but he crossed his arms over his chest and said, "What about him?"

"You've seen what he looks like, right?"

Mason looked in the direction Patrick had retreated and wondered how much time he had to have this out with Odell before Patrick came back. "I sure as hell have seen what he looks like. I like how he looks. Is it the fact that he's white or the fact that he's got funny hair the thing that you object to?"

"I don't give a shit if he's white." Odell glared at Mason defiantly.

"So it's the flamboyant thing, huh? You don't like that he looks gay."

Odell shook his head. "Hey, look, you know I love you. I don't care if you're gay. But you hide it pretty well. I'd never know. You're not like *that*, you know?"

It was like a punch to the gut. Mason swallowed a lump in his throat, and it burned as he choked on Odell's words. This was hardly the first time Odell had made a comment like that, but in the context of Patrick being one of those guys, it hurt more sharply this time.

This was exactly the reaction Mason had feared. It was exactly why he'd never dated anyone like Patrick before, despite Patrick being exactly the sort of guy who got his engine running. It was why Mason had wanted to put off any encounter between Patrick and his family.

He hated that he was right.

"He's not the right guy for you," Odell said.

"Is any guy?"

Odell pressed his lips together.

Mason wanted to shout and scream and protest and tell Odell where he could shove his attitude, but he stayed quiet because Odell was shooting him such an appalled look. He also worried Odell might be right. Maybe Patrick wasn't so great for Mason. Mason's mother would surely hate Patrick on sight. Odell certainly did.

On the one hand, the community Mason had grown up in had some pretty specific ideas about masculinity. Mason upheld all of them—he was strong, he'd had a profession that required physical exertion, he was tall, he was proud. But he was also into men. Perhaps he'd been overcompensating for that, but he was also really fucking tired of all the digs at gay people not being masculine. And okay, Patrick was not the butchest guy ever, but why should it matter? He was still a man.

Odell was still ranting. "I don't get it, of course, but I could see you going after the guys who look like you. I don't know. Women find that beefy thing attractive, right? Who is into *that*?" He gestured toward Patrick, who was on his way back from the bathroom.

"Shut up, he'll hear you," hissed Mason.

Odell shook his head and stood. "Who gives a shit? I'm surprised at you."

"Why, because my date doesn't conform to your idea of a man?"

"Because your date isn't who you belong with. Get real, Mason. I don't know if this is a phase you're going through or what, but this is fucking ridiculous. I'm out."

Odell started to walk to the door just as Patrick arrived back.

Odell turned around and said, "Just… get over it, Mase. I'll call you later."

When Odell was gone, Patrick looked at Mason, confused. "What's going on? Why is he leaving? Did you argue about something?"

"Why do you ask?"

"You're scowling."

Mason sighed. "Yeah. We argued."

Patrick looked at the front door of the bar and then back at Mason. "About me?"

Mason did not want to discuss this, but he said, "Yeah."

"I thought you weren't ready to introduce me to your family yet? Why was he here? Why did he leave? What are you supposed to get over?"

Mason felt sick. There was no good way to answer any of these questions. "Short version? He was here when I got here by coincidence. I don't know exactly why he left, but he didn't really approve of me being with you, I guess."

"Because he saw me for thirty seconds?" Patrick grinned like he was kidding, but then his face fell. "Oh, of course. That's exactly it, isn't it?"

Mason frowned. "I'm so sorry. I wanted to be able to warn him in advance, but he was just here and you walked in and—"

"To warn him?"

Mason realized at once how that sounded and groaned. "Just that you're not like the guys I've dated in the past. Not that he's even met many of them, because he's… well, he's like that."

Mason had hurt Patrick. It was all there on Patrick's face. Mason hated himself a little in that moment. He should have stood up to Odell and defended himself and his choices. He should have defended Patrick, who was just as much a man as Mason. He should have told Odell that he was falling for Patrick harder and faster than he'd ever fallen for anyone.

"I'm sorry," Mason said again, taking Patrick's hand. "Let's sit down."

Patrick furrowed his brow, but he nodded and followed Mason to a U-shaped booth. They sat next to each other. The booth was clearly designed for snuggling, but Patrick kept his distance, sitting about a foot away from Mason and looking at him expectantly.

So Mason explained. "All right. Here's the deal. My family is not the most accepting."

"So you've said."

"My mom's brothers, they're basically the men who raised me. Two of them, Gary and Darryl. And both of them are so caught up in image and masculinity and what it is to be a proud black man." Mason said the words mockingly, but he'd internalized that image so well he still couldn't shake it, even though he knew perfectly well that there was more than one way to be a man.

Patrick sat back with his arms crossed over his chest, not saying anything.

So Mason went on. "I grew up hearing them talk about it." He wanted to disown the lessons he'd learned from his uncles, but the truth was complicated. "I wanted to be like them when I was a boy. I idolized them. But then when I was fourteen, I realized I was gay. And I was horrified."

Patrick's eyebrows tilted in a way that showed sympathy. The ring in his left eyebrow glinted in the dim lighting of the bar.

"I kept it quiet for so long. I felt like such a fraud. I never wanted to let them down. But how could I not? As I got older, they got more candid, let's say. I was in my early twenties the first time I heard Darryl say something like 'A real man doesn't take it up the ass.' And Gary calls anyone he perceives as less than masculine a faggot. Can you imagine how that made me feel?" Mason took a deep breath. "And now they know I'm gay and they still say these things because I'm not one of *those* fags. I'm not flamboyant. I don't, you know, shove it in their faces or whatever the fuck."

"Mason." Patrick took Mason's hands and held them on the table.

"I grew up hearing all of that nonsense, and it never really dawned on me how wrong it was until after I came out. I'd been internalizing it my whole life. And then one day, I don't know, Darryl or Gary or maybe even Odell or my mother said something, and I just got angry. I was so angry for a lot of my twenties because there was just no way I'd ever live up to this ideal I aspired to because, fuck, because I like flamboyant guys and I like bottoming and I am so tired of working so hard to be this thing I will never really be."

Patrick pulled his hands from Mason's and put them on Mason's shoulders. "Mason."

"I'm sorry. I don't mean to shout. I'm just frustrated."

"I know, honey. I know. But I think… I think maybe you have some shit you're still working through."

"Yeah, well."

Patrick ran his hand up Mason's neck and over his cheek. He leaned over and kissed Mason softly. "I'm sorry I was the source of controversy."

"Not you."

"I know. Just… I'm sorry."

"Don't apologize. I shouldn't have let Odell get me riled up." Or let him say all those things about Patrick. Or let him leave without an argument.

"It's what brothers do. Buy me a drink?"

"Yeah, okay." Mason signaled to the waiter. It seemed they were done talking about this for now, but Mason sensed the discussion was far from over.

# Chapter 13

MASON LIFTED his bat as Nate fiddled with the pitching machine.

"You sure about this?" Nate asked, stepping away. "I can throw better than this little machine can."

They were at the Upper West Side Baseball Center, which had batting cages that rivaled the ones Mason had frequented in Florida when he'd been in the minors, and those had been some damn nice batting cages. Scott had been chastising Nate about his swing for the past month, so Nate had finally relented and asked Mason for some pointers.

"National League rules," Mason had said at the time.

"I know, bro," Nate had said. "But even then, pitchers aren't actually expected to hit home runs. If the pros don't have to, I don't see why I do."

And Scott had barked, "Babe Ruth was one of the best pitchers in baseball with the Red Sox before he hit home runs for the Yankees."

Nate had rolled his eyes.

Now he stepped away from the pitching machine and watched it spit balls toward Mason at regular intervals. Mason concentrated and hit eight out of ten of the pitches into the distant net, decent pop flies.

"All right, Mr. Yankee Show-Off," Nate said, picking up his own bat and stepping up to the plate. Mason jogged out to the pitching machine and reloaded it from the basket of baseballs they'd rented.

Once the machine hummed to life, Mason said, "Keep your back straighter. Lean forward slightly. Yeah, like that. Now pull your elbows in. That looks good. Okay, here it comes."

Nate hit half of them. His facial expression alternated between focused and frustrated.

"You're getting better," Mason offered when Nate tossed his bat over his shoulder in disgust.

"Fuck you."

Mason laughed. "No, seriously, you're getting the hang of it. Your stance looked better each time you swung."

"Switch."

Mason picked up his bat as Nate walked back to the machine. "So," Nate said conversationally, "how are things with you and Patrick?"

Mason tested the weight of his bat and gave it a few practice swings. "Good, I think, although we ran into Odell the other night, and Odell was as much of an ass as I predicted he would be."

"In what way?" Nate's attention was on the pitching machine, but his head was tilted in a way that indicated he was listening.

Mason took a moment to examine Nate. Nate typified "average white guy" as far as Mason was concerned, but he had a pretty face, fine light brown hair that had a bit of a reddish tinge, and a soft voice. He was on the thin side, not especially butch but not really effeminate either. He did have a few affectations, mostly gestures, that read as gay. Mason supposed he only tuned in to it because he'd worked so hard to suppress those things in himself.

Well, bottom line, Nate would probably get it. "Odell is only okay with me because I like to fuck dudes but I'm not one of *those* gays."

"Ah," said Nate. "Of course. Poor Patrick. How did he take it?"

"Better than I did."

"Yeah? Did you tell Odell where he could shove his attitude?"

"No. I should have."

The machine started whirring, and Nate took a step back.

It was methodical. Mason swung a bat because he was born to, because he'd been through relentless training under major league coaches, because he had the muscle memory to hit home runs. He thought of Odell and Patrick and what he wanted and what he could have. He thought about his uncles, about every time he'd been called a faggot, about his family, about masculinity. He let his anger and frustration out on those balls as they hurtled toward him. God, he wanted Patrick. His family would never accept that.

He hit what must have been the tenth ball, because Nate stood there, his jaw loose. "Dude," Nate said. "Ten for ten. And those last three are somewhere in Queens now, I think."

"Sorry, I was—"

"That was awesome. You'll never teach me to hit that well."

"I could."

"Maybe I just need proper motivation. Eh?" Nate walked up to the backstop and raised his eyebrows at Mason.

"Proper motivation?"

Nate picked up his bat and used it to point to the pitching machine. "Each ball that comes at me is Aiden's face."

Mason didn't think Aiden was that bad, but then again, Aiden wasn't dating the man Mason was in love with.

"Good luck, man," Mason said, going to refill the machine.


ACROSS TOWN, at the SoHoMos' practice, Patrick lofted his bat and tried to stare down the pitcher, Keith. Keith had kind of a hipster redneck vibe, his hair cut into a fringy mullet that Patrick really wanted to get his hands and scissors on. It was a crime against hair.

But wait, no, he was supposed to be paying attention.

Keith wound up and pitched. Patrick caught the edge of it, but it wasn't exactly a home run. He handed his bat off to Danny and then jogged over to the bench.

"That was good," said Phil, the 'Mos' manager.

"Thanks. You're lying."

Phil smiled. "Is not the purpose of being a coach-slash-manager to be supportive of my players?"

Patrick laughed. "Have you seen that angry guy who manages the Hipsters?"

"Fair point. Er, get back in line!"

"You don't have a mean bone in your body, Phil."

"And the Hipsters win games, so maybe that angry guy is onto something. Although I guess it doesn't hurt that they have an ex-Yankee in their lineup."

Patrick bit his lip to refrain from commenting on that. He retied his cleat and then moved to get back in the line to give batting practice another go.

"You doing anything after practice, Patty?" Phil asked.

"Not really. Why?"

"Come have dinner with me and Ron. Your mother has been on me to spend more time with you. Make sure you're doing okay."

This was the problem with playing for a team coached by a friend of one's mother. Patrick rolled his eyes. "I'm doing just fine."

"I heard you have a new boyfriend."

Patrick sighed. Phil was a good guy, in his fifties with graying hair and a kind face. Patrick was grateful to him in a lot of ways. But talking to Phil about Mason was kind of like talking to an uncle or, worse, his father. Patrick loved Phil and had known Phil his whole life, but there were limits. "Where did you hear that?" he asked.

"People talk to me. Maybe *you're* too cool to hang out with old Phil, but not everyone on the team feels that way."

"Well, I do have a new guy in my life, but… I don't know. I mean, back in the prehistoric times, before you met Ron and dinosaurs still roamed the earth?"

"Ha-ha," said Phil, crossing his arms and raising an eyebrow.

"Back in ancient times, did you ever date someone who was out but not totally comfortable in his own skin yet?"

"That's what you get for dating younger guys," Phil said.

"He's a few years older than I am, actually. I just… no, you know, it's not a big deal. I'll just go try to hit some baseballs again."

"Patty. You can talk to me."

"I know. I'm just… I'm not totally sure what to make of this situation yet, so I can't figure out how to explain it to you. And I mean, we haven't even been dating for that long, so whatever."

Although, "whatever" was pretty much the opposite of how Patrick felt about this. Patrick was starting to really care about Mason, and watching him struggle with his family and with his own self-worth hurt Patrick. He wanted to ease that pain in Mason, but he was worried about the cost to himself. He'd fought long and hard to be okay in his own skin and how he fit into the world, but something about Mason's insecurity threatened to undo all that. To undo Patrick.

"You look troubled," Phil said.

"I'm fine. Just worried about how to hit the baseball."

"Generally speaking, you swing the bat when the ball comes near you."

Patrick let out a surprised laugh. "All right, Uncle Smartypants."

Phil threw an arm around Patrick and gave him a quick hug. "So, dinner with me and Ron."

"Yeah, yeah. But don't think you're getting any information out of me. I'll tell you about my boyfriend when I am good and ready, okay?"

"Sure. But you know you can talk to me about anything, right?"

"I know."

"Good. So now." Phil took a step back and affected a serious expression, his brow furrowed and his lips pressed into a thin line. "Get out there and hit the ball, champ."

Patrick laughed. "Champ?"

Phil laughed too. "Yeah, sorry. Just… go back to batting practice."

# Chapter 14

MASON CLOSED his eyes as the line rang, not really looking forward to talking to his mother but knowing he had to stop stalling. Of course, she was all sunshine when she answered: "Mason! How nice to hear from you!"

"Hi, Mom."

"To what do I owe the honor of this call?"

Mason was home on a Saturday morning, lounging on his sofa. Patrick had had plans the previous night, and Mason was all the sadder for it. "I just wanted to see how you are. I know I haven't been great about keeping in touch lately."

"I know you're busy, baby boy. How are you?"

"I'm fine. How are you?"

She hesitated just long enough for Mason to know something was up, but her reply was upbeat: "I'm great. Never better."

"Mom."

"Well, if you must know, I had a bit of a health scare. It turned out to be nothing, before you worry, but it was a little scary for a few days there."

Mason wondered if this was what she'd been acting strangely about for the past few months. "What happened? And don't brush me off. I'm your son and I love you and you should have said something."

Her sigh hissed through the phone receiver. "I didn't want to worry you. And it really did turn out to be nothing."

"Mom. Please talk to me."

After a long pause, she said, "I guess this was in June. A few weeks before my birthday. I got kind of dizzy when I was at the office. Well, really dizzy. I thought that weird vertigo I had a couple of years ago was back, so I went to the doctor."

Mason hated that she did this. Mason always found out about her health problems after she found solutions for them. One of these days, though, no straightforward solution would work, and then what would happen? "What did the doctor say?"

"It was the anemia. But the doctor changed my medication, and really, Mason, I feel much better now. Good as new."

"This was right around your birthday, you said?"

"Yes. And oh, sweetie, I feel so bad about how that dinner went. I know I was a little distant, and you and Odell went out of your way to give me a nice dinner. But you know, there's nothing like a health scare and a birthday to make you feel old. I guess I was a little depressed."

"Are you really okay? The new medication is helping?"

"Yes. I changed my diet a little too, and I feel great. I promise."

Mason believed she felt better, but he still let the worry overwhelm him for a moment. He felt like an asshole too, for putting off talking.

"What about you, baby boy? How are you doing? You seeing anybody lately?"

"You really want to hear about who I'm dating?"

"Yes. Why wouldn't I?"

Mason sighed. "Because the last time I was dating someone, you and Uncle Gary and Uncle Darryl were awful about it."

Mason couldn't help but recall the terrible family dinner at which he'd announced he had a boyfriend. His mother had seemed excited at first, but as soon as Gary and Darryl started picking on him about it, she'd joined in and made him feel terrible. He'd broken up with the guy a short time later.

He couldn't let that happen to Patrick. He'd found too good a thing.

"I'm sorry," his mother said. "That was terrible, what we did. I… look, I want to be supportive of you, sweetheart. You and Odell, you're all I've got. And I'm so proud of you, I really am."

"Odell said you chewed him out about settling down the last time you talked to him."

She let out another hiss of a sigh. Probably she was just as happy as Mason was that this conversation was happening on the phone, the two of them separated by a river as they talked, so that neither could see the other's facial expressions. "I suppose getting sick again reminded me of my own mortality, all right. And you boys aren't getting any younger either. I'd like to see you settled down, both of you. Your father left when you were so young, and I want better for you, for you to be happy. And if I'm to have grandchildren, I'd like to meet them when I'm still well enough to play with them."

"Even if they were adopted?"

"Of course, darling. Any child of yours would be so loved."

Mason supposed that was a good thing to hear. "I'm just… look, Mom, I'm, well."

"Tell me."

Mason was tired. He was tired of walking on eggshells around everyone. He was tired of taking shit from his uncles, his own blood relations, about his sexuality. He was tired of worrying that his own mother wanted nothing to do with his potential future.

"Honestly?" he said. "I'm worried that you won't like anyone I bring home by virtue of the fact that he's male, and I'm tired of feeling that way, because I can't change who I am."

She paused again, but eventually she said, "I know we haven't always been the most supportive, baby boy, but… I'm sorry you feel that way. I want you… I just want you to be happy."

"You say that, but do you really mean it? Maybe you think you do, but if I brought a man home, how would you feel about that?"

She was silent for another long moment, but eventually she said, "Well, what I feel is that I'm not going to live forever and I want you to be happy, so if you meet someone, and he's what you want, and he makes you happy? Then I will put every effort into liking him too, okay?"

Mason wasn't sure he believed her. He suspected she was like Odell, supportive in theory but less so when confronted with reality. And Mason didn't know what to do with that. She was saying what he wanted to hear, but could he really trust in that?

He kept remembering the look on Odell's face when he first laid eyes on Patrick, and Mason could so easily picture that same expression on his mother's face.

"All right, Mom." All this talk of mortality was worrying him too, so he said, "You sure you're okay?"

"*Yes*. The doctor thinks I wasn't getting enough iron through my diet, so I have to take new supplements. I really do feel a lot better. There haven't been any other incidents since that last one."

"All right. Please promise to call next time something like this happens. I can come with you to the doctor or—"

"I will, dear, I will."

But now Mason definitely didn't believe her, and he hated that.


"THIS IS probably cheating, you know," Patrick said a few hours later as he lifted a bat. "You're aiding and abetting your opponent."

They were in Central Park, taking advantage of the waning daylight hours at the ball fields, thankfully abandoned now of Little League and corporate softball teams. The setting sun cast an orange glow through the trees, and it felt a little bit magic, hidden as they were from the city but aware of its presence as well. Patrick had always found Central Park to be a special sort of magic. In most of the city's parks, the city was plainly visible, full of bustle and surrounded by gray office towers and honking cabs and subway wheels squealing, but here it was just ball fields and trees and the occasional person lounging on a blanket with a picnic dinner. It was kind of like being home in the suburbs, with the manicured lawns and the carefully chosen trees and flowers. And yet if you looked up, apartment buildings towered at the edges of the park and the din of car horns and city noise still hummed in the distance.

Patrick had called Mason a couple of hours before because he'd heard that Mason had been doing secret batting practice with his teammates in his off hours. Mason had demurred, saying it wasn't really secret. So Patrick had made a joke about getting help with his own swing from a real professional baseball player. He'd been a little pouty about it too, though he'd been joking. Mason had called his bluff. That suited Patrick fine, mostly because when Mason had said, "Baseball is pretty much what I live for, so I'd be happy for you to indulge me," Patrick melted a little on the inside. Mason was basically adorable when he got going about baseball.

"Not cheating. I'm not a very good pitcher."

"Honey, you can throw a ball in a straight line. You're already better than half the Rainbow League."

Mason grimaced briefly but recovered. He motioned toward Patrick's legs. "If you widen your stance a little, you'll be more stable and can swing harder."

Patrick looked down as he took a few steps to widen the distance between his feet. He made a few test swings. Mason was right, he did feel more stable.

"All right. Hit me," said Patrick.

Mason shook his head but wound up and pitched. It was a much slower pitch than Patrick was used to, and he couldn't do much more than thunk it back toward Mason. Mason picked up the ball before it rolled by him.

"I prefer to do this with a pitching machine," Mason said.

"Eh, this isn't, like, serious practice, is it? I thought we were just goofing around."

Mason laughed. "All right. Try again."

Mason spent the next thirty minutes throwing meatballs at Patrick. Just as many balls hit the backstop with a clang as Patrick managed to get his bat around, and even then, balls Patrick hit well tended to get lost. When they were down to two balls, Mason called off batting practice but offered to practice fielding.

"Play catch, you mean," Patrick said.

"Sure."

That was fun too, watching Mason concentrate as Patrick threw him the ball. He did take this very seriously. Patrick found that funny, though he wasn't totally sure why; Mason's facial expression showed he was concentrating as if he were practicing with Derek Jeter right before a major league game, not casually hanging out with his boyfriend. There was something cutely endearing about that.

After a half hour of tossing the ball back and forth, Patrick said, "Hey, it's getting dark and I'm starving. Let's get some food."

"Sure."

Mason took care of grabbing all of the equipment and bundled it up in what looked like an official Yankees-issued duffel bag, exactly the right length to hold the bats he'd brought along. As he hoisted it over his shoulder, he pointed west, so Patrick nodded and let him lead the way out of the park.

When they reached Central Park West, Mason said, "You're pretty good at this ball-playing stuff."

"Ha, thanks." Patrick grinned at him. "There's this amazing Italian place on Columbus. I'm in the mood for a dinner drenched in cheese."

"Okay. Lead the way."

They walked, chattering away—well, Patrick did most of the chattering as Mason listened and nodded—and then Mason said, "How did you come to play baseball?"

"How could a guy who looks like me end up on a baseball team, you mean?" Patrick hated this question, hated the assumptions people made about him based on his appearance, and he was disappointed in Mason for asking the question.

Mason frowned. "Did I say that?"

Well, okay. "It's fine. People ask it a lot. I think most of my teammates assume I joined the league to hook up with hot jock types."

"Did you?"

Patrick smirked. Fine, he'd play along. "Maybe a little. Honestly, though, I was on a Little League team as a boy. I played until I was thirteen. I didn't try out for the high school team, though, because by then I'd discovered I liked other boys and I had different concerns."

"Understandable," Mason said.

"My father was pissed, but at the time, I would have rather spent an afternoon at the mall with my friends than have to slog through baseball practice. Dad got over it eventually. Although now I'm wondering if I missed out on valuable locker room time when I was a teenager. All that fantasy fodder. Hot guys all sweaty after practice."

"There was a lot of that," Mason said, "but when you're sweaty and gross and tired too, you tend not to really notice."

Patrick laughed. "Well, anyway. I loved baseball as a little boy. I even had a vintage poster of Mickey Mantle on my wall. Although in retrospect, he was pretty cute, right? Like, in his heyday?"

"He was, yeah." Mason closed his eyes briefly. "I'm trying to picture you as a little boy."

"I was adorable."

"I'm sure you were."

"You played Little League too, I assume."

"Yeah, I was on a team in the Bronx. We were pretty good. Although, it's funny. Nate and Carlos from the Hipsters were on one of our rival teams, so we probably played each other as kids, but I didn't meet them properly until I joined the Rainbow League."

"Wow, really?"

"Yeah. When we figured out that all three of us grew up in the Bronx and we're all about the same age, it took us days to get over it. Their team went to the Little League World Series and everything, but somehow I'm the one who ended up in the majors." Mason laughed and shook his head. "Anyway, then I did go on to play baseball in high school. I was pretty much only baseball back then. I mean, even though I knew I liked other boys, I was terrified of anyone finding out about it."

"I'll bet." Patrick sighed. "It was harder for me to get away with that." He made a few flamboyant gestures to show why. "I decided to embrace it rather than hide from it."

"And you know how I decided to go with that."

"Yeah. And I get it, Mason. It's not a judgment. Believe me, I understand. I embraced my sexuality as a teenager, but I was a kid in the suburbs where I felt like everyone had to fit inside these little boxes. My classmates did not take well to my nonconformity."

"I'm sorry you had to go through all that," Mason said.

"Eh, it's fine. Made me a stronger person. I was always determined to be true to myself after that."

Mason ran his hand down Patrick's arm. "I admire that."

"Thanks, honey. The Italian place is on the next block."

"So you joined the Rainbow League because you had played baseball once upon a time?"

An unspoken question still hovered here.

Patrick had liked Mason's touch and reached for his hand. Mason took it and squeezed gently. That felt like progress, a movement away from Mason's apparent private shame at being seen with a man so flamboyant as Patrick.

"I had just moved to the city," Patrick said. "Was here for beauty school and all that. I grew up in the area, but I didn't really know anyone in the city besides one of my mom's old friends, Phil. He's actually the manager of the SoHoMos. He told me about the league because I wanted to meet other gay guys my own age. It had been a while since I'd picked up a baseball bat by that time, but I still had all that Little League muscle memory. That first year was rough, but I picked it up again quickly enough."

Mason let go of Patrick's hand as they got to the restaurant, but he put a hand on the small of Patrick's back as he guided him inside. It made Patrick smile, how chivalrous Mason was at times. Mason probably didn't even realize he was doing it. Patrick patted his shoulder as they got to the host stand, which earned him a questioning look.

Once they sat and had ordered, Mason picked up the conversational thread again: "The Rainbow League ended up not being what I expected at all."

"Yeah?"

"Yeah. When I joined, I'd been told it could get pretty competitive but was mostly just baseball for fun. It was really hard for me to let go of that old mindset about playing to win at all times. But I was still shaky from my foot injury, and I didn't think I could do much more than play in a hobby league. As I got the strength back in my foot, I thought about joining this one league for retired players, but by then I was having so much fun in the Rainbow League it didn't matter. I could be social and be myself in a way I didn't think I'd be able to be in the retired league."

That was interesting. He reached over and rubbed the back of Mason's hand. "But you would have had plenty in common with those retired players. And those guys would take the game a hell of a lot more seriously than we do."

"Yeah, but that's not really what I want now. And talking to other retired players sometimes reminds me of what I walked away from."

"You miss playing pro ball."

"Yeah. How could I not?" Mason sighed. "That's what I was born to do. I spent my entire childhood and early adulthood working to become a professional ballplayer, and I made it!" Mason leaned back a little and gestured with his arms, throwing them out from his body. "I made it. I did it. But then all that work and training and sweat and tears was all for three years on a job I'd wanted my whole life and like that!" Mason snapped his fingers. "Like that it was over."

Patrick couldn't figure out how to respond.

Mason shook his head. "I don't regret the decisions I made, but I am sad about them sometimes. I mourn the career I could have had if I hadn't been born…." He closed his eyes. "Well, if I hadn't been gay. My life would have been different."

"Sure, but would you want it to be?"

Mason looked up and met Patrick's gaze. He seemed to get stuck there a moment, not blinking or looking away. "No. No, I made the right choices. I'm glad everything turned out this way. I think that's what I like about the Rainbow League too. This group of players represents my new life. The retired league would have been a representation of my old life." He let out a breath. "Being a part of this group is like coming home."

Patrick grinned and took Mason's hand, lacing their fingers together. "For the record, I'm glad you joined the Rainbow League, because it allowed us to meet. This summer has been really great."

Mason smiled back, warming something in Patrick. "Yeah. It has been great."

"I even had fun trying to hit those horrible pitches you threw at me."

"I told you it wasn't cheating."

Patrick laughed. "Well, honey, how do they say it in the military? Providing aid and comfort to the enemy? Helping a player from an opposing team feels like that, yeah? Except I think in this league they encourage comforting the enemy anytime you want."

"I'm happy to comfort you anytime." Mason winked.

A waiter arrived then with the wine Mason had ordered. After he poured it, Mason lifted his glass. "Well, here's to new lives."

"Here's hoping this summer never ends," said Patrick.

Mason smiled and they clinked glasses.

# Chapter 15

AUGUST BEGAN with a whimper, unusually mild for late summer in New York City. It was sunny, at least, but without the sweltering afternoons, something seemed to be missing.

Or maybe Mason just felt that way because, after another rough game, he was on the edge of losing a key part of his summer.

"Well, Mason," Dr. Patterson said as he put up the scans of Mason's legs, "there's a small tear in the muscle here. It's the sort of thing that can heal on its own, but you have to give it time to do that. If you work it too hard, you'll just make it worse."

Mason sighed. He couldn't really see the tear on the scan, but he believed his doctor. "So what I hear you saying is you're benching me."

"You need to take it slow for two weeks." Dr. Patterson held up two fingers and then pointed to the scan. "The reason your leg still hurts and the reason the swelling isn't going down is that you keep putting stress on the tear here before it gets a chance to heal all the way. So yeah, I'm benching you. No baseball at all for at least a week. If it feels better, you can run a little, but be careful not to overdo it. If the tear gets worse, we *will* have to do surgery again."

The news didn't make Mason happy. He thanked his doctor and promised to keep off his left leg as much as practical. When he got back to the lobby of the medical building, Ty was waiting, lounging on a couch.

"Benched?" Ty asked.

"Benched. You better be taking me to lunch somewhere that serves alcohol."

Ty grimaced. "Uh. You want to just go to that microbrewery on the other side of Union Square? I forget what it's called, but anything with 'brewery' in the name surely has beer in great quantities."

"Yeah. Let's go."

Mason couldn't keep from limping as he cut through Union Square with Ty. The park was mobbed, as it seemed to be all the time now, full of summer school students lounging as they studied, political activists holding signs, tourists, and overflow traffic from the farmers' market. The crowd made Mason feel tense and claustrophobic.

"Is the limp worse than it was a week ago?" Ty asked as they dodged a kid running after a soccer ball.

"Maybe. I'm not sure. My knee swelled up like a softball after practice yesterday."

"Yeah, that's what you said on the phone, although I think you compared it to a grapefruit."

"All the beer, Ty. I need all of it."

Ty laughed. "If you plan to drink this place dry, you're paying for lunch."

The restaurant wasn't too crowded—it was after the lunch rush—so they were able to sit right away, which was good because Mason's knee felt like it was about to give out.

Ty hummed to himself as he perused the menu. Mason was glad he'd asked Ty to meet him for lunch after his doctor's appointment; he'd predicted he'd need moral support. What a frustrating summer. Mason rubbed his knee, angry at his body for failing him.

"What if this is my last season playing any kind of baseball?" Mason asked.

Ty waved his hand. "I doubt you're done. You're too stubborn."

That pulled a surprised laugh out of Mason. "Nice of you to say, but wanting to play baseball and being able to play are two separate things."

"True. Have you ever had the burger here? Is it any good?"

Mason surveyed the restaurant. It was generically decorated, like a polished version of every Irish pub in the city, but it wasn't familiar. "You know, I've walked by this place hundreds of times, but I don't think I've ever actually eaten here before."

Ty nodded. "It's a chain. There's one near Ian's hotel, so we grab lunch there sometimes if I can coax him out of his office. I usually get the chicken sandwich. It's fine. Won't change your life but gets the job done for lunch."

Mason chuckled and decided to take his chances with a cheeseburger. Hard to mess that up.

After they ordered, Ty said, "Josh made me swear on penalty of death that I'd ask you about the boyfriend, but I honestly don't care, so you don't have to say anything."

Mason laughed. He suspected Ty did care, which was why he was asking a lot. "He's good."

"Good. That's all you have to say?"

"What do you want me to say? Things seem to be going well. I like him. I would have invited him to lunch today, but he has to work this afternoon. I don't know. What else do you want to know?"

"*I* don't want to know anything. I told you, it's Josh. You know how he is. He meddles in everyone's love life because he's been married so long he misses the first blush of new love or some bullshit. Really, I'm just glad Ian and I are old news."

"Of course. Well, I mean, it's good. Things with me and Patrick are good." Mason couldn't keep the smile off his face as he thought of Patrick.

Ty smiled. "That's good."

"How are things going with your apartment hunt?"

Ty rolled his eyes. "I love Ian, but he is such a pain in the ass sometimes. We've looked at six apartments in the last week and he hates all of them."

"All of them?"

"Well, to be fair, most of them were awful. Never trust a bargain in New York real estate. There was this one apartment, total steal. It was *huge* in a gorgeous building, decent location, but it wasn't quite clean. The bathroom alone would give you nightmares for months." Ty shivered.

Mason laughed. "Are you still fighting about Brooklyn versus Manhattan?"

"I might win that one. Some of the worst offenders in the bad apartment parade were in Manhattan neighborhoods."

"Good luck."

"Yeah. I'll probably need it."

They were most of the way through their lunch when Mason got a text from Patrick: *My last appointment canceled. Want 2 meet up?*

"Your boy just texted, didn't he?" Ty asked.

"Yep. How did you guess?"

"You smiled. Are you going to ditch me to go see him?"

"Maybe. Did you have a better idea for how to spend the afternoon?"

Ty shrugged. "Eh, I should get back to work. I have a commission to finish by the end of the week that I'm kind of stumped on."

"You? Stumped?"

"It's a cover for a fantasy novel. Apparently one of the characters is purple? I don't know. It's not really what I usually do for covers, but the client wants it to look like the cover from one of those midseventies paperbacks with the saturated colors and the half-naked ladies."

"I have no idea what you're talking about."

"That's because you don't read. I like the idea, I just can't figure out how to do it."

"I read."

"Sure, *Sports Illustrated*."

Mason rolled his eyes. So he didn't read *a lot*. He still read books sometimes. He tried glaring at Ty, but Ty seemed oblivious.

After lunch Mason met Patrick at a bar in the East Village, not far from Patrick's apartment. Mason wondered idly if they'd end up there, but then he remembered all those roommates. His desire for Patrick was a powerful thing, but he didn't think he could have sex with Patrick within earshot of three other people.

Patrick's hair looked a little tamer than usual, but he had big dangly earrings with feathers at the end in each ear and he was wearing a black tank top that clung to his body in an alluring way. When they met, Mason leaned in to kiss the smirk right off his face, but then had a brief moment of panic over being affectionate in public, thought better of it, and leaned away. He regretted the move almost immediately—he'd thought he was over this hang-up, and he had no reason to hesitate where Patrick was concerned—and felt awkward as a result.

Patrick frowned briefly but shook it off and ordered a fancy cocktail from the bartender.

"How was your day?" Mason asked.

"All right. Busy. Black Corkscrew Curls is going gray and I tried really hard to talk her into a little color, but she insists that no dye has ever nor will ever touch her precious hair. I was like, hey, just for fun? Hair grows back, right? Whatever." Patrick slid onto a stool. "What was the verdict on your leg?"

"There's a tear in the muscle near my knee. I have strict instructions to minimize the amount of time I spend on my leg for two weeks. That means no baseball at all for a week."

"Oh. Oh, baby." Patrick reached over and grabbed Mason's hand. "I'm so sorry."

Mason appreciated that Patrick didn't say what he'd heard every time he'd been told to take it easy, which was that one week off baseball was hardly the end of the world. No, Patrick understood how devastating this was, maybe even understood how betrayed Mason felt by his own body.

"Well," Patrick continued, "if you need someone to keep you company during your convalescence, I'm your man."

"Thanks."

Patrick leaned forward to kiss Mason, but Mason suddenly had cold feet. This was a trendy bar with a mixed crowd, but Mason wasn't really comfortable with PDAs in places he'd never been before. He leaned away from Patrick and signaled the bartender.

PATRICK WONDERED what gave. Were they still stuck on this weird image thing? Were they not past it yet?

"The hell?" he said.

"I just... I mean, is it safe, in this bar?"

"For what? For me to kiss you? For us to be a weird, mismatched interracial couple?"

Mason frowned. "I don't know. All of it? I've never been to this bar before. I don't know what the crowd is like."

Patrick sighed. "All right. I guess that's fair. You're not holding out on me because you don't want us to be seen together or anything like that, are you?"

"No." Mason squeezed Patrick's hand. "No, of course not. I just felt a little panicky. I'm... I'll get over it."

"I've been here a hundred times, Mason. It's fine to be out here."

The bartender slid their drinks toward them.

"I'm sorry," Mason said. "I really am. I'm... adjusting. I haven't been in a lot of relationships that I could take public before. It's not just... you know... all my issues. It's hard to break out of the habit of being in the closet."

Patrick took a breath, trying to calm down. He understood, but he didn't like it, didn't want to be the one to pull Mason the rest of the way out of the closet.

But then Mason leaned over and kissed him hard full on the lips. He parted his lips and snaked his tongue into Patrick's mouth, and Patrick was so shocked, all he could do was react. He opened his mouth and then relaxed into the kiss, concentrating on how warm and pillowy Mason's lips were, how he tasted of beer and Mason, how his teeth scraped against Patrick's lower lip. The kiss made Patrick's blood rush, made his skin tingle.

When Mason at last eased away, Patrick was breathless.

"How was that?" Mason asked.

Patrick put a hand on Mason's chest to steady himself. He smiled. "That was... good."

Mason's face relaxed into a sly smile. "Just good?"

"Amazing. Oh, honey, that was pretty darn great. I… thank you."

"You're welcome, I think?"

Seeing that Mason didn't quite understand, Patrick said, "I know you're trying and I appreciate the effort. That's what I'm thanking you for. It's hard to change overnight."

"I'd do it for you." Mason moved close and leaned his forehead against Patrick's. "I want to be with you."

Warmth spread through Patrick's chest and his heart kicked up a notch. "Yeah?" was all he could manage to say.

Mason put an arm around Patrick, leaning his head away to take a sip of his beer but still holding Patrick close. "You're worth the effort."

Patrick laid his head on Mason's shoulder. He still had a few doubts about how ready Mason was, how much his family could still sabotage Mason's happiness. On the other hand, he understood Mason's reticence in public and had scars, both real and emotional, to show for his time as the one in the room who didn't fit in, who was dangerous. Patrick had spent enough time in this bar to know it was a safe space, but Mason didn't know that. Patrick got that. And he knew, too, how much Mason had to overcome to kiss him in public.

Patrick nuzzled Mason's neck and reveled in his scent, in his warmth. Mason murmured something Patrick didn't quite hear, but it didn't matter. He was safe here. Cared for. And he cared for Mason a great deal. He was such a strong man, an interesting man, a flawed man.

Mason let go and sat on his own stool. He took a sip of his beer. "So," he said.

"So my mother called me today. One of my sisters is getting married in October, and my mother has decided I should do everyone's hair."

"Okay."

Patrick rolled his eyes. "They're trying to save money. I mean, Mom didn't *say* that, but I can tell that's what she's aiming for. 'Your sister is getting *married*, Patty, you should want to help out.' And I do, but I'd also like to be a guest at the wedding, not the help. And I probably won't even get paid. I was like, 'Mom, you know I do this professionally.' Because, you know, it's my livelihood. I can't just take a day off from work to work for free. And she just goes, 'I'm sure you'll do a great job, honey.'"

"That's rough," Mason said.

"I haven't done a lot of weddings. We've had a few in the salon, and I got hired once to do the hair for the bridal party of one of my clients. I had to take the train out to Long Island for that, but she paid me really well. My sister Maura, she's the one getting married, she has really pretty hair. It's naturally kind of this dark auburn. I'm sure I *could* make it look awesome. But if I have to work at the wedding instead of just attend it, I'd like to get paid for it."

"Understandable. She's your older sister?"

"Yeah. I'm the youngest. I have two other sisters too, and they're both bridesmaids. Actually her fiancé asked me to be a groomsman too, but I think he just did it as a token gesture."

"Do you like him?"

"He's okay." Patrick shrugged. "Kind of a dude bro. He's a nice guy, but he doesn't quite know what to make of me."

"That must get awkward." Mason put a hand on Patrick's knee, which was comforting.

"Eh. It's not so bad. Maura is my great defender. One time when we were all out to dinner, he called something 'gay' in a way that clearly meant stupid and Maura hit him with her handbag. He's been more aware of how he speaks since then."

Mason laughed. "She hit him?"

"Not hard." Patrick grinned. "Just enough to get the point across. Actually, my family had dinner with his family a couple of months ago and one of his brothers started on this rant about gay marriage and how all the queers think they're entitled to this and that, and Kevin, Maura's fiancé, actually corrected him and explained why I deserved the rights they all enjoyed as much as anybody else. It was sweet."

Mason smiled, but the light went out of it. Mason's own brother didn't think much of this relationship, did he?

Patrick touched Mason's shoulder in a way that he hoped would be warm and soothing. "You know," Patrick said, "my father was not so enthused with my plan to be a hairdresser. He's still horrified by the tattoos. I think he always assumed the hairdressing thing was a phase or something I'd do when I was young. When the full sleeve was finished?" He gestured to his arm. "My dad said, 'Well, now you'll never get a corporate job.' Like I would want one. I *like* doing hair. It took him a long time to come around. I still don't think he's all the way there. He doesn't quite get it. When I came out to my parents, my mother was all gushy, like 'We'll always love you, Patty, and we support you,' you know, and I was really happy about that. I was terrified of coming out. My dad just stared at me for a long time and then he said, 'Did we *do* something?' My mom and I had to patiently explain that no, in fact, this was just who I was always destined to be." Patrick took Mason's hand. "Families are hard. They love us but they don't always understand us, you know? My dad wanted a son to walk in his footsteps, to have an important job and wear suits and be wildly successful. Instead he got me. He's coping."

"He must have known."

"Huh?"

Mason leaned forward. "He must have known you wouldn't be... well."

"I'm sure he did, yeah." Patrick went for a smile. Failing, he took a sip of his Cosmo. "Anyway, my point was that, you know, family, can't live with them and so on. I know things are rough with you and your brother, but maybe he'll come around with time."

Mason's face did that thing again where it was clear he was trying to smile but his own pessimism got in the way. He huffed out a breath and took another sip of his beer. "Maybe."

"Oh, baby." Patrick gave Mason a hug. Mason put his big hands on Patrick's back and held him there for a moment.

"Sorry," Mason said when they parted. "It's been a rough day. My doctor just benched me."

"Just for a couple of weeks."

"Yeah, but what if my leg never gets better? What if I hurt it more?" Mason sighed. "I'm so tired. I'm tired of spending my whole life wanting things my body won't let me have."

Patrick could see the pain in Mason's furrowed brow, in the watery look of his eyes. Patrick knew, too, that Mason wasn't just talking about a sports injury, but that Mason's body had been betraying him his whole life, first by desiring men instead of women, and then by giving out on him in a crucial moment on the field. He knew Mason had worked hard to sculpt his own body into what he thought it should be.

"Mason?" Patrick took Mason's hand again.

"What?"

"I just want you to know that I care about you for you, for the man you were destined to be. Okay? It's okay to be who you are. Don't fight against nature so much."

Mason shook his head. "What I am is just baseball."

"That's not true."

"It *is* true. I spent my whole life training to be a professional baseball player. It was the one thing I was most passionate about. I watched games on TV, I played on every team I tried out for, I trained. I collected baseball cards as a kid. When I spent my allowance money, it was on a new glove or a box of baseballs. My mom hated it, told me I should be spending my money on CDs or books or whatever the kids my age were buying, but no, I wanted new equipment. I lived, ate, and breathed baseball for so long that I don't know how to be myself without it. And what my doctor just told me today? Well, he didn't say it, but he implied that if I hurt my leg again, I could be done with baseball for good. And then who will I be?"

Somehow that made everything click for Patrick. He understood Mason's anxieties. Mason had spent his whole life trying to be what others wanted him to be, but baseball was the one thing that was his own. How could he give that up?

"You know who you'll be?" Patrick said, rubbing the back of Mason's head gently. "You'll be a smart, caring, handsome man, and you'll find other things to spark your interest. Maybe you'll write more or have kids or who knows?"

"Kids?" Mason smiled faintly.

"I don't know. Just throwing that out there. Do you want kids?"

"I… maybe." The expression on his face said *yes*.

"Or you could be a coach, maybe. I could see you doing well with a field full of sugared-up nine-year-olds, teaching them how to play baseball."

Mason's smile widened. "Yeah. That could be fun too. I didn't want to coach right after I retired because I didn't think I could handle being on the sidelines, but if I can't play, then… yeah, I could see that."

"See? Don't worry. You'll figure it out."

Mason nodded. "Thank you. I… you made me feel better."

"Kinda my job."

"Yeah?"

Patrick sipped his drink and smiled at Mason. "Well, usually I try to make people feel better about themselves with a snazzy haircut. I try to make people feel beautiful. But since you have no hair on your head, and since I'm your boyfriend, I figure I can make you feel better on the inside."

Mason leaned forward and rested his forehead on Patrick's again. "Thank you." He took a deep breath. "I hope that I make you feel as good as you make me feel."

"You do, baby, you do. You just listened to me prattle on about my sister's wedding and never once looked bored."

Mason leaned away and laughed. "You are never boring."

"Don't I know it! But you would be forgiven for thinking so."

"I am never bored when I'm with you. It's part of your charm."

Patrick laughed too. "See that? You make me feel swell too."

Mason sipped his beer. "Glad I could be of service."

MASON WALKED with Patrick to the subway the next morning. As Patrick babbled about… something—a movie he'd seen recently, maybe, but it was hard to pay attention—Mason looked around and saw one of those twin couples holding hands and staring at each other all googly-eyed in front of the diner on the corner. Mason recalled a number of late-night meals at that very spot when he'd first moved to the neighborhood. The point of moving to Hell's Kitchen was to be in a neighborhood that had a big enough gay population that he felt comfortable being outside and being himself.

Well, that had been the plan. It didn't always play out in reality. He had woken up that very morning to a phone call from Davis, who told him he had another endorsement deal lined up, but the company was on the conservative side. Davis assured Mason this was nothing to worry about and everyone involved knew about Mason's sexuality, but Mason was still thinking about what he'd wear to that client meeting to make himself look as normal and heterosexual as possible.

But what did a straight guy even look like? Mason had never had to tone himself down before. He'd never been even a little flamboyant, in fact. His whole image was a carefully constructed lie, essentially, showing the world that he could blend in with the crowd.

He blended in, but Patrick didn't. This morning, Patrick had on a pink T-shirt with a purple unicorn on it that had come out of a stash he'd left at Mason's apartment. Mason thought it was cute and totally the sort of thing Patrick would wear. It made Mason realize that his whole wardrobe epitomized bland, that it had been cultivated to render Mason unnoticeable. There was nothing in Mason's wardrobe, in the way he presented himself, that gave anything away. But Patrick just put everything out there.

"I'm beige," Mason said as he steered Patrick around the twin couple, who were now pretty much just making out under the awning of the diner.

"Those boys should get a room," Patrick said. "Not that I don't like the show, but it is too early in the morning for slobbery kisses." He shook his head. "What were you saying?"

"I feel like the color equivalent of oatmeal."

Patrick tilted his head. "Maybe it's just because you brew your coffee too weak, but I have no idea what you are even saying."

Mason stopped walking and turned toward Patrick. He backed up toward the diner window to not be in the way of passersby in the sidewalk, though this had the unfortunate effect of putting the kissing couple right in his line of sight.

He had a passing thought that two guys that into each other—and who looked so much alike, and so clearly had things in common—belonged together in a way Mason and Patrick didn't.

Ugh, why wasn't he past this yet? They'd had such a nice time the night before.

He took a deep breath. "I was just thinking, you know, if you were a color, you'd be, like, magenta. Or chartreuse. But if I were a color, I'd be beige."

"Do you think you're boring? Because I don't."

"No. It's not quite that." Mason had a hard time coming up with the words to express what he meant. "So, you present yourself to the world in a certain way, right?"

Patrick balked but said, "Uh-huh."

"It's not a bad thing. All of this is you, right?" Mason waved his hand over Patrick.

"Yes."

"So I was just thinking, you know, I spent so much of my life very carefully being what everyone else wanted me to be that I'm not really sure I know who I really am anymore."

Patrick sighed. "It is too early in the morning for an existential crisis, but okay." Patrick put his hands on Mason's shoulders. "You're a good guy, Mason. A sweet guy. Nerdy about baseball, sure, but that's to be expected."

"No, I mean, I don't know how to express myself. You do. You're all bright and colorful and you don't give a fuck what other people think, but I'm so worried about what other people think that I lost myself somewhere. So now I'm just... beige."

Patrick nodded. "Okay. But on the other hand, I don't think you should go out and get all pierced and tattooed, either, if that's what you're thinking. That's not you either."

"How do you know?"

Patrick shrugged. "I just do. I mean, the first time I dyed my hair, I looked in the mirror and thought, 'That's me. That's what I'm supposed to look like.' Can you picture yourself with, like, a nose piercing?"

"No." Mason really couldn't. He wasn't even sure what he'd change about himself.

"Me neither."

"But I could… dress less plainly."

"Sure," said Patrick. He smiled. "That would be a good start."

"Maybe you could go shopping with me."

"I would love to." Patrick pulled his phone from his pocket and glanced at the display. "Well, honey, I have an appointment in less time than it takes to get downtown on the subway, so I better run. Are you okay?"

"Yes."

"Are you sure? Because if you are having a crisis, I can come back after my last haircut today."

"I'm fine." But even Mason didn't think it sounded like he meant it. Still, he resumed walking and Patrick fell into step beside him.

"Of course you are."

They arrived at the subway entrance. Patrick put his hand on the railing and leaned up toward Mason. "Kiss me good-bye?"

Mason gave him a quick peck. The vision of the twin couple in front of the diner had brandished itself in his mind, and he didn't want to put on too vulgar of a display, but when he pulled back, Patrick was frowning.

"I'll see you later, all right?" Patrick said, starting to go down the stairs.

"Yeah. Later," said Mason, unable to shake the image of Patrick's frown from his mind.

# Chapter 16

WAS IT easier to walk away or easier to stay? Patrick wondered about that as he sat at Barnstorm after a game. Partly it was a hypothetical exercise, just thinking about which would be more challenging when you were falling in love with a man who had such deep insecurities. His relationship with Mason seemed to be going well, but Patrick sensed that there was a deeper issue lurking beneath the surface. Was it easier to fall all the way or easier to leave before putting your heart on the line? There was risk involved either way. Patrick didn't know.

His teammates were being especially loud—the hapless SoHoMos had eked out a win over the all-female Bronx Bombshells—and though their record made it seem unlikely they'd make the play-offs or anything, it was nice to win something.

So Patrick had texted Mason to say *We won, we're coming for you*, which had gotten him a *LOL* in response and then an *Are you at the bar? I'll come meet you.*

That was a no-brainer, although Patrick still felt wary. He understood now more about Mason's shame and insecurities, about what made him hesitate sometimes even when they were alone together, but understanding didn't make it easier to cope with. And still sometimes the way Mason looked at him made him feel like dog crap on the bottom of a Ferragamo loafer.

But on the other hand....

Mason appeared at the doorway to Barnstorm and turned the considerable force of his wide, charming smile on Patrick. A zippy thrill went through Patrick. Man, he really liked Mason. And he knew Mason liked him a lot, cared about him even, in return.

So would it be easier to stay or to walk away? Which option was better? Patrick didn't know. They hadn't been together very long, so now was the time to get out before he got more invested, but… it might be too late for that.

As if to match his mood, the soundtrack on the Barnstorm speakers seemed to be all teen angst anthems tonight. Patrick glanced at his teammate Paul, who was manning the jukebox. Paul closed his eyes and swayed with the music for a moment. "You guys remember this song?" Paul asked. "Aw, man, soundtrack of my youth!"

Patrick mentally balked. This song was twenty years old. It was only the soundtrack of Paul's youth if he counted his toddler years.

Mason arrived at Patrick's side and greeted him with a kiss. "So you won? Is this a celebration?"

"Apparently. I don't know why we're trying to relive the nineties on the jukebox, though."

Mason grimaced in a comically exaggerated way. "This song was a huge hit when I was a freshman in high school. I could not escape it." He laughed. "You guys are all, like, a decade younger than me. I feel like an old man sometimes."

"Aw, honey. Age is but a number. Besides, I'm only five years younger than you. *Hardly* a whole decade." But Patrick didn't doubt that Mason sometimes felt old. Mason had been limping a lot lately, especially when he didn't think anyone was watching. More evidence of his body betraying him, Patrick imagined.

The thing was, Mason was getting there, but he wasn't all the way there yet. He hesitated just a moment too long sometimes. Still, he was here now, and it felt like progress.

"This your boyfriend, Patty?" Paul asked.

Patrick hated when people called him Pat or Patty, but Phil had revived the hated childhood nickname and now everyone on the team called him that. Bad enough when his parents called him Patty, but Patrick was more or less resigned to this fate when he was with his team.

He chose to ignore it now. "Yeah. This is Mason. He plays for the Hipsters."

Danny and Steve were looking on, and both of them had reverence in their expressions, so clearly they knew who Mason was. Mason eyed them warily.

Patrick believed that Mason had the capacity to overcome all those years of being told what a man was, all of his own expectations and shame, but if he had the will remained to be seen. Right now he looked so unhappy at being recognized that Patrick wished a trapdoor would open under his teammates.

"Come on, honey, let's get you a drink," Patrick said, hooking his arm around Mason's and pulling him toward the bar. "How's your leg?"

"All right. Not so bad now. I'm still benched, so that's not so great, but it doesn't hurt as much today as it did a few days ago."

"That's good. I'm glad to hear that."

When they got to the bar, Mason greeted Tom amiably. Tom looked like he'd been flirting mildly with Phil. Phil smiled at both of them.

"What brings you here on an off night?" Tom asked Mason.

"Came to see Patrick."

Tom smirked. "Do we have another Rainbow League love connection?"

Patrick rolled his eyes. "Please. As if the league were created as anything other than a means for New York's slightly athletically inclined gay men to hook up with each other."

Phil's eyebrows shot up. Patrick groaned inwardly. Phil had long been a parental figure to Patrick, and he'd grown up with Patrick's mother besides. Patrick regretted his comment now that word was more likely to get back to his parents.

Patrick glanced at Mason, who was looking back at him with a puzzled expression.

"Yes, we're dating," Patrick said. "Okay, Phil? You can go call Mom now and tell her that her son is dating an ex-Yankee."

The puzzled expression made a deep groove appear between Mason's eyebrows.

Tom chuckled. "I knew it."

Mason frowned. "What did you know?"

"That you two would make a good couple."

Patrick guffawed. "Really? Because Mason and I... I mean you've met us. Could two people be any different?"

"Doesn't matter," said Tom. "I saw you making eyes at each other last summer. Being hot for each other is one thing. You two have more in common than you think. I'm always right about these things."

Patrick sighed. "Okay. But can we not talk about this in front of Phil?"

Mason glanced at Phil. "Have we met?"

"I'm Phil." Phil grinned. "I manage the SoHoMos. And I'm Patrick's godfather."

"Really?" Mason's inflection was unreadable. Was he amused? Was this bad news?

"Phil and my mother were BFFs all through school," Patrick explained. "So he's, like, a family friend. And hey, you know, I pretty much came out of the womb in a haze of glitter or whatever, so my mother must have guessed that Phil would be a good person to, ah, see to my spiritual guidance."

Phil laughed. "Now, see? Who did you come to the first time a boy broke your heart? I'd say I gave good spiritual guidance."

Patrick put his hands on the bar. "You also bought me my first box of condoms, which, by the way, would have horrified Dad if he'd found out. I don't know if that's exactly in keeping with a good Catholic lifestyle."

Phil waved his hand dismissively. "Look, kid, I've known you since you were born. I knew you were gay when you were six. Your father is a good man, but he's always been uncomfortable with… nonconformists, let's say, so I figured I needed to get in there and be a role model for you. Did I ever steer you wrong?"

"No," Patrick said grudgingly. He slid onto the stool next to Phil and gestured for Mason to sit on his other side. "So riddle me this, Obi-Phil-Kenobi. I've been seeing Mason coming up on two months. I haven't told Mom and Dad yet because I'm not totally sure how they'd react. Do you think Dad would have a heart attack?"

Phil narrowed his eyes. "Because Mason is an ex-Yankee or because he's black?"

Mason bristled.

"Either. Both," said Patrick.

"Your parents aren't quite that closed-minded, are they?" Phil asked.

"I don't know. You tell me."

Phil narrowed his eyes and tilted his head and appeared to consider the issue. "Well, I think if it's serious, you should introduce them."

That was the question, wasn't it? Was this thing with Mason serious? All that they'd established was that they were in a relationship, a "real thing," but would it last the summer?

Could Patrick walk away if Mason's shame got to be too much?

"Dad has said some things to me over the years," Patrick said. "I don't know. Maybe I'm worrying over nothing, but I wonder sometimes how accepting Dad really is."

Mason stared unfocused at an indeterminate point on the bar. He was biting his lip as if he were mulling something over. Probably this conversation was making him uncomfortable.

Patrick turned to Mason. "Bad enough to your family that you're gay, right? But now you're dating one of *those* gays, and that's just beyond the pale. That's how your family feels. Am I right?"

Mason sighed. "Odell seems to feel that way, yeah."

"On top of being gay, we're dating people our families may not approve of. I mean, I don't know, maybe my parents will be so overjoyed that I'm in a steady relationship that they'll welcome you to the family. Or, you know, Dad's a pretty big Yankees fan. Maybe he'll be starstruck. They'll see in you what I see and think you're pretty darn great. Mom will make a big dinner and Dad will ask you about your intentions and it'll all be *Leave It to Beaver* normal. But maybe they won't."

"You won't know until you talk to your parents," Phil pointed out.

Mason's expression was rueful. "I spend a lot of time wondering how much I care. If the happiness I get from being with you trumps whatever nonsense my family's going to give me."

"Being with me makes you happy?"

Mason smiled and put his hand on the side of Patrick's face briefly. "Yeah. It does. I'm… less happy about how Odell is acting, and it's hard to even think about how my mother will react, but it's… it's not you, Patrick, it's their own stupid nonsense. I wish… well, I wish a lot of things. But I can't change any of it, so here we are."

"Oh, honey."

Mason rolled his eyes. "Don't get patronizing. All I was trying to say is that I want to be with you no matter what my family says."

"Well." Patrick turned away, not wanting Mason to see his face. He liked the words but didn't quite believe them. Something about Mason's tone wasn't quite as enthusiastic as Patrick wanted, or maybe he was projecting. He shook it off and said to Phil, "Since you're going to call Mom tomorrow anyway, I guess you might as well scandalize her. Maybe make it surreptitious. 'Oh, Andrea, darling, I ran into your boy at the bar last night and you'll never believe who he's dating now.'"

"Your parents love you, Patty. All of you. Your father is maybe not the most open-minded man in New York, but he accepts you."

Patrick sighed. "I know."

"It'll work itself out," said Phil, standing. He put a few bills on the bar and smiled at Tom. "I need to be getting home. I didn't intend to stay out this late tonight. Ron is out of town on business, so the dog is home alone. He's probably ripped the sofa by now."

"Good night, Phil," said Tom. "When Ron gets home, say hi to him for me."

"I will. Night, Patty. Mason."

When Phil was gone, Patrick put his forehead on the bar. Mason rubbed his back gently.

Patrick sat up. "I love my family. I do."

"Can I buy you a drink?" Mason asked.

"Yeah. Cosmo, Tom. Can you make it a double? Can you make Cosmos double?"

Tom laughed. "I'll see what I can do."


THEY ALWAYS went to Mason's place, and definite signs of Patrick were strewn about all over the apartment now. Mason had been buying almond milk because Patrick was lactose intolerant. Patrick kept a toothbrush in Mason's bathroom. He'd left clothes behind, which Mason had washed with his own laundry and kept in what he'd come to think of as Patrick's drawer in his dresser. The living room was a little less tidy than usual, as Patrick had a tendency to leave detritus in his wake. He liked to pull the old afghan Mason's grandmother had crocheted off the back of the sofa and wrap it around himself when they watched TV together, so it was never in the right place anymore. He left granola bar wrappers and dirty coffee cups all over. One of the purple water bottles Patrick brought with him to games was currently drying in Mason's dish rack.

Mason didn't mind. He kind of liked having Patrick's stuff around, having the evidence of their relationship everywhere.

Patrick picked an earring up from the coffee table. "That's where this went. I've been looking for it all week."

"Your godfather calls you Patty. Just like you always call yourself Patty when you're imitating your mother."

Patrick rolled his eyes and pocketed the earring. "Ugh, don't remind me. I hate that name. It makes me think of that lesbo Peanuts character."

"Peppermint Patty? Lesbian?"

"You know she and Marcie are living out their days in connubial bliss on a sheep farm upstate where they spin their own yarn and wear clogs."

Mason laughed. "When he was talking, I kept trying to imagine you as a kid."

"I was just as sparkly, I promise." Patrick grinned.

"Did Phil really buy you your first box of condoms?"

"Yep. When I was, ah, seventeen maybe? I had this unbearable crush on a guy at the salon where I was working at the time. I just answered the phone and swept up hair after school, nothing glamorous. But one of the stylists had a client who was just smoking hot. Maybe twenty-five and all muscles and scruffy hair. I wanted him bad, but I turned into jelly whenever he talked to me, so that was never gonna happen. I mentioned to Phil in a totally offhand way that I had a crush, and the next time he came to the house, he pulled me aside and handed me the damn box. 'Be safe, okay?' he said to me. I was mortified."

"It's nice that you had someone like that in your life, though."

"Yeah." Patrick smiled faintly. "I love Phil. I'm grateful to him in a lot of ways, actually. My father is so awkward about the gay thing, but then again, sex generally seems to give him hives. How my sisters and I came into being remains a mystery."

Mason couldn't keep the smile off his face. Patrick was just so funny and adorable. And gorgeous. And sexy. And everything.

Mason took a step closer to Patrick and put his hand on Patrick's waist. He ran it up Patrick's side, felt the warmth of Patrick's body under the fabric of his uniform T-shirt. "How old were you when you lost your virginity?"

"Really?"

"I'm just curious."

Patrick sighed. He put his hands on Mason's shoulders. "Eighteen. Freshman year in college I dated this guy who was a bit older and wiser than I was. He, uh, showed me the way. How old were you?"

"Nineteen. He was a football player."

"Look at us late bloomers. A football player?"

"I wasn't really in the closet in college, but I wasn't very vocal about my sexuality either, so it suited me fine to sleep with a closeted football player who was bound for the NFL. Incidentally, he currently plays for Green Bay and is still very much in the closet."

"Your life is very weird."

Mason barked out a laugh. "Look, I had a type for a long time, okay? Or, not really a type, but you spend enough time in locker rooms and jocks become the easiest guys to hook up with. I always figured I should be with someone athletic and masculine like me."

Patrick frowned. "Well, sure. You had a standard to maintain."

"The real honest truth is that I have always been attracted to guys who look like you. Who are thinner and look kind of subversive. I think you are just sexy as fuck. And the first time I saw you, I had no idea what to do with that."

"I got that. But thank you for sticking with me."

"I want to be able to just shrug off all my old nonsense. I want to stop caring what other people think."

Patrick ran a hand over Mason's head. "At the end of the day, when no one else is watching, what is it you want?" He dropped his voice to a whisper. "What do you think about when you're alone? What do you want? Who do you want?"

Mason closed his eyes. Lately, when he was alone at night, he'd thought only of Patrick. It was Patrick who he jerked off thinking about, who was on his mind as he fell asleep at night, who was in his thoughts when he first woke up. He often went to bed wishing Patrick was there in bed next to him, that he had Patrick's smile and energy with him every day instead of just a few times a week.

What he wanted was to tell Odell, his family, the whole fucking universe to go fuck themselves, because who Mason wanted shouldn't matter. He didn't spend his twenties in the closet, fretting about his future, enduring homophobic slurs and bullshit from his coaches and teammates, for this; he didn't give up his career to stay in any kind of closet. Everything he did, every article he wrote, every Pride parade he marched in, every interview he gave, every time he spoke out or acted up, all of it was so that other professional athletes could have the right to love whoever they wanted to. Mason should have claimed that right for himself.

If he couldn't love Patrick fully and without shame, all of it was for naught.

He pulled Patrick into his arms. "You," he said. "I only want you."

Patrick shifted his hand from his shoulders to his shoulder blades to his back, rubbing the long length of Mason's body. He let out a little breath near Mason's ear and said softly, "I'm glad to hear that. I want you too."

"Not just sexually," Mason said. He needed to make this clear. Maybe it was too early for the L word, but he needed Patrick to know that Patrick was not currently in Mason's living room only because Mason wanted to fuck him. "I really care about you. I want to be with you. I want to spend time with you in and out of bed. I want you to be here with me."

"Yes," Patrick whispered. "Yes, Mason. I want to be with you in all those ways too."

Warmth swelled in Mason's chest. It felt so good to just hold Patrick, to feel Patrick's body against him. But he needed to be closer suddenly. And the proximity of Patrick, his scent and his warmth, made Mason's body tingle.

If the hardness against Mason's thigh was any indication, Mason was not the only one.

"Come to the bedroom," Mason said, reluctantly pulling away from Patrick to take his hand and lead him down the hall.

He decided the time for talking was over. He maneuvered Patrick so that he stood at the foot of the bed. Then Mason slowly, lovingly divested him of his clothing. He carefully uncovered every bit of pale and tattooed skin, letting his fingers float over the ink. When Mason tossed Patrick's undershirt aside, he trailed his fingers down Patrick's chest. He pinched Patrick's nipples, which made Patrick gasp.

Patrick kissed him and slid his hands into the waistband of Mason's jeans, his fingers dancing against the skin there. Patrick, in just a pair of bright blue briefs now, slowly unbuttoned Mason's shirt, then his jeans. Patrick peeled away each layer of clothing as if he were unwrapping a present, his expression excited and expectant.

When they were both in just their underwear, Mason lifted Patrick and laid him on the bed. Patrick smiled and immediately reached for Mason, pulling him into his arms. Patrick ran a hand over Mason's head, down the back of his neck, across his shoulder blades. Mason kissed Patrick, massaged his chest, his hip. He hooked his fingers into Patrick's briefs.

Mason's body came alive. His skin tingled everywhere, his blood rushed through his limbs, his heart pounded in his chest. He touched Patrick's body because it was beautiful, because it was precious. Because he loved Patrick but had no way of telling him, no words that would make it sound as amazing as it felt.

Because in this moment, it was just the two of them in bed together and it was perfect.

"Mason," Patrick murmured. "Oh, baby. God, I want you so bad."

Mason slid his hand into Patrick's briefs and squeezed one cheek of his perfect round butt. Man, Mason loved the feel of Patrick's skin under his hands, how smooth it was. He loved the contrast of their skin together. He loved how colorful Patrick's body was, the swirling tattoos on pink skin contrasted with Mason's simple brown complexion. Mason could stare at those tattoos all day and never see all of the detail. He could look into Patrick's eyes all night and never know all that Patrick was thinking.

He pulled off Patrick's briefs and then wriggled out of his own boxers. He took Patrick back into his arms and buried his face in the crook of Patrick's neck. He licked and nibbled the skin there as Patrick threw his head back. Mason loved being this close to Patrick, but he wanted—he needed—to be closer.

*I love you*, he thought. *I love you, I love you, I love you. Please let this moment go on forever.*

"Let me…." Patrick panted, digging his fingers into the skin of Mason's back. "Let me be inside you."

"Yes," Mason said. "Yes. Over me. Inside me. Me on my back."

"Okay."

Patrick reached for the side table with practiced hands and grabbed what he needed from the drawer. He nudged Mason onto his back and bowed his head. He kissed each of Mason's nipples and then ran his tongue along the groove of muscle that went down the center of Mason's abs. Mason snaked his fingers into Patrick's crazy, colorful, disheveled hair. He loved the look of his hand there, and he loved Patrick's little cat tongue licking the sensitive skin near his groin, and he loved the devious expression Patrick shot him before he licked Mason's cock from base to tip.

Mason moaned. How could he not? This assault was entirely unfair. Patrick was so fucking sexy down there sucking on the tip of Mason's cock, his pink lips doing unspeakable things. Patrick wrapped his manicured fingers—blue nail polish today—around Mason's cock, and that looked and felt perfect too. All of it amazed him.

*Please let this go on forever.*

Mason spread his legs and opened for Patrick. Patrick took that as the cue, as Mason intended. He sucked on his own fingers for a moment and then placed them near Mason's entrance. Patrick made lazy circles with his fingers as he began to suck Mason's cock in earnest, and Mason had to close his eyes to keep from coming, because the scene combined with the physical sensation was too much. He didn't want to come yet. He couldn't come yet.

Patrick poured lube on Mason's balls, let it trickle down. It was cold and it tickled, but soon enough Patrick's fingers warmed it up and spread it where it needed to go. With aching slowness, Patrick sank a finger into the entrance to Mason's body. He kissed Mason's hip and ground his cock against the mattress as he finger-fucked Mason. He moved his mouth to just inside Mason's thigh, trailing kisses from Mason's balls to his knee, teasing Mason, making him want to beg.

So he did beg, because this was not a time to hold back from what he wanted. "Please, Patrick."

Patrick lifted his head and reached for a condom. "Please what?"

"Please, I need you inside me or I will lose my mind."

Patrick grinned. "Can't have that."

Patrick rolled on the condom and stroked himself a few times with his lubed fingers before he lined up his cock with Mason's hole.

"You want me?" Patrick asked.

"More than anything."

"Mmm."

Patrick pressed forward, sinking into Mason with careful slowness. That was perfect too, the sensation of Patrick filling of him, of that big cock stretching him, of the quick searing pain that would soon give way to pleasure. Mason let out a breath and relaxed, sliding into the pain, pushing back against Patrick.

Patrick kissed him and slid home.

"Oh, that's good," Mason groaned against Patrick's mouth.

*I love you. Please let this go on forever.*

Mason put his arms around Patrick as he shifted his hips up to encourage Patrick to move. Patrick took long, lazy strokes at first, but when Mason looked up at his face, it was screwed up in concentration.

"Let go, baby. Let go," Mason whispered.

"It's too good. You're so tight against me. I won't last very long."

"I'm close too. Come on, Patrick."

Patrick nodded slightly and then increased his pace, sliding in and out of Mason. Mason held him close so that Patrick's body rubbed against Mason's cock as he moved. It wasn't quite enough friction to bring Mason off, but it felt good as it prolonged the inevitable.

Mason kissed Patrick, petted his hair, traced his fingers over the tattoos. Mason gazed at Patrick's face, his collarbone, his shoulders, the dancing ink on his arms. Patrick was it for Mason, Mason knew it then. No one else would make him feel this way, no one would inspire him this way, would fit inside him this way, would belong with him this way.

Love and arousal spread across his chest, his body. He pushed back against Patrick, who started slamming away, seeking his own orgasm. They both shifted their hips at the same time, which was just right, because now Patrick hit Mason's prostate on every upstroke, and all of Mason's blood seemed to rush to his cock.

All sensation concentrated where their bodies met. This combination of them was the only thing that mattered, the only thing that existed.

Patrick propped himself up on his hands and fucked Mason hard and fast as Mason wrapped his own hand around his cock and started to stroke as he loved being stroked. He was close, his balls pulling up, everything churning and tingling.

"Oh, Patrick," he moaned. "Patrick, Patrick. Come inside me."

Then everything went white. Mason's blood rushed in his ears, what had been tingly seemed to explode, and cum poured out of his cock onto his stomach as he gasped and groaned against Patrick.

"Shit," Patrick grunted as Mason was coming down. "God, oh, God, Mason." Patrick grasped at Mason's shoulders and held Mason close as he pumped a few more times into Mason and then went stiff and shuddered. His body jerked as he came, as he lost his mind, and that was perfect too.

Patrick grabbed the base of his cock and pulled out, but he dropped his forehead on Mason's chest instead of getting up.

"Dear Lord," Patrick said. "What you do to me."

Mason laughed softly. "Hand me a tissue?"

Patrick grabbed a handful of tissues and wiped up the spill on Mason's belly. Then he tossed the tissues and the condom in the trash can near the foot of the bed. He came back and crawled next to Mason and snuggled up to him.

"Did you know," Patrick said, "your nose scrunches up right before you come. It's really cute."

Mason couldn't remember the last time someone had called him cute. "Really?"

"Yeah. I was watching your face this time to see if you'd do it again. You did." Patrick sounded smug.

Mason laughed and hugged Patrick against him. "That's good to know, I guess."

Patrick yawned. "Now I'm sleepy."

"So sleep." Mason stroked Patrick's hair and held him close. "Stay here with me."

"Mmm. I will."

# Chapter 17

IN PATRICK'S dream, the neon yellow bird in the window chirped happily but then started screaming. Come to think of it, the scream sounded a bit like Mason's phone's ringtone.

And with that, Patrick woke up. When he turned to see if Mason was awake, Mason was already reaching for his phone. Patrick took a moment to admire Mason's broad back, all that acreage of smooth skin that would have been perfect for a tattoo. Patrick could see something black and gothic, maybe "Patrick" stamped across those shoulders so that any passersby would know to whom that beautiful man belonged.

Mason grabbed his phone and lay back down on his back. He answered it with a huffy "Morning, Odell."

Oh, Lord.

Patrick didn't know if he should give Mason privacy to talk to his brother. He figured he'd go take care of his morning ablutions and moved to get out of bed. Before he got up, though, Mason grabbed his wrist and pulled him back.

All right, then.

Patrick got comfortable again, settling against the pillow on his side of the bed. He curled his hand around Mason's forearm and awaited further instruction.

"Yeah, I think so," Mason said into the phone. "Today's Wednesday?"

Patrick smiled and shifted to lean against Mason's shoulder. Mason put an arm around him. So Patrick put his arm across Mason's big chest.

He felt warm. Safe. Loved.

That last thought gave him pause. He believed that Mason cared about him a great deal, and he certainly cared about Mason in return, but love? Had they really gotten there already?

For a moment the night before, when Patrick's cock had been buried in Mason's body, when Mason had breathed Patrick's name, Patrick felt something stir in his chest. It was like the cracks that happened when ice melted. In that moment, any defenses Patrick had melted away, and he felt open to Mason, and Mason was open to him, and they were in love.

Patrick didn't know if that feeling was the result of a sex-induced haze of intimacy and closeness and pleasure or if it was real. He supposed he could sort that out when Mason got off the phone.

"Yes, I'm still dating him. He's—"

That got Patrick's attention. He leaned up, propping himself on his elbows on Mason's chest, and looked at Mason's face. Mason's expression was troubled.

"Did you really just say— No, I won't— Christ, really?"

Patrick could hear Odell's voice on the other end of the call but not what he was saying. It was just deep murmuring.

Mason's face fell. He looked completely miserable.

"Please don't. No, it should be me who— Dude, really? Where do you get off? I—"

Patrick gazed at Mason, wondering why he couldn't get a word in. Was Odell really that pushy or was Mason caving to him without putting up enough of a fight?

"Look, just… I can't talk about it right now, okay? I— yeah. He's here with me if you must know."

Oh, this was bad.

"I'll meet you for dinner tonight, okay? I can't tomorrow because I have that thing my agent is making me do. Yeah, okay. I'll be there at seven. You can yell at me then." He pulled the phone away from his face and hit the End Call button so hard Patrick feared he'd crack the screen. Instead, he put the phone on the side table and sighed.

"Your brother?"

"Yeah."

Patrick was close enough to feel how hard Mason's heart was pounding.

Mason said, "He wanted to tell me some more what a big mistake I was making by continuing to date you. He threatened to tell my mother."

Patrick balked. "What would she do?"

"I don't really know."

Patrick thought that might be the end of it. Mason pulled Patrick into his arms and hugged him tightly. This hug was for Mason; Patrick imagined it placated Mason, made him feel better. But Mason's heart still pounded and he still had more to say.

"Odell said that if he told Mom, she'd tell my uncles, and they'd make my life hell. That's very likely true."

"But what can they really do to you, Mason? Your family's in the Bronx, right? You're here in Manhattan. I know that's not that far, but it's a big city. You have your own life. You're an adult man in your thirties. You can make your own decisions."

But Mason didn't seem to be listening. "It's like I'm a little boy again and Darryl's yelling at me for picking up a pink T-shirt in the store. I liked the color, but he told me only faggots wore pink. Or Gary telling me no nephew of his would be on the cover of *People*, showing his face and admitting he was a fag. You know, he wouldn't speak to me for nearly a year after I did that. Wouldn't take my calls, wouldn't come to family parties if he knew I would be there. When he did talk to me again, it was mostly to tell me how much I'd shamed the family by being such an embarrassment of a man."

Patrick wanted to tell Mason that those men were not worthy of Mason's love, that real family didn't say things like that, but the pain in Mason's voice was palpable. Mason's uncles had hurt him as though they'd stabbed him with knives.

"What about your mother?" Patrick asked instead.

"She's… she's always supported me. She's great, she really is. But she'd ask her brothers for advice. And they always tell her the same nonsense they said to me, and then she comes to me and is all, 'Honey, I love you, but Darryl said blah blah and Gary said blah blah blah and I really think we should listen to them.'" Mason sighed heavily.

"Mason, baby, don't… it's going to be okay, you know."

"Is it?" Mason asked. "I *am* a fucking embarrassment, aren't I?"

"To who? Not to me. Honey, you're a hero! There are hundreds, thousands of people who saw you come out. Do you know how many people you've probably helped by doing that? How many people saw you on the cover of that magazine and thought, hey, if it's okay for Mason Brooks to be gay, maybe it's okay for me too? And I, well, I think you're great just as you are. So don't listen to that bullshit."

"But you said yourself. Your father would have a heart attack if he found out we were dating."

"I was kidding mostly. I doubt he actually will. If he does, I will defibrillate his ass, because I love him, but he has no say in my love life. If I want to be with you, I'll be with you. My father will have to deal with that on his own time."

Mason shook his head. "I wish it were that simple."

"It is."

"No. No, I love my family. I need them. If they tell me… I mean, I'm not what they wanted in a son, not what I should have been, not a real man. It was okay for a while, you know, because I only dated guys who seemed like real men the way my family defined them, and I pretended I didn't want what I really did want, and it all fucking sucked. It sucked. I just… I want to be with you and I want them to shut up."

Patrick laughed softly and let Mason paw at him a little. Mason's grasp on Patrick's body felt a little desperate.

"I lost so much when I came out," Mason said softly. "I lost friends. I lost my career. I can't lose my family too. But I don't know how to tell them that the man I want to be with is you."

"Odell knows. Tell them the truth."

Mason seemed half out of his mind now. Tears shimmered in his eyes. Part of Patrick was disgusted with all of it and wanted to storm out of the bedroom, out of the apartment. He did extricate himself from Mason's grasp and sit at the edge of the bed. Since he was still naked, he pulled the sheets up over his lap.

Mason lay on his back and rubbed his eyes. "I'm not flamboyant. If I don't draw attention to myself, to them, I'm not a fag."

"Not a fag like me, in other words," Patrick said. "Not a queeny twink with tattoos and weird hair and colorful clothes, eh? Not a lady boy born with glitter in his hands. Not anyone who has any pride."

Mason closed his eyes. "It's bullshit. All of it's bullshit. The way I look. My body. You. Your hair. It's all fucking bullshit. It's window dressing. The people we are underneath are what's important. I'll just have to say that."

It was a good sentiment, but it didn't sit well with Patrick. "Actually," Patrick said, gesturing to his body, "this is me. Each line of ink, each streak of color in my hair, it's all me, an extension of me, an expression of myself. This is who I am, Mason. I'm not going to change any more than you are. I don't care if people just see a faggot when they see me walking down the street, because that's what I fucking am. I fought to be myself, for years I did, and I live how I want to live. Isn't that what you want too at the end of the day? Didn't you give up what you did, didn't you make that sacrifice, so that you could be who you are openly, so you could love who you love?"

Mason furrowed his brow but opened his eyes and gazed at Patrick. "Yes," he whispered.

"You told me last night that you wanted only me. So that's what you tell your family. If they can't respect that, they don't deserve to be your family."

"I don't know if I can."

Patrick got out of bed. He went to his drawer and pulled out a change of clothes, clean underwear, jeans, and a T-shirt, so he didn't have to put his grody uniform back on. As he got dressed, he said, "Last night, before you got to the bar, I was wondering if I should just leave. Walk away. Leave you behind because I don't need this nonsense."

Mason made a strangled sound in the back of his throat.

"It should be easy, right? If this were still just a sex thing, it would be. But it's not, because I've come to care about you. I can see you're really struggling with this. I can see how it tears you apart. I want to help you, I do. But I can't let you tear me apart too, okay?"

"Patrick. I would never—"

"I know you don't want to hurt me. You'd never do it on purpose. I know that. I know you're trying. But at the end of the day, I need you to make a decision. Take me as I am, Mason, and I'll take you, flaws and all." Patrick let out a breath. "You've never asked me to change. I appreciate that. But I can tell that sometimes when you look at me, you question yourself. I can't... I can't be a part of that."

"I understand. I'm really trying."

"I know. And that's why I'm... I'm going to go for now. Let you work out whatever it is you have to work out. Go see your brother. Figure out how to tell him what you need to tell him. Do that big interview tomorrow and say what you need to say. Then when it's all over, come back to me and we'll talk, okay?"

"Patrick, please don't—"

Patrick pulled the shirt over his head and ran his fingers through his hair. "Think about everything. Decide what you want. And most importantly, be honest. Be honest and don't hold anything back. Okay? Then come back to me if I'm what you want."

Mason nodded. He looked miserable, but he seemed to understand. "You're benching me too."

The image was apt, though Patrick understood, too, how it must have been a significant loss for Mason, to have baseball and Patrick taken away from him within a week. "Just for a few days. Just till you get your head screwed on straight."

"What about you?"

"What about me?" He walked over to the mirror above Mason's dresser. Lord, his hair was a horror show. Mason had a Yankees beanie hanging from a set of hooks that held a number of other hats. Patrick commandeered the beanie and pulled it over his hair. Maybe a beanie was not the way to go in the summer, but he'd fix his hair when he got home.

"What do you want?" Mason asked. "You keep asking me what I want, but you've never said what you want."

"Oh, honey. I thought that was clear by now."

"Not to me."

"I want you. I want those moments when you don't think about what other people think, when you're all the way with me. I want to keep having that feeling I get when you walk in a room."

Mason nodded. "Please just don't let this be good-bye."

"It's not. Not yet."

"Good. Because Patrick?"

Patrick gave up trying to fix his appearance. He turned around and faced Mason.

"Patrick, I love you."

Patrick's heart raced. He almost melted right there. He wanted to crawl back into those big arms, the ones that made him feel safe and loved, because he *was* loved.

And he loved Mason in return. He must have, or his heart wouldn't ache the way it did when he thought about what he had to do.

So he said, "Prove it, Mason. Prove it. If you love me, work out your shit and come back to me and be honest and I'm all yours, okay? But if you stay steeped in this nonsense with your family, it will only tear us both to pieces. I don't want that for us. I want us to be better than that."

"Okay," Mason said softly. "I'll… I'll prove it."

Patrick walked to the bed. He dropped a kiss on the top of Mason's head. "I have to go. Call me in a few days, after you've thought everything over. I have to think about some things too."

"I will."

Patrick kept it together until he got back to his apartment. He held his breath most of the trip downtown on the subway because it gave him something to concentrate on that wasn't crying or his heart breaking. The tears threatened, though, as he unlocked his front door, as he waved at whichever roommate was in the kitchen—he couldn't even tell—and then he full-on sobbed as he threw his bedroom door shut. He dove onto his bed and wept.

# Chapter 18

MASON SEETHED with resentment at Odell as he sat at the bar of the restaurant Odell had chosen, a seafood place near Odell's store where they'd eaten a few dozen times over the years. Mason liked it fine—the food was pretty good; he'd probably get to eat some if Odell ever fucking showed up. Mason was pretty well into his second whiskey sour by then.

The whiskey wasn't doing much to erase the constant loop of what Patrick had said that morning.

*Prove it. Be honest.*

So, fine, Mason would prove it. If he had any idea how.

If Odell ever fucking showed up.

"Another," Mason told the bartender, feeling a little fuzzy around the edges.

He understood the dilemma he faced. The judgment of his family versus the man he loved. Gary and Darryl and Odell and Mom, they were all related to Mason by blood, they all had their own ideas about who Mason should be, and none of them reflected who Mason actually was. He loved his family, but it was getting harder to be who they wanted him to be.

That was really the issue, wasn't it? Mason had been skating by, barely holding on to his family's approval, because he didn't seem obviously gay. But Patrick was a walking, talking reminder of everything Mason really was underneath. And Mason was tired of covering that person up.

Mason remembered being about sixteen and going to Odell and screwing up his courage enough to say, "I think I'm gay." It wasn't a proud statement. It was a wishy-washy, maybe, sort-of statement. Mason had known good and well that he was totally, 100 percent gay by then, but he couldn't say so with any force. Because Mason had never, in his whole goddamned life, stated anything unequivocally. He was maybe gay, and then when he was gay, he wasn't one of *those* gays....

But he *was* one of *those* gays, because he was *gay*, full stop, and he was in love with a man, and he had come out on the cover of a magazine so that he could be his whole self, but he had never let himself do it.

His family hadn't been the ones holding him back. That was what Patrick had been trying to tell him, wasn't it? His family wasn't forcing him to be anything. He let them keep him in a box, but he was ultimately in charge of himself. He was holding himself back because he sought their approval. But what had trying to gain his family's approval gotten him but misery?

Maybe Patrick had the right of it. Maybe Mason should grow out his hair and pierce something and get a tattoo.

Well, maybe those things were not Mason, exactly. But the idea was the same. No more holding back. Be honest. Prove it.

Odell finally showed up when Mason had drunk about half of his third drink. He was now full of whiskey and indignation. Odell eyed him warily as the host led them to their table.

"Forty-five minutes late," Mason pointed out once they sat.

"Is that why you're drunk?"

"What makes you think I'm drunk?"

"Your eyes are bloodshot and you're talking a little too loud."

Mason closed his mouth and picked up the menu.

Now that he was a little drunk, he couldn't remember the exact purpose of Odell's invitation to dinner besides to yell at Mason. So he said, "You're forty-five minutes late and you pretty much only called me here to make fun of me, so yeah, that's why I'm drunk."

"I'm not going to—"

"Why are we here, Odell?"

A waitress coming by to take their order saved Odell. Odell hastily glanced at the menu and seemed to pick something at random, so Mason did the same, not remotely hungry. Instead he was angry and frustrated and tired and, well, a little drunk.

When the waitress left, Mason leveled his gaze at Odell.

Odell crossed his arms over his chest. "Well, I may have mentioned to Mom that you had a new boyfriend and that I'd met him but didn't like him. That's all I said, by the way. I'll let her decide what she thinks about that little flamer."

"That's it? You invited me to dinner to tell me you mentioned to Mom I had a boyfriend?"

"I thought maybe you'd come to your senses. I hoped we could talk this out like adults."

"I'm not the one acting like a child."

Odell grunted and crossed his arms. "You're my brother, Mase. I hate that we're not talking to each other right now. I miss talking to you. I thought we could find a way to work this out."

To work this out on Odell's terms, of course. Odell wanted Mason to break up with Patrick, to go back to being the guy he was before he met Patrick. But that guy had never really existed.

Mason sighed, though he wanted to punch Odell right in his snarling mouth. "You want to work things out between us?"

"Yes. That's why I invited you to dinner."

That this was his opportunity to say everything he'd wanted to say since the last time he'd seen Odell. This was when he could finally have it out. He'd be honest. He paused and sipped his drink, tried to work out how best to go about this. He started with "Can I ask you something?"

"Of course."

"When you told me you would be my brother no matter what, did you mean it?"

Odell balked. "What?"

It had been a deliberately argumentative question, but Mason felt like being argumentative. He loved his brother, but he was done letting Odell off the hook for being an asshole. "You came to me after my first surgery to see how I was. When I first hurt my foot in the ALCS game. Remember?"

Odell nodded.

Mason had been lying in that hospital for a day by then, and he'd already made his decision, and then Odell came by that same afternoon to see him. Mason had said, "My career's over. I'm coming out of the closet." Odell had tried to talk him out of it at first—"Are you even sure you're gay?"—but once Mason had made it clear he'd made up his mind, Odell backed off.

Now Mason said, "You said that if I was really gay—which I am, by the way, no *if*—then it was okay and you'd support me. You'd always be my brother. Do you remember that?"

"Of course. You don't have to repeat my words back to me. I was there."

Mason sat back and looked Odell over. Odell looked irritated now.

"All right," Mason said. "Pop quiz, then. Would you still be my brother if I were one of *those* fags? The ones you make fun of? The flamers? Patrick?"

"But you're not," Odell said warily.

"Here's the thing, Odell. There aren't different boxes to check off. There aren't really categories of men. I mean, sure, we put ourselves in boxes, even us gay men. Twink, bear, whatever. But at the end of the day, we're all just men. All of us. The only difference between me and you is that I'm into men and not women. The only difference between me and Patrick is that he's not afraid to express himself. He's not any more or less gay than I am."

"So what are you saying?"

Mason took a fortifying sip of his whiskey sour. "Would you still be my brother if I got something pierced? If I talked with a lisp? If Patrick moved in with me? Hell, if I married Patrick? Would you still support me? Because it seems to me that your support has depended on the fact that I'm not obviously gay, even though I came out on the cover of a magazine and will very likely go down in history not as a solid home run hitter or an essential part of the Yankees lineup for three years. No, I'm going to be remembered as Mason Brooks: That Gay Baseball Player. That's my legacy, Odell."

Odell shook his head. "But Mason—"

"I'm one of *those* fags," Mason said, probably raising his voice more than was appropriate. "And I'm tired of pretending otherwise."

Odell's gaze darted around the room and he looked stricken. "Mase, you can't be serious. Are you really—"

"You want to tell Mom that I'm dating a flamboyant white man, that's fine. I'll introduce him to her very soon because I'm pretty sure I want to spend the rest of my life with him. If Gary and Darryl feel it's necessary to weigh in, that's fine, I don't give a shit about their opinions anymore. Because I'm tired of being careful."

Odell's shoulders dropped. "Mason."

"I didn't lie there in a hospital with my goddamn leg in traction, contemplating the end of my career and hearing that my brother was going to be supportive, did I? Oh, no wait, I did. I assumed you would be there for me no matter what. I gave up my career in baseball, Odell. I quit being a Yankee. I did it because being true to myself was more important to me than that dream. Can you appreciate that? Can you appreciate the sacrifice I made, everything I gave up? And after all that, was your support conditional on my behaving a certain way? Are you only my brother if I behave in a way *you* deem appropriate?"

Mason couldn't believe he'd said all of that to Odell. He was surprised, too, that Odell seemed rendered speechless. The silence was only interrupted by the waitress plopping their plates down in front of them. Mason thanked her and she left them alone again.

Eventually Odell said, "I guess you had some things to say."

Mason was about ready to walk out. He put his silverware down and pushed away from the table.

"Did you say you think you want to spend the rest of your life with this guy?" Odell asked. "*This* guy?"

"Yup. And if you took the time to actually get to know him instead of making a snap judgment based on seeing him for thirty seconds, you'd see that he's a sweet, funny, kindhearted guy, and he's good for me. He makes me happy."

That is, if he took Mason back. It wasn't a breakup. Patrick said to take some time to think about things. So Mason was thinking. But what if Patrick came out the other side of this separation and didn't want to put up with Mason anymore? The idea made him panic.

But it wasn't the first time Mason had faced a tough decision head-on, not the first time he'd had to change his life. So he'd just prove that he was worthy of Patrick, that he loved Patrick, and he'd hope everything would work out.

Odell grunted. "I don't get it."

"I'm in love with him. What's to get?"

Odell kept shaking his head. "He's so effeminate. If you wanted someone that feminine, why not date a woman?"

"Because I like cock?" Mason tried.

Odell screwed up his face, clearly disgusted.

"Look, Odell, you support me or you don't. You're my brother and I love you, but I will end this right here if you can't find a way to get behind me 100 percent. Because if you say you're supporting me but you don't support Patrick, then your support is meaningless. You're no brother to me then."

God, if Patrick could see him now. It was like everything he'd thought or felt for the past few months, or really since he'd come out publicly, was coming to the fore. He was telling Odell everything he'd wanted to say for years. He was done holding his tongue. His heart pounded and he was sweating, but it felt amazing. It felt great to finally say all of this out loud.

Except that Odell looked like he might throw up. He pushed back from the table. "How can you do this?" Odell asked. "How can you be this way?"

"You really expect me to answer that? Maybe I should do a musical number. Bring in Lady Gaga."

The joke was clearly lost on Odell. "It's not true. You weren't—it's that guy's fault."

"That guy's? Patrick's? He has a name, you know."

"Why are you acting this way?" Odell's face became confused and horrified.

"I've always been this way," Mason said, sitting up. "I just hid and suppressed it for a long time. But I'm done with all that. So get on board, Odell, or get lost."

Odell stood. "Guess I'm going, then." He walked out of the restaurant.

# Chapter 19

CARLOS WONDERED if Aiden knew he snored. The sound didn't compare to a freight train or anything, more like a gentle saw-whistle repetition, like the way people snored in cartoons.

Carlos had only noticed it a handful of times before, but that included right now, because it was the middle of the night and he was awake, unable to get his brain to shut up and, therefore, unable to sink into sleep. They were cuddled together in Carlos's bed, even, which usually helped him fall asleep, but no, one of his rare bouts of insomnia had struck. So now he lay on his back, a little too hot, his skin slick with sweat, while Aiden had a heavy arm thrown over his chest and was snoring in his ear.

The situation with Nate was wigging him out a little, and he had a work project he couldn't seem to stop obsessing over, and he thought deep in the recesses of his mind that even though Aiden was a great guy and sexy as fuck, he and Carlos had no business being with each other, let alone for a year. It was just a nag, a sense that while Aiden was a great boyfriend, he wasn't The One.

Oh, and Aiden had asked him to move in with him.

Carlos had demurred, saying he still had another few months on his lease and wasn't it awfully soon? He'd said confidently that they'd still be going strong in six months, or twelve, so really, why rush? Anyway, Aiden's only reason for wanting to cohabit seemed to be so they could have sex more regularly. Carlos might not have a wealth of experience when it came to long-term relationships, but he knew even awesome sex could not sustain a relationship.

"You love me, though, right?" Carlos had said.

"Of course I do!" said Aiden, though it had rung a little hollow.

But that could come with time.

Still, they were coming up on their one-year anniversary, the invitation to move into Aiden's Brooklyn apartment—which, granted, was bigger and nicer than Carlos's little studio in Manhattan—hung in the air between them, and Carlos was abjectly terrified to take that step toward more permanent coupledom.

What did that say about their relationship?

On top of all this was Nate, who had always had sharp instincts when it came to men. Nate thought something was off about Aiden. Carlos couldn't figure out what Nate saw in Aiden that Carlos didn't, though he trusted Nate's judgment.

Aiden stirred and snorted, rolling away, his arm sliding across Carlos's chest until it flopped on the mattress on Aiden's other side. Carlos closed his eyes, figuring Aiden would go back to sleep, but instead Aiden rolled again and whispered, "You awake?"

"Yup."

Aiden stretched and then curled up next to Carlos again. "I was just having a sexy dream about you."

"Yeah?"

"Yup. We were on a beach together, and your hot little ass was in only a red Speedo."

"I don't even own a Speedo, let alone a red one."

"Hey, I don't question my dreams." Aiden reached over and started playing with Carlos's chest hair. "It was sexy. You got all hot and bothered and you were just lying there on a lounge chair, but the fabric of the Speedo was stretching over your big cock."

Carlos laughed, but he was getting aroused too. He reached for Aiden and ran a hand through his hair. "I didn't know you had a Speedo fetish."

"I didn't either. I think my brain was doing some of the work for me. Like, I saw this thing on TV last week about Spanish soccer players?"

"You watched something about sports on TV willingly?"

Aiden propped himself up on his elbows and looked down at Carlos. "Hey, I'm trying. You like sports, right?"

"I do, yes."

"And anyway, these soccer players were hot. One of them kind of looked like you. All tan and dark hair. So I think I was thinking about you being Spanish and Speedos are kind of a European thing, and that's how my brain got there."

"I'm Puerto Rican."

"Huh?"

"I'm Puerto Rican, not Spanish."

Aiden shrugged and flopped back on his back. "Same thing."

"It's really not."

"Well, whatever. Semantics. It was a hot dream."

Carlos sighed, annoyed now, not just because of Aiden's apparent casual racism but because the thought *Nate knows the difference* popped in his head. Because Nate was practically family. They'd grown up on the same block in the South Bronx. Nate's mom had worked two jobs, so Nate had spent nearly all of the time she wasn't home with Carlos's family. Nate came to all of the Ruiz clan's many family events. Nate texted with Carlos's sister Marisol nearly as much as he texted with Carlos. And since the beginning of time, the two of them had been a pair. Carlos and Nate. Nate and Carlos.

Carlos loved Nate, but in a brotherly way. It had surprised Carlos's family—well, except for Marisol, who was shrewd—that Carlos and Nate had both turned out gay. Carlos had always just figured that the thing they had in common had brought them together as friends even before they knew they had it in common. When they both came out, Lourdes had asked if they were a couple, and they'd both laughed and laughed.

It didn't seem so funny here in the middle of the night.

Except Carlos was with Aiden, whom he really liked. And Nate was, well, Nate.

Nate was cute, more now that he was older. He'd been an awkward teenager, all long limbs and acne and untamed blond hair. He'd filled out a little in college, though he was still on the thin side, and his hair had darkened to kind of a reddish caramel color as he'd gotten older, and his skin had cleared up. Nate had really nice skin now, come to think of it, clear and pink and smooth-looking. He worked out periodically and had a defined chest. His arms were solid from throwing all those pitches. He had a tight butt, round and asking to be grabbed, actually. Carlos had never let himself look that closely at the rest because they weren't friends in that way, but truth be told, Nate was pretty sexy, all things considered. Not a solid block of muscle like Aiden, and he didn't have the thick, dark body hair or the piercing blue eyes that Aiden had. But he had something, that was for sure. Why there weren't pretty boys lined up around the block to fuck him, Carlos had no idea.

The fuck? He was in bed with Aiden. Why was he thinking about how sexy Nate was?

He rolled over to Aiden. "In this dream of yours, did I take the Speedo off? Did I show you my big cock? Did I fuck you with it?"

"Oh, baby." Aiden licked his lips. "No, but it could have gone that way."

"Do you want me to fuck you right now?"

"God, yes." Aiden's legs fell open to demonstrate how much he wanted it. He tore the sheet off and dropped it on the floor. Aiden's hard cock lay there, red and ready.

Carlos reached for the lube. "Let's make your dreams come true.

PATRICK WALKED into Dimensions Thursday morning feeling… everything. Sad, happy, angry, all of it. He didn't like when his emotions got this out of hand. He knew he'd done the right thing in telling Mason to get his shit together, because he couldn't see their relationship proceeding if Mason still let his family dictate how he behaved, if Odell still made him feel ashamed. Patrick had no room in his life for shame.

Of course, Patrick had been assuming Mason *would* work everything out, but what if he didn't? What if Patrick was asking to get his heart stomped on by staying with Mason instead of walking away?

Mason loved him. Patrick could see the two of them together, living in the same space, facing the world side by side. Neither of them fit neatly in the box designated for them, which was perhaps why they got along so well. And Patrick loved Mason. He hadn't really walked away from Mason, because he couldn't. He just hoped Mason came through. It was a terrible place to be stuck, not willing to compromise what he found essential in himself but knowing that putting everything on the line with Mason could mean his heart would get broken.

He set up his station and then took a long look at his clippers. He wanted to do something drastic to his hair.

"Step away from the clippers," Valerie said.

Patrick turned around and held up the wireless clippers near the edges of his hair. "I'm gonna do it, Valerie."

"Oh, dear God, no!" Valerie clutched her hair and screamed like a horror-movie virgin.

Patrick laughed. "Okay, I won't shave my head or anything, but maybe it's time for a change."

"What color is your hair naturally?"

It had been a while since anyone in the real world had seen it, Patrick supposed. "Dark brown."

"Wow! I assumed you were blond. It works with your complexion. You're really on it with the roots retouching."

"I work in a salon."

Valerie shook her head. "That doesn't mean jack. You know stylists have the worst hair. I used to work with this woman who dyed her hair like you, pink one week and green the next, but it was always a frizzy, dried-out mess. I don't know how you use so much peroxide without killing your hair."

"Good products."

"You seriously want to shave your head?"

"I don't know. No, not really. I think it's like... you know those women with crazy long hair who come in here about once a week and are like, 'My boyfriend and I are through! Chop it all off!'" Patrick made a cutting motion near his neck with his hands. "I think that's what I'm feeling."

Valerie gasped and took the clippers out of Patrick's hand. "Did you and Mason break up?"

"No." He reached for the clippers, but Valerie, who was a little taller than Patrick, held them just out of reach. "No, we didn't break up, but we had kind of a weird nonargument, so we're cooling off for a few days." He reached for the clippers, but Valerie hopped away. "Valerie, honey, give me the clippers back."

"I need a promise that you won't do anything drastic."

"I won't, geez. Maybe I'll just dye my whole head blue. Do we have any of that midnight blue left?"

Valerie squinted. "Huh. That actually might work on you."

Patrick jumped and grabbed his clippers back. "I'm willing to compromise if you just give me a trim, okay? Maybe shorten these bits in the front." Patrick touched the fringe of hair that fell over his forehead.

"Sure. That I can do. Are you okay, sweetie?"

Patrick let out a breath. He put the clippers back in their place at his station. "I don't know. I don't think... well. I didn't realize how much I really cared about him until I walked out of his apartment yesterday."

Valerie gave Patrick a kind smile. "I hate when that happens."

Patrick couldn't help but laugh. "Yeah, well. This is a man who holds my heart in his hands. He... I care about him so much that he has this power now." Patrick had a hard time voicing it, but he knew Mason had the power to break him. That if Patrick fell well and truly in love with Mason—which he was certain was happening—that a Mason who was not fully committed would tear Patrick to pieces. One more of those looks, one too-long hesitation, and Patrick would be finished. He couldn't put himself out there like that without trusting Mason to take care of his heart.

Valerie gave Patrick a hug. "Oh, sweetie. Falling in love is the worst, isn't it?"

"Tell me about it."

MASON WAS still thinking about Odell as he arrived at the Midtown hotel at which his interview was supposed to take place. He hadn't actually expected Odell to walk out on their dinner. He'd expected to say his piece, for Odell to be enlightened, and then for them to carry on so Mason could deal with the rest of the family with some support. He'd always assumed he could do anything if he and Odell were a united front. And he'd always assumed that Odell had his back.

But no, Odell, his brother, a guy who had always come through for him, had walked right the fuck out of the restaurant.

That had stunned Mason. It had hurt like a punch in the stomach. Odell could be an asshole, yeah, but he'd never been *that* much of an asshole.

But Mason had to shake that off if he was going to give a positive, coherent, endorsement-deal-earning interview with this reporter from a weekly sports magazine.

He missed Patrick too. It had been less than two days, but he ached with the need to hold Patrick in his arms again. He'd barely slept the night before as he'd stared down the possibility of never having another night with Patrick.

So it was hard to pull it all in and not be a mess in front of Alison Lowe from *All Sports Weekly.*

She was pretty in a generic newscaster way, and she wore a dark red suit and had her wavy brown hair styled in such a way that it would never move again. She shot him a toothy grin as he sat in a big plush chair across from her. They had privacy, at least, with a small conference room reserved just for them. Mason didn't think he'd be able to do this in public.

Ms. Lowe pulled a small recorder from her bag and placed it on the table. "Mind if I record us?"

"Not at all."

She nodded and got right to it. The first volley of questions was easy: Where did you grow up? What have you been doing career-wise since you left the Yankees? How are you enjoying living in Manhattan? Easy, softball questions. By the time they wrapped up that portion of the interview, Ms. Lowe had told Mason to call her Alison.

Then she said, "Do you still play baseball?"

"I do, yeah. Really low key. I play in an LGBT sports league. Just for fun."

Alison paused just long enough for the moment to feel significant. It was the first time anything gay had been brought up. "What's that like?" she asked.

"Great. It's mostly social and I've made some great friends." And one boyfriend. Maybe. Hopefully. "There's just enough competition to keep it interesting but not enough that it feels too stressful."

"It's all LGBT?"

So Mason spent the next few minutes explaining the particulars of the Rainbow League, and he and Alison chatted amiably about how the mechanics of the game differed in a professional league and an amateur one. She knew the game cold, and she was smart and quick to make connections. Mason enjoyed talking shop with her.

She looked up and met Mason's gaze. "So, this social league. Any love connections?"

This was nerve-racking to talk about, but Mason's continuing evolution depended on his ability to be frank, didn't it? He must be honest, and he must be willing to be open in a public forum. "Yes," he said. "Lots of couples meet in the league."

He spoke slowly, and as he did, he got an idea. He tried to push it away, to dismiss it entirely, but the more they chatted, the more it seemed just crazy enough to work.

"I met my boyfriend through the league, actually," he said.

That snared her attention. "Really?"

Mason began to tell her that he wanted to keep things vague to respect Patrick's privacy, but he realized as he spoke that the truth was that he wanted to sing Patrick's praises from the rooftops. Because the bottom line was that the ache Mason had been feeling since Patrick had walked out of his apartment the day before meant that Mason needed Patrick, wanted Patrick in his life like no other. Mason wanted to spend the rest of his life with Patrick, and it didn't matter what his mother or Gary or Darryl or even Odell had to say about it. Mason planned to do whatever it took to make that happen. What had been a fleeting idea now crystallized in his mind, and he knew what he had to do.

As they continued to chat, Mason gave her the pull quotes she wanted, invigorated now by his excitement over his new plan to keep Patrick. He even gave her what he thought was the money quote. Her eyes lit up when he said it.

Alison told him that because of a story that had gone belly-up, she was going to try to rush this into the next Monday's issue, which Mason found nerve-racking. Still, he couldn't deny that the timing would likely be very good. Perfect, even. If everything went the way he hoped.

After the interview, he took the subway downtown because he needed to tell Patrick about what happened with Odell in person, but then he realized the odds of Patrick being home on a Thursday evening were slim. He tried to remember where Patrick's salon was. He couldn't remember, but he knew it was called Dimensions, so he searched for it on his phone and then successfully located it after twenty minutes of wandering around.

A quick glance through the front window told him Patrick wasn't there, but he strolled inside anyway. A pretty woman with long auburn hair sat at the front desk reading a romance novel. She looked up as Mason approached.

"Uh, no offense, but are you really here for a haircut?"

Mason touched his recently shorn head and said, "No, I suppose not. Is Patrick here?"

"No. He has baseball practice on Thursdays. Are you Mason?"

Practice, of course. In the two months they'd been dating, Mason had gained some sense of Patrick's schedule, but apparently not enough to realize he had team practice on Thursdays.

This girl was staring at him. "Uh, yeah. I'm Mason."

"Oh, my God." The woman hopped off her chair and ran around the desk. She put her hands on Mason's upper arms. "So good to meet you!"

"I take it Patrick has mentioned me?"

She grinned. "I'm Valerie. I'm another stylist here. Patrick and I are old friends. It's a shame he's not here right now. I'll definitely let him know you stopped by, though."

The postinterview euphoria had worn off, so Mason was no longer sure coming here was a good idea. Patrick had been clear about giving it a few days. He probably shouldn't have been so presumptuous.

"No, don't say anything. I'll call him later. But maybe while I'm here…."

Valerie raised one eyebrow. "I don't know if you noticed, but you don't have any hair."

"Patrick's been trying to talk me into a mani-pedi for a month."

"Oh." Valerie grinned. It looked a little evil. "Well, in that case, I'm at your service. Come over here with me and pick out a color or three."

# Chapter 20

NOW THAT her children were grown and had money of their own, Mason's mother was down to one job: she was a receptionist at a publishing company in Midtown, reasonable walking distance from Mason's apartment. When he'd first gotten his apartment, he'd drop by and take her to lunch periodically. It had been a while, though, months at least.

He figured Odell would have gotten to her first, but when he arrived in the reception area at lunchtime on Friday, she smiled broadly.

"Oh, baby boy, what a surprise!" She stood and walked around her desk. She hugged him tightly and rocked a little.

"Hi, Mom. Can I take you to lunch?"

"Sure, let me just find someone to man the phones for an hour."

While she secured a replacement, he waited in the little reception area, flipping through the publisher's catalog.

When she was ready to go, she smiled at him and introduced him to the twenty-year-old intern who would be answering the phones in her absence. She referred to Mason as "My youngest, cutest son."

"I won't tell Odell you said that."

She grinned and they walked to the elevator together.

He chose a cute little French bistro two blocks from her office, and they sat at a quiet table together. He watched her peruse the menu, and when she decided what she wanted, she put it down and looked at him.

"How are you, Mom? How are you feeling?"

"Pretty darned good, actually. The new medication is working. In fact, I saw the doctor last week, and all the tests came back with good results."

"That's great, Mom. I'm really glad."

She smiled. "Now what did you want to talk to me about? I know you didn't just ask me to lunch because you had an afternoon free. And please don't tell me we're only going to talk about my health, because I'm *fine*."

He could have demurred, but instead he said, "Have you talked to Odell since Wednesday?"

"No. Why?"

He wondered if he should just have it out with her. That way if she walked out, at least he didn't have to pay for another uneaten meal.

"I'm dating someone," he said.

His mother's eyes lit up. She smiled. "Oh, that's wonderful. Why are you looking at me like you just confessed to killing a puppy?"

"Well, I just… I mean, I didn't know how you would react."

"Honey, I told you I just want you to be happy." She unfolded her napkin and placed it in her lap. "Who is he? What's his name?"

Mason took a deep breath. "His name is Patrick. Mom, I think he's the one."

She gave him a knowing look. She reached across the table and rubbed the back of his hand. "I want to hear everything about him, then. When do I get to meet him?"

"Soon, I promise. But there's something you should know."

"All right." She leaned forward, apparently all ears. "Odell knows already, eh? That's why you asked if I talked to him? You boys always were so close, I'm not surprised you told him first. What do you want me to know?

The waitress came by, but Mason held up his hand and she left again. "Well, Patrick is… he's white."

Mason's mother nodded slowly. "All right. You've dated white men before, though."

"Yes. That's true. But Odell kind of implied—"

"It's okay, baby boy. It's the way of the world, isn't it? And if he's the one, it doesn't matter. Did you really think I would shun you for that? You're all tense."

"No. No, actually, the bigger issue is that he's kind of unusual-looking. Not in a bad way. I mean, I think he's very attractive, but he… he's a hairdresser, right? He doesn't have the sort of job where he has to wear a suit or anything. So he has crazy hair and a lot of tattoos and he's got piercings in both ears. Actually, hang on, I have a picture."

Mason's heart pounded. He was so nervous and shaky that after he pulled out his phone, he had trouble navigating the screen. Eventually he brought up a photo someone else had taken one of the nights Patrick had met Mason for a drink at Spokes after practice. In the photo, he and Patrick were smiling, their heads leaning against each other, their arms around each other. Mason liked the photo enough that it had briefly been his phone background, before he lost his nerve. They looked happy and coupled in the photo. This was the photo he showed his mother.

"Oh, he's a cutie, Mason."

Her reaction was not at all what he expected. He was so surprised he couldn't speak for a moment.

Eventually he said, "Odell hates him. They only met for, like, a minute, but Odell hated him on sight."

"Why? Did Patrick do something?" She handed back the phone.

"No. He didn't do anything. He was just himself." Mason paused to take a deep breath and gather his thoughts. "He's kind of—no, he's *very* flamboyant. But I really like that about him. He's so great, Mom, and he has this amazing energy, and he's fun to be around, and I really, really like him."

"Then that's what matters, sweetheart."

Mason didn't get it. He shook his head. "You're not upset?"

She looked at his phone for another moment before handing it back. "I will admit that I never pictured you with someone like this. You're right, he's not... the hair is a little... but you know what?" She smiled. "You look so happy in that photo. Does Patrick make you happy?"

"Yeah. He does."

"I'd still like to meet him."

"Okay. I... soon. I'd like for him to meet you. But, I mean, Odell kept saying... he threatened to tell you... he said it wasn't okay for me to date a guy like Patrick. Because he's so flamboyant. And I told Odell that if he didn't support Patrick, he didn't support me, because I'm gay and he needed to accept that."

"Is that what all this fuss is about?" she asked. "You and Odell had a fight?"

It sounded stupid when she put it that way. "Odell doesn't want me to date a guy like Patrick. He was so mad at me, he walked out of the restaurant where we were having dinner a couple of nights ago. I thought you'd feel the same."

Mason's mother glanced at the waiter hovering about ten feet away, as if she understood now why Mason had put off ordering food. She turned back to face Mason. "Odell doesn't want you to date anyone." She shook her head. "Probably least of all someone who talked you into painting your nails purple."

Mason looked at his hands. "It was a weird idea. I don't know. Does it look strange?"

She laughed. "Oh, sweetheart. If dating Patrick helps you loosen up, then I am all for it. You've always been far too uptight."

This was news to Mason. She'd never said anything like that before. "You think I'm uptight?"

"I know I haven't always been the most accepting of everything. When you told me about... that you're gay...." She said the words slowly, as if she still had trouble wrapping her lips around them, even all these years later. "It was hard for me. I knew it was true, deep in my soul I knew, because I'd raised you and I saw it when you were growing up. But I was in denial. Then when you just said it… I know it took me a long time to come around, and I'm sorry for that. But I've been thinking a lot lately. You know, ever since the… well, since I got sick a few months ago. I think it made me really see what's important in life."

"You said you were okay."

"And I am! But I can't waste time fretting about everything. I know I haven't always been accepting of you, but you're a grown man now, and in the end, I want you to be with the best person for you. I just want you to be happy and settled, okay?"

Mason leaned forward. "Really?"

"You're my baby boy and I love you. As long as you are a good person, it shouldn't matter who you love."

Mason's chest tightened as she spoke. He wanted to reach across the table and hug her, but it was awkward in the restaurant. "Thanks."

"I know I've made mistakes. I've tried to make it up to you these last years. Did you really think I wouldn't approve of your relationship just because he's white and has funny hair?"

"I don't know what I thought."

She tilted her head. "It's not easy for us, I think. There were always expectations of us. You and me, I mean. Your father left us, and I had to improvise. My father wasn't having it. He didn't think I should work so much. He wanted me to find another man, become a housewife. But that wasn't the right path for me. If marrying a woman isn't the right path for you, it's okay. I understand. You have to pick the path that's best for you, not the one everyone else thinks is best for you. I understand that better than anybody."

Mason believed that she did. He nodded. "So it's okay?"

"It's okay. As long as you're healthy and take me to lunch sometimes."

Mason couldn't help but smile at that. "But what about Odell?"

"Oh, well, Odell. He tried, I know he did, when you first came out, but I've seen him struggle with it. With you. It's hard for him to accept it."

"I just thought… he's always had my back."

"He's your brother and he loves you. This is hard for him."

"It's hard for him? Mom, he walked out on me in the middle of a restaurant! He won't return my calls. And need I point out that *I'm* the gay one?" He refrained from giving her his whole canned speech about everything he gave up, because she'd heard it before. That, and he was tired of defending himself.

"He'll come around. Just give him some time."

"Mom."

Mason wanted to crawl across the table and into her arms. He wanted her to hold him as she had when he was a little boy, or when he was in the hospital and struggling with what to do. He still felt abandoned by Odell, and it would take him a good long while to forgive Odell's recent behavior, but at least his mother was there to support him.

"What about Gary and Darryl?" he asked. "The rest of the family?"

"They already know not to say a bad word about you in my presence, and I intend to keep it that way, no matter who you date. If they're jerks, they can't come to your wedding."

He laughed. "My wedding? So if I wanted to marry Patrick, you'd be okay with that?"

"I really would like to meet him first. I worry, you know."

"I know. You will meet him. He's a good man, I promise." He picked up his menu, the butterflies in his stomach finally calming enough that he thought he could eat. "Thanks, Mom. I really appreciate it."

"Of course, sweetie. Now, I'm starving. What shall we eat?"

# Chapter 21

PATRICK EXAMINED his part in the mirror, thinking he probably should have touched up his roots the day before after all. Then again, he was kind of over being a blond. He thought about letting his hair grow out, about how he'd style it if it were darker. Even if he went natural, he still had the tattoos, so he wouldn't look normal, exactly. The colored streaks in his hair and the piercings and the tattoos, it was all a lot.

Mason hadn't asked him to change. Mason was struggling with whether he could be with someone like Patrick, but he'd never asked Patrick to be anything other than who he was. Patrick was grateful for that.

After he'd decided his hair was satisfactory that Saturday morning, he went into the kitchen for breakfast. He stared forlornly at the empty carton of almond milk someone had left in the fridge when Wendy came into the kitchen and said hello.

"Morning," Patrick said. "I have to kill Keith now."

"Did he leave an empty carton in the fridge again?"

"I don't know who he thinks he's kidding. Like, if he leaves the carton in the fridge it will fool us all into thinking there's still milk left. What does a half-gallon cost these days? A couple of bucks? I know he's broke, but maybe don't drink my milk if you're not going to replace it." Patrick tossed the carton in the trash and shut the refrigerator door. "That was the good almond milk too. Bobby keeps buying soy milk instead. That shit tastes like chalk."

He was tired of sharing his space with three other people. He was tired of Keith eating the food Patrick or the other roommates had bought and leaving empty cartons in the fridge. He was tired of fighting everyone for the one bathroom in the morning. He was tired of petty squabbles over who owed which fraction of the utility bill when Wendy had an air conditioner in her bedroom and Patrick had all those hair appliances. He'd liked the quiet of Mason's apartment, the absence of all this chaos.

"Oh, by the way," Wendy said with a sly smile, "Bobby has a new boyfriend. He stayed over the last time you were at Mason's."

"Really? Our Bobby?" Patrick's other roommate was terribly shy. Of course, leave it to Wendy to keep track of his romantic comings and goings.

"Yup. The guy's name is very British sounding, Nelson or Neville or something like that. He's got a nice face but the body of a toothpick. Bobby's totally smitten."

"Aw. That's cute."

"You'd be able to see it for yourself if you were home more."

Patrick raised his eyebrows. "I'm home right now."

"Yeah, because you and the boyfriend are taking a break."

"It's not really a break. Just a few days apart. And I'm not going to live here forever, you know. Once baseball season ends, I plan to start working more nights again and save up to move out of this dump."

Wendy frowned. "Or you'll move in with Mason."

"It's kind of early for that." Although Patrick couldn't deny he found the idea appealing. "Anyway, whatever, if I moved out, I'd find a replacement. Half my teammates are under thirty and in various complicated roommate situations. There's always someone looking for a cheap room in Manhattan with a woman, a gay guy, and a straight guy."

Wendy laughed. "This place really is a sitcom set, isn't it?"

"I'd laugh harder if there were some damn milk for my cereal."

He gave up and decided he'd get breakfast from the bagel shop on the corner before he went to the salon. He looked down at himself and questioned his own sartorial choices, not liking how the green in his shirt was probably clashing with the new blue streaks in his hair. He went into his room to change.

He hadn't done much in the days since he'd told Mason they should take time apart. Well, he'd gone to baseball practice, same as every week, and he picked up a lot of extra shifts at the salon because he needed the distraction so as not to wallow in his feelings about Mason. The goal of the break was still not entirely concrete in Patrick's mind. He wanted some time to decide what he really wanted without Mason's sexy influence, because it was hard to think straight when Mason was in the room. When they were together, Patrick mostly just wanted to reach out his grabby hands and say, "Mine!" and hold Mason and pet his bald head. It was hard to resist Mason's essential magnetic appeal, his too-serious but not humorless demeanor, his goodness. Mason was beautiful and had been through so much and Patrick really liked him.

So he wanted to keep Mason. It was too late to walk away unscathed now; his heart was too invested. But he couldn't be with a man who couldn't give himself freely, couldn't be with a man who felt any shame where Patrick was concerned. Patrick deserved better. So he hoped that

Mason had worked out what he needed to work out in their time apart, hoped that Mason came to a similar decision, but he knew what he had to do if Mason let him down. It would be hard, but Patrick could do it.

As he was pulling on a new shirt, Mason called.

Patrick almost didn't answer. He wasn't sure if they'd spent enough time apart. He both looked forward to and dreaded whatever Mason had to say. And could Mason even say anything that would satisfy Patrick and the itchy uneasiness he felt about this situation? Patrick had told Mason to prove his love, but how could he do that? In an ideal world, what could Mason say that would convince Patrick everything would work out for the best?

No sense in wondering if the man himself was calling.

When Patrick answered, Mason said, "Hi." Just like that.

"Hi," said Patrick.

Then Mason let out a long sigh. "Man, I miss you. Do you realize that we at least texted every day for the last month? No contact at all for a few days was harder than I expected."

"For me too," Patrick said, because it was true. "I miss you as well. It's good to hear your voice." And it really was. Just hearing that soft baritone sent the same zippy thrill through Patrick that he felt whenever Mason walked into a room.

"So much has happened," Mason said. "I kept wanting to call you and tell you, but I also wanted to respect your wanting to keep your distance."

Mason's tone sparkled with excitement. Patrick melted a little at it. It made him optimistic. "Thanks. I appreciate that."

"Can we have dinner? This weekend?"

"Oh, honey." Patrick closed his eyes. He wanted that badly. He wanted to hold Mason, to be held by Mason, to be able to hope that everything would work out. "I want to, but I picked up a bunch of extra appointments at the salon this weekend. I'm basically working nonstop. The salon closes at eight tonight, but I'm always so tired and brain-dead after a long shift. I'll be useless."

"Monday, then. That might be better actually."

Patrick laughed despite himself. He glanced at his alarm clock and saw he was already late. So much for breakfast. "All right, Monday. I need to get going, but I hope things are well with you?"

"I told off Odell and he's not talking to me, but my mother wants to meet you at your earliest convenience. I showed her a photo and she thinks you're a cutie."

One could have knocked over Patrick with a feather. He sat on his bed with a thunk. "You told—"

"And the interview went better than I could have hoped for, and man, I want to see you so much."

Patrick swallowed. "I know, me too, but I have hair to cut. We'll have dinner Monday."

Patrick was about to hang up when Mason said, "I was serious, you know. I do love you. That wasn't a heat-of-the-moment thing."

Patrick's chest ached. He rubbed his forehead, and he hurt for a moment because he wanted to be with Mason in person. He wanted to pull Mason's big body into his arms and run his hand over Mason's head and breathe in his warm scent. He didn't want to be having this conversation over the phone, a few miles apart, and he didn't want to feel this terrible yearning he felt at Mason's absence.

It was stupid. It was two and a half months of dating. They'd been apart for all of three days. How could his feelings be this intense?

"Yeah," Patrick said. "Yeah, I know. I...." He sighed. "I feel the same. But I want to tell you in person. You and Odell had a fight?"

"I told him that if he didn't accept you, he didn't accept me. He got mad and stormed out of the restaurant."

Patrick's chest warmed. This was what he wanted, wasn't it? Had Mason really figured out how to live for himself?

Patrick realized he'd been preparing to be let down.

"Oh, Mason. I want to give you the biggest hug right now."

"On Monday you can give me all the hugs you want."

"Deal. *All* the hugs."

"Have a good weekend, okay? I'll text you where to meet me."

"All right. Soon, Mason."

"Soon."

But *soon* didn't feel soon enough.

NATE TOSSED a ball in the air. Carlos didn't think he knew anyone was watching as he practiced throwing it. Nate really was a brilliant pitcher. Carlos imagined he could have made the majors if he had that kind of ambition. But he didn't. Their Little League team had kicked ass and taken names across the Bronx, but when Nate aged out, he'd stopped playing baseball for a while. He swore up and down that he only ever wanted to play for fun, but Carlos sometimes thought all that natural talent was wasted on an amateur league.

Somehow they'd both arrived at Hipsters practice early, and everyone else, even Scott, seemed to be running late. So Carlos made a show of taking his sweet time lacing up his cleats and fiddling with his bag. Nate was pretending to throw fastballs.

"Hey, Carlos," Nate called out. "Want to try to hit my curveball?"

"You throw a curveball?"

"I do now." Nate frowned. "Well, not well. I'm still trying to get it right."

Carlos stepped up to the backstop. "Don't bean me."

"I'll try, but I can't make any promises."

Carlos ran back to his bag and pulled out a batting helmet. No sense in risking brain injury. He patted it down on his head and then walked up to the plate again. He lifted his bat and settled into a stance.

Nate threw the ball. It went wide and clanged against the chain-link behind the backstop.

"Bro," Carlos said.

"I know. I can throw it fast, but not with any kind of accuracy." Nate picked up a ball from the basket at his feet. He wrapped his pitching hand around it and twisted his wrist experimentally. "I've been watching videos online that are supposed to teach you how to throw pitches. I've got the hold right but haven't figured out how to throw it so it stays fair. Let me try again."

So Carlos got ready for another pitch. This one was better but still went outside the strike zone, whizzing by Carlos's hip.

"Forget about not hitting my head," Carlos said after he jumped back. "Don't hit me in the junk."

Nate kicked the dirt on the pitcher's mound and grunted. "One more. Third time's gotta be the charm."

He wound up and pitched again. This time it looked like a fair ball, so Carlos swung for it. His bat clipped the edge of it, sending a grounder back toward Nate. Nate bowed to scoop it up as it got to his feet.

"Not bad," Carlos said.

"Not really game-ready yet, but it might be fun to throw a few of those at Ty during batting practice to see him get flustered."

Carlos laughed. He couldn't help but think about how nice it was for just the two of them to goof around together, surrounded by baseball, the glue that held their childhood together. They'd both been insane Yankees fans as boys, one of many things that had brought them together.

Scott appeared at the edge of the ball fields and made his way toward them, so Carlos supposed their reverie was over. Nate tossed a ball in the air before jogging around the field to pick up the stray balls. He put them all in the basket and carried it over to the bench.

"You might be happy to know," Nate said, "that I have a date tomorrow night."

It was like Nate had reached into Carlos's chest and squeezed it. Which was nuts, because Nate had dated plenty in the years he and Carlos had known each other, and also, Carlos had a goddamned boyfriend.

"Oh yeah?" Carlos tried sounding interested. "Anyone I know?"

"I don't think so. It's this guy who is also a regular at that coffee shop near my apartment. The one with the scones you like?"

"Yeah, yeah."

"We kept showing up there at the same time every morning, so he suggested we drink our coffee together yesterday. He's incredibly smart. Chemistry professor at NYU."

"Wow." That was... interesting. Carlos hated it, but it was still interesting. He didn't think he could compete with a chemistry professor.

"Yeah. I felt totally outclassed, but he was actually pretty down-to-earth. We talked for, like, an hour yesterday. I was late to work. Then he asked me out. And I was like, you know, he seems nice. I'm single. What the hell?"

"Sure." Those were all true things. Why did it bother Carlos so much? He shrugged, trying to shake it off. "You'll have to let me know how it goes."

"I will."

"I mean, I hope it goes well. You deserve to be happy, Nate."

Nate smiled sadly. "Yeah. Thanks."

They left something unsaid there. Carlos wanted to ask what, but then Ty and Ian and Mason arrived all at once, as did most of the rest of the team, so Scott started yelling at them to get their shit together to start practice.

Carlos patted Nate's shoulder and walked away.


NATE HAD already pretty well shredded the cardboard sleeve around his coffee cup by the time Mason arrived at the little coffee shop near his apartment.

"So," Mason said as he sat down, "what I hear you saying is that you have a problem."

Nate looked over the little pile of cardboard shreds. "You could say that."

Mason glanced at the counter, trying to choose between something practical, like a cup of coffee, or a sugary latte. Then he looked back at Nate. "I'm beginning to think getting coffee instead of going to a bar was the wrong choice."

Nate shook his head. "I think booze will only make it worse."

"That bad, huh? Well, hold tight. Let me just get something to drink."

When Mason came back with his latte and a couple of cookies, Nate had moved on to shredding a napkin. Mason handed him a cookie. "What happened?" Mason asked.

Nate pursed his lips. "You go first."

This whole coffee date had started when Mason had, in a panic, started calling friends to see if he could get another perspective on the situation with Patrick. When Patrick had left his apartment and said he'd needed time, Mason had wondered if this was a break or a breakup or what the hell was going on. He'd had time to sleep and think and had gained some perspective, but when he'd called Nate and Nate had sounded completely despondent, Mason reasoned he wasn't the only one with problems.

He took a sip of his latte. "Well, Patrick and I are... on a break."

Nate furrowed his brow. "Geez. What happened?"

Mason shrugged. "Insecurity isn't sexy, I guess."

"What the hell does that mean?"

The coffee shop was unusually crowded for this time of day; usually the neighborhood bars were more attractive to the after-work set. Activity buzzed around them, which made Mason feel like it was safe to talk. There was too much going on for anyone to pay attention to them. "Turns out I have some hang-ups that Patrick thinks I need to get over before we take our relationship further."

Nate looked dubious, but then he said, "Gee, Mason Brooks has hang-ups. I *never* would have guessed."

"You don't have to be sarcastic, you know."

Nate smiled softly. He started putting the little shreds of napkin and cardboard into his empty cup. "Look, man, I get it. Probably every gay man does. You spent a lot of time hiding in the closet because of your job. I understand that. My mom is super Catholic. That didn't keep me in the closet, of course, but there are only so many times you can hear you're going to hell before it starts to give you a complex, you know?"

Mason nodded.

Nate said, "But what's the verdict? You like this Patrick fellow, huh?"

"I do. A lot. I think… I think what I need is a grand gesture."

"You'd do better to have coffee with Ty or Josh. I'm no good at romance."

Mason nodded, watching Nate closely. They'd been friends for a long time. When Mason had first joined the Rainbow League, Nate and Carlos had both gone all super fanboy on him, but once he convinced them he was a regular guy, they bonded over loving the Yankees and growing up in the Bronx and other common ground.

Still, it was because they'd been friends for so long that Mason could clearly see the emotions Nate was unsuccessfully masking, and knew that something was going on with Carlos. Because who else but Carlos would make Nate this mopey while talking about romance?

"I think I know what I'm going to do," Mason said. "So what's going on with you?"

Nate frowned. "I went out with a chemistry professor last night."

"And?"

"It was… nice. I dunno. He's cute and interesting and I don't know what my problem is, because on paper, he's the sort of guy I could really fall for, but in reality?"

"He's not Carlos," Mason said.

"He's not Carlos." Nate sighed. "I wish I didn't feel this way. If I knew of a way to make it stop, I would do it. Instead, do you know what I did? I told Carlos about this date in great detail, both before the date and after I got home last night. I hoped to make him jealous, because I'm insane and stupid, and at first he seemed happy for me. But then he said…"

Mason waited. Rather than speak, Nate blinked a few times and took a deep breath.

"He said…," Mason said.

"He got angry. He asked if me rubbing in how well my date went was revenge for him always talking about Aiden." Nate shook his head. "I mean, if I was home alone after the date, it couldn't have gone *that* well, but I didn't point that out to Carlos. Instead, I said that he sure did talk about Aiden a lot, and then we got into a big stupid fight about I don't even know what, and then he said maybe we shouldn't hang out for a while."

Mason could practically see Nate's heart breaking, but he couldn't think of anything more comforting to say than "That sucks, man."

"My own fault. I dug this damn hole. I've been a jerk about Aiden, which is pissing Carlos off, so it's no better than I deserve."

"So maybe the chemistry professor is a good thing. I know he's not Carlos, but maybe it's time to move on."

Nate started shredding the lip of his coffee cup. "Yeah. But you can see why I am not the one to advise you about grand romantic gestures, because any romantic advice from me is bound to blow up in your face."

"Nate."

"Sorry. I know I'm being a sad sack." Nate took a deep breath. "Maybe what everyone needs is time and distance. If Carlos and I avoid each other for a bit, maybe what I feel will cool off. Or maybe I just need to fuck the chemistry professor. His name is Todd, by the way. He has two PhDs. He's way smarter than me, but hasn't figured that out yet."

"He sounds great."

"Yeah. As great as all the empty-headed beefcakes you dated before Patrick."

# Chapter 22

MASON HAD been to the intimate little bistro in SoHo once before with a few of the guys from the Hipsters because Ty had read a review of it in the *Times* and wanted to try the food. Four guys in that restaurant had made for some awkwardness because everyone else there had been on a date. Mason remembered thinking at the time that it would be a great date spot, given the small tables, the flickering candlelight, and the menu full of plates meant for sharing. It was a good spot for a grand romantic gesture. Mason made a reservation for Monday night.

He was a few minutes early and had clearly beaten Patrick there, so he sat at the table, pulled out the new issue of *All Sports Weekly*, and ordered a glass of wine.

Part of him felt confident that he was about to do the right thing. Part of him worried it was colossally stupid.

Patrick walked in a few minutes later and Mason's heart skipped a beat. He smiled wide and stood, happy to see Patrick. Patrick smiled back and opened his arms, so Mason hugged him. He closed his eyes and savored the feeling of Patrick pressed against him, Patrick's arms around him. Patrick was warm and smelled sweet—well, and kind of astringent, thanks to all the product in his hair—and Mason did not want to let him go.

"It's going to be hard to eat if you don't let me sit," Patrick said. "This is wonderful, but I'm starving."

Mason kissed Patrick's forehead and backed away.

They sat and a waiter immediately appeared to ask Patrick what he wanted to drink. Patrick said he'd have whatever wine Mason was drinking, so Mason ordered a bottle of the wine.

"You trying to get me drunk?" Patrick asked.

"I'm trying to celebrate. I haven't seen you in almost a week."

"Five days."

"Still."

Patrick laughed. His smile was radiant. He looked great; he'd cut his hair in a way that flattered his face, and he was dressed nicely in a short-sleeved button-down and navy cropped pants. Mason took a moment to take in the whole picture: the sleeve of tattoos, the spiked hair, the rings in his ears and in his eyebrow, his pale skin, his pink lips, his wide shoulders, his slim body. Looking at Patrick made Mason want to smile for days. Mason loved this man. If Patrick returned the sentiment—the grin on his face made Mason optimistic that he did—then Mason was about to make a very wise decision.

When the waiter came back, Mason ordered a small feast: two appetizers and a shared entrée. He already knew Patrick didn't really care for fish, so he ordered chicken and tofu and lots of vegetables.

"So tell me about what happened with Odell," Patrick said after they ordered.

Mason related what had happened at dinner. He watched Patrick's face as he spoke, measuring his reactions. Patrick had such an unconsciously expressive face, with brows that furrowed and a mouth that curved and cheeks that dimpled when he smiled. When Mason described his dinner with Odell, Patrick's eyebrows rose and fell in concern, indignation, surprise.

"You really said all that?" Patrick said when Mason finished speaking.

"Yup. And it felt really good. *Really* good. Until Odell walked out, that is."

"Have you talked to him since then?"

Mason let out a breath, not pleased with this memory either. He didn't want to let Odell's bullshit rain on his celebration with Patrick. "He called yesterday to say he was sorry for storming out, but he wasn't quite ready to apologize yet. We started arguing again and I... I just hung up on him. I didn't want to fight anymore. I was surprised that he called at all, actually. I think my mother got to him."

"Your mother?"

So Mason explained about taking her to lunch and everything she'd said. How her having a little bit of a health scare had shifted her perspective. Patrick smiled through a lot of the story. He winked when Mason repeated that his mother had called Patrick a cutie.

Mason concluded, "You asked me to think about us, and I did. I really did. And what I decided is that I'm done being ashamed. I didn't make the sacrifices I did to play it safe. I gave up a career so that I could love who I wanted to. And who I love is you. That's all that matters."

Patrick grinned widely. "Oh, Mason, sweetie. I'm really thrilled to hear that." He glanced at Mason's hands. "Did you know your nails are purple?"

Mason laughed. "They're kind of chipped now. I, uh, met your friend Valerie. She taught me about nail polish." Mason looked at his nails. They really were horribly chipped all these days later. "My toes still look good anyway."

"Look at you!" Patrick laughed, an ebullient, joyous sound. "You *have* been busy in our time apart."

The waiter served appetizers then. The smell was intoxicating. Mason's stomach grumbled. He supposed he'd been so busy thinking about today that he hadn't gotten around to eating. Now that Patrick was smiling at him, his nervousness faded, replaced with a deep hunger, albeit not just for food. One thing at a time, though. He sampled a piece of chicken, which was juicy and exploded with flavor in his mouth.

"So tell me about this interview." Patrick's gaze settled on the magazine Mason had left on the table. "Is that the issue you're featured in?"

"It is."

"That's awfully fast."

"I was a last-minute story replacement. I'm starting to think my agent greased some wheels so that he could close out this endorsement deal."

"Can I see it?"

"Yeah," Mason said, his heart beating faster again. "But first, I have to tell you something else."


PATRICK'S HEART had been racing since he'd left his apartment. The anticipation of seeing Mason and what it meant this time had sent butterflies dancing in his chest. When Mason said, "I have to tell you something else," he worried he might be in the middle of some kind of coronary incident. Everything felt light and fluttery and crazy in his body.

Mason picked up the magazine. He was not on the cover, at least; a handsome tennis player holding his racket in a somewhat suggestive way graced the cover instead. Mason flipped through the pages and then folded them around, presumably because his interview was on that page. He held the magazine to his chest.

"I need you to know," Mason said, "that I love you and I'm proud to have you at my side and that when I gave this interview, we'd been apart for all of twenty-four hours, but that was enough for me to decide that if I had to choose one person to spend the rest of my life with, I'd choose you a hundred times, the hell with anyone who disagrees."

"Did you talk about me in your interview?" Dear Lord, what was happening? Why was Patrick's heartbeat so erratic? Why was he so nervous?

Because the stakes were high. Because he loved Mason, even though he hadn't said so aloud yet. He knew in his heart, deep in his soul, when he looked at this man with a silly grin sitting across the table from him, that Patrick could easily picture many dinners like this. Well, maybe ones that were not so emotionally fraught. He could picture waking up in Mason's big bed together with the sun streaming in through the wide window that faced Ninth Avenue, and lounging lazily in front of the TV. He could see them hanging on each other at a bar with their friends, and gently teasing each other when their teams played games.

He could imagine Mason coming by the salon when Patrick was working so that Valerie could do his nails while they all chatted about TV or celebrity gossip. He could imagine buzzing around the apartment when Mason was working, maybe suggesting ideas for stories or helping Mason through writer's block. He could so easily picture the two of them making a life together, their day-to-day stuff entangled.

Yeah, he loved Mason, and he could not imagine a better fate for himself than that life he'd just pictured. He wanted that life. He needed it. And if Mason had stood up to his family, if Mason had shucked off his old shame and his stupid ideas about gender and masculinity and who he should date, then Patrick was in. Because Mason should be with the person he most wanted to be with. He deserved it. He deserved Patrick. And Patrick deserved him.

Patrick was pretty sure Mason was about to do something really brave but really stupid. Patrick wanted him to do it, though.

He reached for the magazine.

Mason held it just out of his reach.

"I may have mentioned you in the interview," Mason said.

Patrick shook his head. "I don't know what I was thinking when I told you to prove you love me. I believed you did at the time. I was just upset and confused. But you've gone so far beyond what I expected, and I—"

"I wanted to make a grand gesture."

Patrick reached across the table and took Mason's other hand, the one that was not clutching the magazine. "I know. I'm trying to tell you that I appreciate it. I never expected you to go to these lengths. I am happy you did, but honestly? This is kind of a 'you had me at hello' moment."

"I love you. I want to be with you."

Patrick couldn't keep the smile off his face. "I love you too."

It was out there now. Mason smiled.

"Seriously, though," Patrick said. "I walked in here and you smiled at me and I was yours."

Mason intertwined his fingers with Patrick's. "So what do you think? You and I are pretty different. Think we could make a go of something bigger than just 'a real thing'?"

Patrick laughed, remembering how awkward that conversation had been. "Mason, do you know why I love you?"

"Tell me."

"Because you are sweet and caring and really sexy, but also because you never once tried to change me or make me be something I'm not. You've always been interested in me for me. You love me just as I am."

"Yeah. How else could I love you?"

"You wouldn't have been the first man who tried to get me to calm down. When you were having your crisis, though, you never tried to make me change to make me better suited to your family. And trust me, honey, I've dated plenty of guys who told me to cut my hair or stop painting my nails or were like, 'Ugh, Patrick, do you have to be that way *all* the time,' and yes, actually, I do, because this is who I am."

"I would never. If anything I want to be more like you."

"I know. That's why I love you. You're a swell guy, but you also love me."

"A swell guy?"

"You know what I mean. I'm not selfish enough to like you just because you like me."

Mason grinned. "That was a very sweet speech."

"Enough to see the magazine?"

"Yes. I've, ah, highlighted the relevant passages." Mason handed it to Patrick.

Patrick turned the magazine over in his hands. There was a huge picture of Mason standing at what looked like a Manhattan street corner in broad daylight, a happy smile on his face and a somewhat wistful look in his eyes as he stared off into the distance. He was at his fashionable best in a blue-and-white plaid button-down and tight dark-wash jeans with tan oxfords that looked very expensive. He was strikingly handsome in the photo. *Life After Baseball*, read the headline. There was a subtitle that read *Mason Brooks talks about love, sports, and coming out of the closet.*

Okay. Not the most clever headline.

Mason had indeed drawn a box around a few paragraphs. Patrick skipped straight to those.

*Brooks has been an outspoken advocate for LGBT athletes since coming out of the closet himself. He says he wants it not to matter if a player is gay or straight. He's been forthcoming about the fact that the foot injury that prompted him to leave the major leagues probably wasn't career-ending after all, but that it was more important to him to lead an honest life than to keep playing while in the closet. Does he regret this decision?*

*"Not at all," says Brooks.*

*So I had to ask if part of what made it worthwhile was a special someone.*

*"Yes," he says. "That is, whether I'm in a relationship or not shouldn't matter because the fact that I'm gay doesn't change if I have a boyfriend or I'm single. But it's definitely nice to have someone in my life. I'm dating a guy named Patrick, and he's the love of my life. I'm going to marry him someday. He makes me so happy. And none of it would have been possible if I'd kept playing baseball, at least not at the time I was playing."*

Patrick was probably going to be diagnosed with some kind of heart condition, the way this evening was going. But he looked at Mason, who was leaning forward and looking a little anxious now. His smile was uneasy, but it did seem hopeful.

*I'm going to marry him someday.*

"Mason," Patrick said. "Are you asking…?" He held up the magazine. "Is this a proposal?"

"Ah, well. Not exactly. Unless you want it to be."

If one's life flashed before his eyes right before something traumatic, Patrick wondered if one's potential life could flash before his eyes before something like this. Because Patrick could see all of it laid out before him, a lifetime with Mason, of them holding each other, and talking, and laughing, and waking up together, and just being so joyously happy that they could make it over any hump life tried to put in their way.

And leave it to Mason not to ask in a straightforward way. It was probably too soon for any kind of talk of forever, and Patrick didn't know if he was ready for that either, but he did know that he wanted Mason for the long haul.

"You were right," Patrick said, holding up the magazine. "You are going to marry Patrick someday."

Mason scooted his chair around the table so that they sat next to each other. Then he put a hand on the back of Patrick's head before pulling him into a kiss. It was probably a little vulgar for the restaurant, but Patrick didn't care. Patrick put his arms around Mason's neck and kissed him back.

"That was… wow," Patrick said as they parted. "I'm surprised."

Mason moved his seat back, glancing warily at the disapproving waiter. "I'll admit I didn't think this through completely. I just said what was on my mind. Which was that I want to spend my life with you. I know it's kind of soon for talk of marriage, but it's nice to know it might be in our future."

"It's okay. We'll work it all out together. Maybe we could start with living together?"

Mason smiled. "I like the sound of that."

A burst of laughter broke out of Patrick because he was just so happy suddenly. This probably also was not good for his heart, but who cared? He and Mason could soon be together every day. They'd get married eventually. He couldn't think of anything he wanted more.

"It was awfully presumptuous for you to have put it in a magazine that way, though," Patrick said. "What if I turned you down flat?"

"If I've learned nothing else, it's that you don't get far in life by keeping quiet and safe. Sometimes you have to make the bold move."

Patrick just smiled. "I hope you keep on making bold moves, babe. For the rest of our lives."

"I plan to." Mason winked.

# Chapter 23

THE END-OF-SEASON party for the Rainbow League was a raucous event held at Barnstorm. Members of all eight teams and a handful of significant others crowded together and bumped against each other and competed for space. Mason kept a firm hand on Patrick at all times, worried about losing him in the crush. It was loud too, the cacophony of voices ringing and thrumming through the space, making it impossible to hear anything even though the music was low.

They got drinks at the bar and made their way back to the table Ty and Ian had commandeered. Ian was a little drunk already and smiling stupidly. He positively beamed at Ty, who was trying to pry the pint glass out of his hand. Patrick sat in the one empty chair, put his glass on the table, and shook out his hands.

"I don't know why they serve martinis in these dumb glasses," said Patrick. "It's impossible not to spill."

Mason stood behind him and put a hand on his shoulder as he sipped his beer. He supposed that since Patrick was sitting, he couldn't get lost, but Mason just liked touching him.

"Good news!" Ty said. "We finally found a place we both agree on. Big doorman building near Grand Army Plaza."

"So you're staying in Brooklyn?" asked Nate. "Or Ty is."

"Yeah." Ian smiled. "I didn't want to move, but this apartment is really nice. Rent is reasonable given the location and the size of the apartment. Killer view of the park. And it's walking distance from my mother, which I guess is not terrible."

Ty grinned. "Once you go Brooklyn…."

"That doesn't even work because it doesn't rhyme," said Ian. "And we could move to Manhattan sometime in the future. The only reason I even entertained the idea is that it's close to a lot of train lines."

"It has two bedrooms and they allow pets. We're going to get a dog!" said Ty.

Ian frowned. "We're not getting a dog."

"An apartment near the park is the perfect place for a dog."

"We'll talk about it," Ian grumbled.

Mason chuckled. He put his glass on the table and then leaned down to kiss the top of Patrick's head. All that spiky hair tickled his nose. He smiled and then hovered near Patrick's temple. "Should we tell them *our* news?"

Patrick cupped the back of Mason's head with his hand. "Oh, honey. I guess now that I've met your mother, it's official, huh?"

Patrick had gone with Mason up to the Bronx for a big Italian feast on Arthur Avenue with Mason's mother. She had adored Patrick almost on sight, which had shocked the hell out of Mason. Then she mortified him by confiding that she had a tattoo on her thigh. When Patrick asked conspiratorially if he could see it, she consented; Mason had declined to look, but apparently it was a black rose on a vine that went around her thigh. It must have been fairly new if Mason had never seen it.

So that was traumatizing, but the bottom line was that she approved whole-heartedly. She conceded that Gary and Darryl would be harder to convince, but she reiterated to Patrick that if they couldn't get over themselves, they were not invited to the wedding. Patrick's eyes went wide at that, probably because Mason hadn't explicitly told his mother there would actually be a wedding. Mason had told her it was a possibility down the line, but for now they were just planning to move in together. And his mother had given them her blessing. Mason couldn't remember ever being happier.

Of course, Odell was still a problem, but he had at least deigned to speak to Mason. He grudgingly apologized for overreacting and admitted their mother had chewed him out. He still didn't seem totally okay with Patrick, but Mason was optimistic he'd come around. Eventually.

For now, though, Mason had what felt like a bubble about to burst in his chest, an unprecedented level of excitement about the future and all it would bring. He couldn't keep the smile off his face.

Nate narrowed his eyes at Mason. "Considering we stank out loud this season and lost in the first round of play-offs, you seem awfully giddy."

Mason shrugged and stood back up. "I like winning, but there are more important things in life."

"Like twinky boyfriends," said Jim, who was sitting on his boyfriend's lap in one of the other chairs.

"Hey, I am not a twink," said Patrick. "I think once you're over twenty-five, they don't let you be one anymore."

Mason laughed. "I don't care what you are. I love you just the same."

Ian said, "Aww." Nate made gagging sounds.

"You're probably next, single boy," Ty said, pointing at Nate. "Law of averages. Ten bucks says next season we get some hot new recruit and you turn to jelly at the sight of him. You won't be gagging then."

"Doubtful," said Nate.

"What's with the necklace?" asked Paul.

Patrick fingered his new necklace. It was a gold 17 on a thin chain, a weird memento from Mason's Yankee days that he had been keeping in a box on his dresser.

"It's Mason's Yankee jersey number," Patrick said. "I decided to keep it for myself. It's kind of a symbol."

Ty laughed. "Of what?"

"Like a promise ring?" Patrick tilted his head as if he were still working out what it all meant. "Is that cheesy? Has anyone had promise rings since 1955?"

Mason just shrugged and kissed the top of Patrick's head.

"Well, anyway," Patrick said. "Number Seventeen and I are moving in together too. As soon as I find a replacement for my room in my apartment, my little butt is moving uptown." He hummed a few bars of the theme from *The Jeffersons.*

The table let out a few collective excited cheers. A few of the other Hipsters standing nearby patted Mason on the back. Everyone hugged and kissed and someone made Mason and Patrick pose for a couple of photos. Mason might not have been a fan of getting his photo taken, but he was happy to show off his relationship with Patrick. He couldn't have kept the smile off his face for anything.

Then the music kicked up a notch and the mood turned celebratory and everyone started dancing and laughing, and it was one of the best season-ending parties in Mason's memory. The bar was loud and crowded, alcohol flowed freely, and everyone seemed to be in a genuinely good mood, even the teams who hadn't fared so well that season.

In all the chaos, Patrick grabbed Mason and gave him a big kiss, everything they felt for each other right there where their lips met, and it was perfect.

Keep reading for an exclusive excerpt from

# *The Long Slide Home*

The Rainbow League: Book Three

By Kate McMurray

Nate and Carlos have been the best of friends since their childhood playing baseball together in the Bronx. For the last few years, Nate's been in love with Carlos, though he's never acted on it, and Carlos has never given any indication that he returns Nate's feelings. Nate has finally given up, determined to move on and find someone else, especially now that Carlos has shacked up with his boyfriend Aiden.

Carlos doesn't understand why Nate has suddenly gotten weird, acting cold and distant at team practice for the Rainbow League. But if that's how things are going to be, Carlos is done trying to figure Nate out. But then Aiden starts to show he might not be the man Carlos thought he was, and Carlos needs his best friend's support. Worse, he starts to realize his feelings for Nate might not be limited to friendship. But in the aftermath of his relationship with Aiden, and with Nate having problems of his own, the timing is all wrong to make a real relationship work. As emotions run high, both have a hard time figuring out what is real and what is just convenient.

## Coming Soon to
## http://www.dreamspinnerpress.com

# Chapter 1

NATE HAD pressed the buzzer for apartment 4D several thousand times in his life, but it felt different now. He took a deep breath and pressed it with his thumb, waiting for the telltale static squawk of the ancient intercom system. Eventually Mama Lulu called out, "Hello?"

"It's Nate."

"Come on up, *mi hijo.*"

When the buzzer sounded, Nate pushed through the door and went up the stairs, the same way he had nearly every day from when he was six until he was eighteen. By the time he got to the fourth floor, he was out of breath, a little out of shape after being lazy all winter, but he dutifully knocked on the door. Luisa Ruiz—Mama Lulu to everyone—answered, waving her arms to welcome him into the apartment, her round body resplendent in a floral dress.

It was chaos inside, but then, it always was. Even though all of the Ruiz children had fled the nest, here were two more. Nate recognized them as Lourdes's kids, Lulu's grandchildren. Mia was not quite two, toddling around in a frothy pink princess dress complete with a little plastic tiara. The baby—Nate couldn't remember the baby's name and hated himself a little for it—wore a onesie covered with footballs, having a grand old time in his bouncy chair on the kitchen table. The baby also sucked on a blue pacifier. No gender ambiguity for these kids.

"Uncle Nate," Mia said, opening her arms to give him a hug.

He knelt to hug her back. "Hi, sweetie."

"I'm babysitting," Lulu explained.

"Ah." Nate stood back up and patted Mia's head.

"What brings you here, Nate?" said Lulu. "No, wait, sit at the table."

This was part of the ritual too. Nate would come in and sit at the kitchen table, and within moments some sort of food would appear before him. Mama Lulu was never happier than when she was feeding people. This time, it was a bowl of paella, yellow rice with bits of chicken and chorizo and maybe some kind of fish in it. Nate's mouth watered, so he took a forkful. It was salty and savory and delicious.

Mia toddled over and climbed onto one of the other chairs. When she sat, the table came up to her nose, but this didn't seem to bother her.

"Now," said Lulu, plunking down a glass of lemonade in front of Nate, "talk to me. It's bad news, yes?"

Nate sighed. Just being inside the Ruiz home had made him feel many times better, so much so that he almost didn't want to bring up his reason for visiting in the first place. But he'd come here seeking comfort, so he said, "I was in the neighborhood. Mom's in the hospital."

"Oh, Nate. What happened?"

He rubbed his forehead. "The cancer's back."

Mama Lulu's face fell.

"I'm not sure how I feel about it," Nate said.

Mama Lulu rubbed the back of Nate's hand. He loved that he didn't have to explain. Lulu already knew that Nate's mother, Rebecca, was cold and stoic, that she and Nate weren't very close, that her working so many hours when Nate had been a boy had driven Nate into the Ruiz home to begin with. The cherry on top was that Rebecca was devoutly Catholic and Nate's homosexuality had never quite sat well with her.

Of course, the Ruiz family was Catholic too, but matriarch Lulu was everything Rebecca was not: she was warm and welcoming and loved her children fiercely and without condition. When her son, Carlos, Nate's best friend since first grade, had come out, she'd given him a hug and carried on with her day. And Nate had never felt unwelcome here, had been a part of the family since his elementary school days, even though he wasn't blood related.

So now Nate's mother was in the hospital being treated for breast cancer that the doctors had apparently not completely excised the first time. Now it had spread to other parts of her system. Of course she hadn't told Nate about it, not at first. Only when she started coughing up blood did she decide it might be a good idea to call her son and ask him to take her to the hospital.

He put his fork down. Mama Lulu stroked his head.

"I don't want bad things to happen to her or anything," Nate said, "but we're so distant these days that, I don't know. I think I should be sadder than I am?"

"You feel how you feel, *mi hijo*."

"Yeah. Well, anyway. The prognosis is not good. The doctors are saying she may not last the summer." He shook his head, more frustrated than sad. "Her doctor won't say it, but I get the feeling this might have been more treatable if she'd gone to see him sooner. She has insurance now. I don't understand why she would wait so long. The oncologist told me she must have felt unwell for months while the cancer progressed. Months!"

Mama Lulu smiled sadly at Nate and stroked his hair some more. "Maybe she thought it was just the flu. Maybe she did not want to admit to herself that the cancer was back."

Nate swallowed and picked up his fork again. He ate a piece of chorizo. In many ways, he was grateful to his mother, who had always kept a roof over their heads even if it meant working two jobs; who had helped pay for his college; who bought him new clothes every year. But Lulu Ruiz continued to show Nate every day that there was a lot more to being a mother than paying for stuff.

Rebecca had once come to Ruiz family functions. The big Puerto Rican family certainly knew how to throw a party. Often Rebecca would arrive quietly and then sit on the edge, awkwardly eating and not talking to anyone. Around the time Nate turned sixteen, she'd started begging off, and once Nate left home, she stopped going entirely.

Bottom line was that Rebecca may have been Nate's mother, but he'd long felt that the Ruizes were his real family.

"She has a few months left," Nate said. "Then I'll have to say good-bye."

"That's never easy."

"No."

"Abuela!" little Mia said.

"You want some *arroz con pollo*?"

Mia screwed up her face in confusion. Nate guessed that Lulu's Spanish dishes were not in her diet or vocabulary yet.

"How about some animal crackers?" Lulu offered.

Mia nodded enthusiastically. Lulu got up to fetch the box from the counter. She offered Mia her high chair, which Mia adamantly refused. So Lulu put some animal crackers on a plastic plate and then placed it in front of Mia. Mia had to reach above her head to pick them off the plate, but she sat there, crunching happily.

As Mama Lulu walked around the table and settled back in her chair, she asked, "Have you talked to Carlos about this?"

"Ah, well. I haven't really talked to Carlos much at all since he moved in with Aiden."

Lulu made a disapproving guttural noise and pushed back from the table. "Why is that?" she asked, her voice wary.

"I may have let it be known that I don't really like Aiden and I thought Carlos was making a mistake, and now Carlos hardly talks to me. You must know that."

She nodded. "He hasn't said as much, just that you had an argument. You really told him you thought moving in with Aiden was a mistake?"

"I did."

That hung in the air. Nate supposed he didn't need to explain why. Lulu had always been extraordinarily intuitive.

"I worry about him," Lulu said. "Carlos loves Aiden, I know that, and Aiden seems like a decent man, but I just don't...." She shook her head. "There's nothing wrong with him."

"No. There isn't." Well, except that Aiden was the man Carlos went to bed with each night, not Nate. And Nate just got a bad vibe off him, but Nate was so crazy with jealousy that he didn't trust his instincts. Carlos had never really shown bad judgment with men in the past—his exes were mostly good guys with whom things just hadn't worked out, or that was how it seemed before Nate's heart decided he and Carlos should be together. So Nate should have trusted Carlos's judgment, but something about Aiden.... "I've never been able to put a finger on why I don't like him, but I don't. Besides the obvious reason. I don't know. And probably I'm saying too much."

"It's all right, Nate. I appreciate your honesty."

He ate a few more forkfuls of rice and watched Mia carefully chew on her animal crackers. The baby—was his name Jorge, maybe?—had fallen asleep in the bouncy chair and looked serene, his little pacifier bobbing occasionally as he sucked on it in his sleep.

"It's funny," Lulu said. "I always thought you and Carlos would end up together."

It hurt Nate to hear that, like a punch in the stomach. It was a recent thing, wanting Carlos, and it had sprung on Nate quite suddenly two summers ago when they were both single for the first time in a while and Nate started thinking, *Maybe*.... Carlos had been his best friend forever, his family, and they cared about each other deeply. Nate had always thought Carlos objectively attractive—he had that tall, dark, and handsome thing going for him, for one thing, and he was in good shape and a little obsessed with proper grooming. He wore too much cologne, but Nate had come to miss the cloud of it that always surrounded Carlos.

One day, though, Nate and Carlos had been tossing a ball back and forth in Central Park and Nate had noticed how much Carlos's brown eyes sparkled, how neat his eyebrows were, how plush his lips looked; he'd seen musculature he hadn't noticed before, strength, physique. He noticed that Carlos actually had quite a nice ass, that the swishy way Carlos walked was kind of seductive, that Carlos's husky voice could sometimes make Nate hard even if he was talking about unsexy things, like baseball or work.

Of course, within weeks of Nate discovering all of these things, Carlos had discovered Aiden.

"I thought we would end up together too," Nate said.

He realized suddenly he'd spoken out loud and put a hand to his mouth. Mama Lulu stared at him.

"I'm so sorry," said Nate. "That was an inappropriate thing to say to his mother. I swear, I've never even made a move on him."

Then Lulu laughed. "Oh, Nate. No. It's all right. Carlos loves Aiden, but something nags at me when I see them together. I don't know what. Aiden may be a good man, but I do not think he's the right one for Carlos. But Carlos will not be dissuaded. I had made my peace with it. If this is what Carlos wants and Aiden makes him happy, who am I to stand in the way?"

"And arguing with him just makes him more stubborn."

Lulu balked but then nodded slowly. "Yes, he is that way. These are matters of the heart, though."

Still, Nate hadn't been able to shake the idea that this was his fault somehow. Instead of talking about his feelings like a mature adult, he'd lost hope and let Aiden claim Carlos. Then he'd acted like such a pill about it that Carlos had stopped talking to him. He worried that being an ass about Aiden had spurred on Carlos's stubborn streak, and even though Carlos himself had been having second thoughts about moving in with Aiden, Nate agreeing it was a bad idea had seemed to inspire Carlos to do it anyway.

"It's too late now," Nate said. "They have happy domestic bliss and I have nothing."

Lulu sighed. She put some more animal crackers on the plate in front of Mia. Then she said, "So dramatic, *mi hijo*. You have plenty. You are just having a rough year. No matter what your relationship with your mother, it can't be easy seeing her sick. And I know you care about Carlos, so stop picking fights and make up with him."

Nate nodded. "No, I should. I will."

"You boys have been such good friends for so long. I do think you could make each other happy, but this is the way life has dealt the cards. It is hard for me to talk about since you're both my boys." She tilted her head. "I would not give up hope just yet. But there are other fish, Nate. I know there is a man out there who will make you very happy."

"Thanks, Lulu."

"And if you need anything, you obviously know where to find me. We'll get you through this, okay?"

"Yeah." Nate couldn't tell if she meant his mother's illness or his feelings for Carlos. Picking Door Number Two, he said, "I mean, you know, I care about him, but he's made his decision."

Lulu frowned. "It seems that way."

"So I'm dating. I'm moving on." Although that was an exaggeration. He'd been on a lot of first dates in the past year. None of the guys measured up, though.

"Good. Eat your rice, *mi hijo*."

Don't miss how the
story began!

*The Windup*

The Rainbow League:
Book One

By Kate McMurray

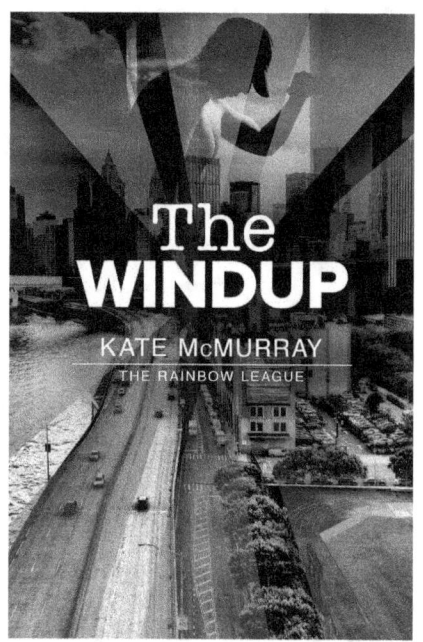

Ian ran screaming from New York City upon graduating from high school. A job offer too good to turn down has brought him back, but he plans to leave as soon as the job is up. In the meantime he lets an old friend talk him into joining the Rainbow League, New York's LGBT amateur baseball league. Baseball turns out to be a great outlet for his anxiety, and not only because sexy teammate Ty has caught his eye.

Ty is like a duck on a pond—calm and laid-back on the surface, a churning mess underneath. In Ian, he's found someone with whom he feels comfortable enough to share some of what's going on beneath the surface. The only catch is that Ian is dead set on leaving the city as soon as he can. Ty works up a plan to convince Ian that New York is, in fact, the greatest city in the world. But when Ian receives an offer for a job overseas, Ty needs a new plan: convince Ian that home is where Ty is.

http://www.dreamspinnerpress.com

KATE MCMURRAY is an award-winning romance author and fan. When she's not writing, she works as a nonfiction editor, dabbles in various crafts, and is maybe a tiny bit obsessed with baseball. She is active in RWA and has served as president of Rainbow Romance Writers and on the board of RWANYC. She lives in Brooklyn, NY.

Website: http://www.katemcmurray.com
Twitter: http://www.twitter.com/katemcmwriter
Facebook: https://www.facebook.com/katemcmurraywriter

# Blind Items

By Kate McMurray

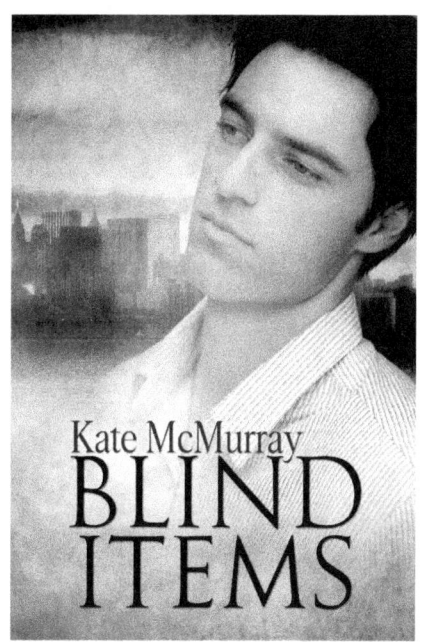

Columnist Drew Walsh made his career by publicly criticizing conservative, anti-gay politician Richard Granger. So when a rumor surfaces that Granger's son Jonathan might be gay, Drew finds himself in the middle of a potential scandal. Under the guise of an interview about Jonathan's new job teaching in an inner-city school, Drew's job is to find out if the rumors are true. Drew's best friend Rey is also Jonathan's cousin, and he arranges the meeting between Jonathan and Drew that changes everything.

After just one interview, it's obvious to Drew that the rumors are true, but he carefully neglects to mention that in his article. It's also obvious that he's falling for Jonathan, and he can't stay away after the article is published. Still, Jonathan is too afraid to step out of the closet, and Drew thinks the smartest thing might be to let him go—until Jonathan shows up drunk one night at his apartment. The slow burn of their attraction doesn't fade with Jonathan's buzz, but navigating a relationship is never easy—especially in the shadow of right-wing politics.

## http://www.dreamspinnerpress.com

# *Four Corners*

By Kate McMurray

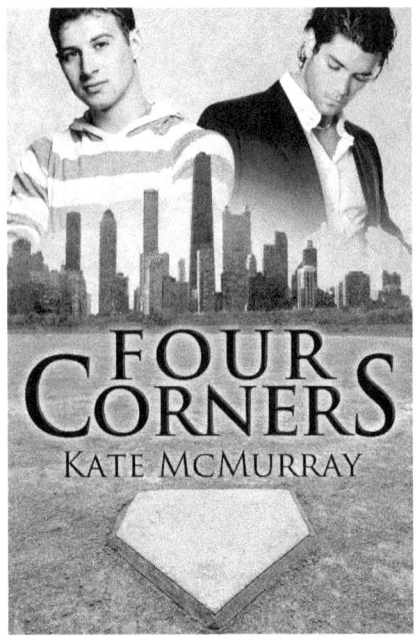

Since childhood, Jake, Adam, Kyle, and Brendan have been teammates, best friends, brothers. Then one day, when they were twenty-five, Adam disappeared without a word, devastating his friends—none more so than Jake, who had secretly loved Adam since they were teenagers.

Now, five years later, Adam is back, and he has his mind set on Jake. But those years of anger, hurt, and confusion are a lot to overcome, and Jake doesn't find it easy to forgive. He isn't sure they'll ever fit together the way they did. Jake, Kyle, and Brendan have moved on with their lives, but Adam's high-profile career keeps him in the closet—the same place he's been for years. Still, his apologies seem sincere, and the attraction is still there. Jake desperately wants to give him a chance. But first he has to find out why Adam left and if he's really back for good.

# http://www.dreamspinnerpress.com

# Kindling Fire with Snow

By Kate McMurray

Weathermen are predicting an incredible blizzard for New York City, but with old snow melting on the sidewalk, Seth Roland is a little skeptical. Despite moping over his ex-boyfriend Evan, who recently dumped him, Seth pretends all is well as he steps into his regular local bar, where he's surprised by a blast from his past. Enter Kieran O'Malley, Seth's very first boyfriend, in the city for a conference.

It might have been just a chance meeting, but first a train derailment and then the predicted blizzard keep Seth and Kieran in close proximity. It's enough time for old feelings to surface, rekindled attraction to take hold, and new hopes for a future together to fill them both. But once the storm passes, the real challenge begins. Will Seth and Kieran work to make the relationship last, or will they let it melt away like snow in the sun?

# *Playing Ball*

By Shae Connor, Kate McMurray,
Marguerite Labbe, & Kerry Freeman

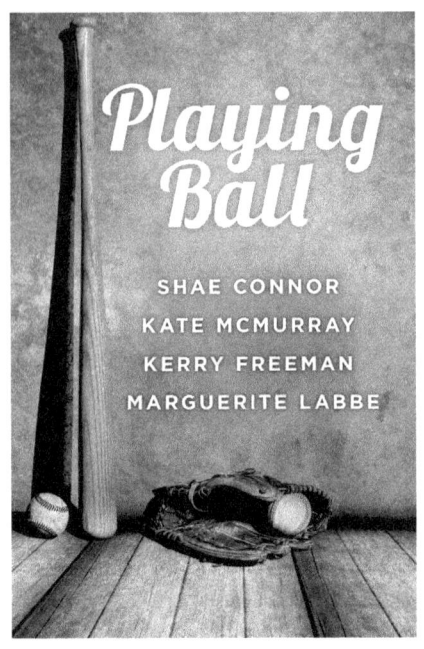

Baseball—America's favorite pastime—provides a field wide open for romance. A *Home Field Advantage* may not help when Toby must choose between the team he's loved all his life and the man he could love for the rest of it. In 1927, Skip hides his sexuality to protect his career until he meets *One Man to Remember*. Ruben and Alan fell victim to a *Wild Pitch*, leaving them struggling with heartache and guilt, and now they've met again. And on *One Last Road Trip*, Jake retires and leaves baseball behind, hoping to reconnect with Mikko and get a second chance at love.

*Home Field Advantage* by Shae Connor
*One Man to Remember* by Kate McMurray
*Wild Pitch* by Marguerite Labbe
*One Last Road Trip* by Kerry Freeman

http://www.dreamspinnerpress.com

# The Stars that Tremble

By Kate McMurray

Giovanni Boca was destined to go down in history as an opera legend until a vocal chord injury abruptly ended his career. Now he teaches voice lessons at a prestigious New York City music school. During auditions for his summer opera workshop, he finds his protégé in fourteen-year-old Emma McPhee. Just as intriguing to Gio is Emma's father Mike, a blue-collar guy who runs a business renovating the kitchens and bathrooms of New York's elite to finance his daughter's dream.

Mike's partner was killed when Emma was a toddler, and Gio mourns the beautiful voice he will never have again, so coping with loss is something they have in common. Their initial physical attraction quickly grows to something more as each hopes to fill the gap that loss and grief has left in his life. Although Mike wonders if he can truly fit into Gio's upperclass world, their bond grows stronger. Then, trouble strikes from outside when the machinations of an unscrupulous stage mother threaten to tear Gio and Mike apart—and ruin Emma's bright future.

http://www.dreamspinnerpress.com

# The Silence of the Stars

By Kate McMurray

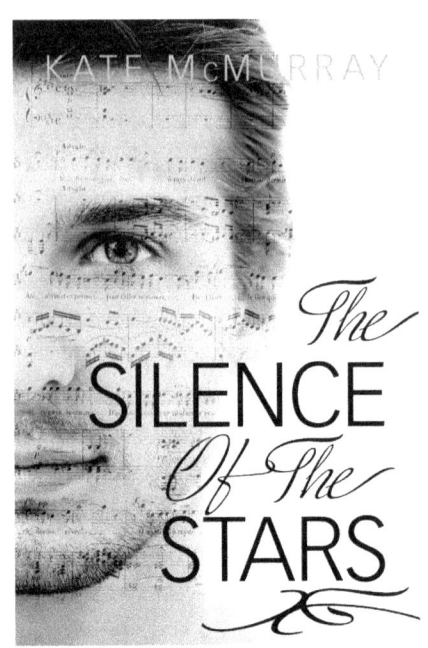

Sandy Sullivan has gotten so good at covering up his emotions, he's waiting for someone to hand him an Oscar. On the outside, he's a cheerful, funny guy, but his good humor is the only thing keeping awful memories from his army tours in Afghanistan at bay. Worse, Sandy is now adrift after breaking up with the only man who ever understood him, but who also wanted to fix him the way Sandy's been fixing up his new house in Brooklyn.

Everett Blake seems to have everything: good looks, money, and talent to spare. He parlayed a successful career as a violinist into a teaching job at Manhattan's elite Olcott School and until four months ago, he even had the perfect boyfriend. Now he's on his own, trying to give his new apartment some personality, even if it is unkempt compared to the perfect home he shared with his ex. When hiring a contractor to renovate his kitchen sends Sandy barreling into his life, Everett is only too happy to accept the chaos… until he realizes he's in over his head.

http://www.dreamspinnerpress.com

# What There Is

By Kate McMurray

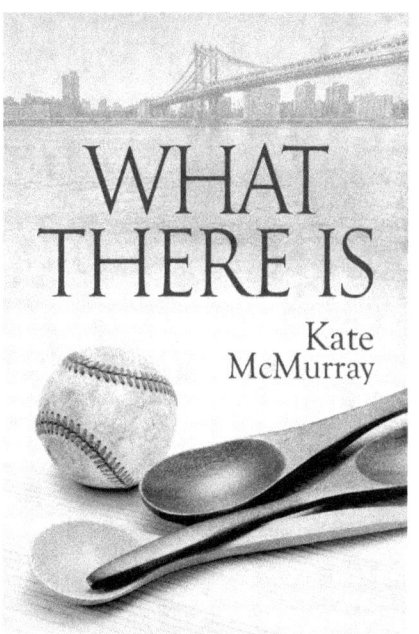

Former professional baseball player Justin Piersol needs a new life after a career-ending injury, and his job as a high school baseball coach isn't exactly fulfilling. Still, things are looking up: he finds the perfect room in an apartment in Brooklyn with Mark, who writes a popular column on sports statistics.

Mark is nerdy and socially awkward and intensely shy, and he immediately develops a terrible crush on Justin, who barely seems to notice him. As they get to know each other, Justin admits he misses playing baseball, that coaching doesn't scratch the itch. Mark confesses he thought he'd be married by now, that he wants a serious relationship. So they make a pact: Justin will help Mark find a man, and Mark will help Justin find something he loves more than baseball.

They put their plan into action… and then life gets complicated. Mark meets a nice guy named Dave, and Justin is suddenly crazy with jealousy. Justin realizes he wants to let go of the past and focus on the present, but as Mark and Dave become an item, Justin fears he's too late.

http://www.dreamspinnerpress.com

# When the Planets Align

By Kate McMurray

Best friends Michael Reeves and Simon Newell always lived within ten minutes of each other, but somehow they're never in the same place at the same time.

Brash, outgoing Michael's unwavering confidence that he and Simon are meant to be carries him through some hard times. When Simon moves to New York, Michael dutifully follows. Quiet, practical Simon loves Michael as a dear friend, but he's not ready for anything romantic.

Several years and several failed relationships later, Simon realizes he's been in love with Michael all along. Only now Michael has moved on. Though Simon offers everything Michael's ever dreamed of, the timing is all wrong. Confusion, betrayal, and secrets from the past threaten their friendship until it might be time for them to go their separate ways. Or maybe the planets will finally align, and Michael and Simon will find themselves in the right place at the right time to take the next step.

## http://www.dreamspinnerpress.com

The
# ESKIMO
## SLUGGER

Brad
Boney

DAYS

8

http://www.dreamspinnerpress.com

www.ingramcontent.com/pod-product-compliance
Lightning Source LLC
Chambersburg PA
CBHW070123260626
47160CB00004B/1593